Midlife Fairy Hunter

THE FORTY PROOF SERIES

SHANNON MAYER

Copyright
Midlife Fairy Hunter
Copyright © **Shannon Mayer 2020**
All rights reserved
Published by Hijinks Ink Publishing
www.shannonmayer.com

Midlife Fairy Hunter

THE FORTY PROOF SERIES

SHANNON MAYER

ACKNOWLEDGEMENTS

Weirdly enough, I have very few words for this section. Not that there aren't people who helped this book come to life. There are editors, copy editors, beta readers and ARC teams. There is my real life friends, my online friends, my author besties.

But this book came together in a time of upheaval not only in the world, but in my life and so it gives me pause in how to acknowledge the process this time around.

All I can HOPE is that it provides those who read it with the escape it gave me. I can HOPE that you find your smile come back a little.

I can HOPE you enjoy and savor each chapter as it was written to give not only me, but each of you a place to find yourself.

#LiveWithHope

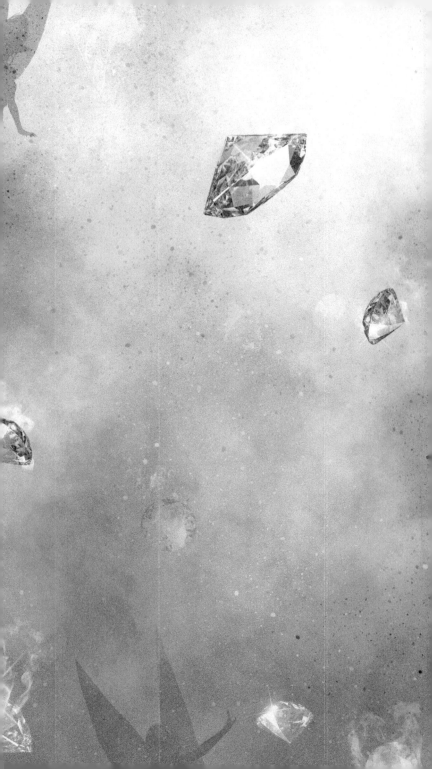

1

The mirror in front of me was most certainly not magical, or if it was, it was kind of a dick. It gave me a crystal-clear view of the fine lines around the sides of my eyes and the sunspot on my left temple, whose existence I'd been steadfastly ignoring. I rubbed at the darker shade of skin as if it would wipe it away. It didn't, of course, and when I grimaced, a severe line etched into the side of my mouth, one that never totally went away anymore.

I blew a raspberry at myself. "Falling to pieces, girl."

A tinkling like small bells rattled against the too-small window to my left. The bathroom was not very big, too narrow for more than one person and littered with Corb's stuff. Like his hair cream that smelled a bit like spice and musk, which I may or may not have opened and inspected. I'd never heard of the brand, but it seemed like something I could steal the next time I needed cream for my own hair. A girl had to make do with what she had—or could take—when she was dealing with a vindictive ex-husband and trying to buy her gran's house back.

The window rattled again, and I turned to see a bug smacking against the glass repeatedly. I frowned and narrowed my eyes because the bug had legs— feminine legs that ended in tiny feet. I closed my eyes hard as if I could reset what I was seeing. Quite possibly I just had a floater in my eyes—courtesy of middle age—but I had a sneaking suspicion that what I was seeing was real.

Sure enough, when I opened my eyes, the bug with the nice legs was still there, now standing on the ledge of the window and rapping on the glass with a miniature fist.

Let me be clear, this was not my first brush with the shadow world, so seeing a tiny fairy was not exactly shocking. *Unexpected* is a better word for it. You see, I'd barely just dunked my toes back into Savannah, Georgia, the place I'd grown up believing in every bogeyman that lived in the darkness. My gran had raised me to know about them and, when necessary, to fight them.

But her teachings had faded over the years because Gran had put a spell on me before I left Savannah. I'd fallen in love with a man who didn't believe in magic, you see, and she'd ensured I could start over by making me blind to the monsters in our world. Most humans don't even realize supernatural creatures live among them, but I was born with the ability to see them.

For twenty years, I was as blind as most humans.

But then Himself—my a-hole of an ex—gave me a surprise divorce, and some underhanded dealings, which were just screwy enough that I suspected magic, had allowed him to steal the house Gran had left me on her death six months prior. I'd come to Savannah to see if I could save the house, and maybe save myself along the way.

What I'd found was a new job working for the Hollows Group, a mishmash of people who did odd jobs for people in the shadow world and also helped police them. They hadn't wanted to take on a woman who was over forty, had extra weight hanging off her, and let's be honest, doesn't take crap from anyone.

Obedient, I am not.

And yet, they had brought me on all the same.

So here I was, living with Corb, Himself's black sheep cousin, in his loft in downtown Savannah. I'd found myself here by several weird twists of fate, including the fact that Corb also worked for the Hollows Group, but here I'd stayed.

Today was the auction for my gran's house—the house she still haunted—and unless I managed to win, I'd probably be sharing this apartment for a while.

I rubbed my hand over my face again, focusing on that sunspot, then lifted onto my tiptoes to open the window. The latch stuck, and I had to pull hard to open it. The screech of paint peeling and ungreased hinges made me wince.

Corb was still asleep as far as I knew, and while I didn't mind him waking up, the truth was I wasn't sure what to do about him.

You see, he'd kissed me. Not like a peck on the cheek but an open-mouthed kiss. He'd done it in front of Himself, and it had almost certainly been nothing more than a favor to make him jealous, but it had confused me. Because Corb was younger than me, hot as sin, related to my ex, and I'd thought he barely tolerated me. Oh, and the kiss had been hot. Like hot-flash hot.

Not complicated at all, right?

The little fairy stumbled in and stayed on the sill. Her skin tone was the color of rusted metal, and her hair was a close match. Deep orange eyes stared at me from under long black lashes.

"Oh! Can you see me?"

I wondered how many windows she'd flown by before she'd found mine. At least a few, by the look of exhaustion written all over her. "I can see you," I said.

"Can you help me?" Her voice was a bit breathy, and even though my eyesight wasn't what it had once been, I could see that she glistened with sweat as if she'd either been flying for a long time or was terrified.

A freaked-out fairy was not the way to start the day.

I paused with my hand halfway between the window and the sink as I tried to remember if Gran had ever told me anything specific about dealing with fairies. Making deals with them was dodgy, I did recall that much, and that alone slowed my hand. "What do you need?"

She pointed at something behind her with both thumbs. I lifted my hand up to her and she hopped onto my palm. I turned her around to see a wad of gum stuck between her wings. She could still fly, but the gum tore at the delicate material every time she pumped them. That explained all the sweat. She would have had to work twice as hard to go half as far.

"Yeah, I think I could do something for you." I paused and raised an eyebrow. "What have you got in payment?"

The shadow world didn't run on empathy, and fairies were infamous for taking advantage of others. She eyed me up. "I can do your makeup."

"Done," I said without trying to haggle for more. I needed all the help I could get in that department. "Stay here, I'll get something to get the gum out."

If I remembered right, a good olive oil would get gum out of hair, so why not little fairy wings? I put her on the edge of the bathroom sink, and she cowered under the bumped out mirror, the bright pink gum a gaudy contrast to the earthy hues of her body and wings. I found myself wondering which plant she most resembled, as most of the fairy folk had a flower or a tree they were more closely connected to than others if I was remembering right.

I headed for the kitchen, my steps quiet on the original hardwood. A quick search of the cupboards produced not a single jar of oil. "Damn it." There was peanut butter, but it was the super thick kind with crunchy bits. Terrible stuff that would tear at her wings too.

I bit the inside of my lip thinking. Maybe Corb's hair cream would work? It had seemed exceptionally slick.

I let myself back into the bathroom. "Here, let's try this." I scooped up the jar of hair cream, glancing quickly at the label. *Boy Butter.* I popped the lid off and scooped out a tiny amount on my fingertips, rubbing it together experimentally. Pretty greasy for hair pomade, but it should work for my purposes. I sat on the toilet lid and motioned for her to turn her back to me, then began to work the cream into the edges of her wings and around the gum, using my fingers and finally a couple of Q-tips.

"How did you manage this?"

"A ghoul caught me and spat his gum at me," she muttered. "I'd just woken up, so I was slow. Fairies are always slow in the morning." Morning being closer to noon, unless she'd been flying for a lot longer than I'd thought.

Her wings were like gossamer lace and I found myself sweating as I did all I could to be careful, to not put a single tear in them. My concentration was so intense that when she spoke to me again, I had to get her to repeat herself.

6

"The Hollows Group turned down our offer today." She looked over her shoulder at me. "But really, we didn't want them to help us." The weight in her stare said it all, but she went on anyway. "Or at least not all of them. My lady would like to hire *you*, Breena. She'll pay well."

I grimaced as I continued to rub the greasy hair cream through her delicate wings. So apparently it wasn't just happenstance that she'd stumble-flown to my window. The whole *can you see me?* thing had been a ruse. I should have known. "Tell me if that hurts."

"It's fine, a little tingly."

She wasn't wrong. My fingers were tingly too. "Is that your magic?"

"No, I think it's whatever you're using." She cleared her throat. "Would you be willing to meet with my lady? To at least hear the offer?"

My own brain was still trying to work through the morning fog. Yes, it was closer to noon, but when you worked till three in the morning, noon *was* morning. "Why did the Hollows Group turn you down?" It seemed exceptionally strange to me that they would turn down any job. Especially given the last job they'd *almost* turned down had ended up paying so well, both financially and as a PR opportunity.

The door to the bathroom opened and Corb stood there in nothing but shorts, his dark hair mussed up, eyes at half-mast as he stumbled toward the toilet on which I was sitting. Every muscle in his torso was defined as if they'd been sculpted, and it looked

7

like he'd woken up in a sweat. Damn it, I think I was actually drooling. My hormones had gone into overdrive when I hit forty, and I really, *really* liked to window shop. Fortunately for me, the men I was around gave me a good amount to look at.

"Move, I gotta pee," he grumbled. A one-bathroom loft had its disadvantages.

I rolled my eyes as I fought my suddenly raging libido and the urge to reach out and swipe my hand across his abs to see if they really were that hard. Instead, I held out a palm for the fairy and picked up the hair cream with the other hand. "Manners, Corb."

His eyes shot to the container in my hand. I held it up. "Your hair cream is helping me get the gum out of her wings, seeing as you don't have a lick of cooking oil in the kitchen." Classic bachelor pad if you asked me.

He swallowed hard and slowly looked at my hand and the petite woman who sat there, seemingly enjoying the view of his naked torso as much as I was. She leaned forward and pointed a finger at him. "He's hot. Do you really live with him?"

Yup, she was a window shopper too.

I laughed. "I live in the closet, not his bedroom."

His eyes shot to the hair cream. "That's not hair cream."

I held the container up. "It's *Boy Butter*. What else would it be?" I lifted my eyes to him, making a pitiful attempt to raise one eyebrow, which always ended with me lifting both of them. "You maybe need to go back to bed."

His jaw flexed and he turned on his heel.

"I thought he had to pee?" the fairy girl asked.

"Me too." I sat back down on the lid of the toilet, and she hopped off my hand and onto the sink edge, where I kept working the cream through her wings. "It smells nice."

The fairy let out a giggle. "Oh my lady of the stars! I think I know why he was upset."

I pulled the long string of bright pink gum off and put it on a piece of toilet paper. "Why?"

"That isn't hair cream."

I grabbed the container and flipped it over so I could read the label.

"*Boy Butter*, best cream around."

She was giggling; I was staring at the picture of a large arm grabbing a stick as it churned butter on the yellow label.

Churning. Butter.

I put the container down, unable to stop the blurt of laughter that ripped out of me. "CORB! You should keep this in the bedroom, not the bathroom!"

Heavy footsteps and then the front door slammed. I couldn't stop a fit of giggles, and the fairy laughed with me until tears streamed down both our faces.

"Do you think he has more?" she finally managed.

My hands were covered in exceptionally greasy lubricant, which made it hard to open the cupboard under the sink because my fingers kept sliding over the handle. But when I did...all I could do was stare. "Jaysus, it's like he's stockpiled enough to outlast the apocalypse. Oink and Boink? Tastes like Bacon?" I

9

fell back laughing, unable to help myself. Was this real? Maybe I was dreaming.

The fairy flitted in front of me, flicking lube around with each flutter of her wings, and read off the rest of the names until I was laughing so hard I had to lie on my back so I could still breathe.

I held up my hands in surrender. "Stop, stop! Whatever makeup I had on is gone, and as you correctly determined, I need all the help I can get." I swiped my eyes, forgetting that I had the heating lube on them. "Ahh, that's not good!" I sat up, eyes pinched shut and tearing, and smacked my head on the bottom edge of the sink as I scrambled to get a wet cloth.

The water helped, but the lube wasn't water-soluble, which only made me giggle more. I mean, I'll admit part of me was totally intrigued. Corb was a hottie. I liked looking at him, and he'd kissed me.

But that was a helluva lot of lube he had going on. Like there had to be at least thirty bottles under the sink! Who needed that many? Was he planning on an orgy in the near future, or maybe an old-fashioned key party?

My eyes tingled, and I rubbed at them with the cloth, which only made them redder and intensified the feeling of heat. "Crap." This was not going well.

"Here, I can help." The fairy flitted up around my face, the fanning of her wings cooling the heat rushing across my skin. I could only imagine what it would feel like to have that lube somewhere else, with someone leaning in close to blow on it.

My face fanned hot again as images blasted through my mind like an out-of-control race car heading straight for a wall and a supernova explosion. I only needed to keep it from crashing into the wall.

Crash.

Damn it, if I wasn't thinking about one guy, I was thinking about the other. Nope, no thinking about Crash. He was one of the bad guys. A *bad* guy. But a really, terribly hot and nice-to-look-at bad guy with muscles and a bit of silver in his hair that just added to the hotness factor.

I sighed. "You think you can help me with my face now?"

The mirror showed my eyes were slightly swollen and red around the edges, like I'd been playing in the stinging nettle patch. I was a bit red all over from the laughing and the sudden hot flash, which hadn't helped the heat index at all. Sighing, I took out my makeup bag.

"Difficult, but not impossible," she said as she fluttered around my head, tilting her chin as she did so. "You should use a little more cover-up." Her voice wasn't as high-pitched as I would have expected a fairy to sound. Musical and sweet, like the tinkling of the bells I'd heard at the window, but it wasn't ridiculously perky.

"Cover-up looks crappy on me."

Her smile flashed super sharp canine teeth. Fairies were omnivores—just like humans—but they had a tendency to like their meat a bit more than most.

"Eric has been talking about you non-stop the last few days. So when my lady asked me to come see you, I knew you wouldn't be like the Hollows. Will you talk to her? Will you consider working for her?"

I didn't answer her, at least not right away. Eric was the bigfoot I'd saved from a ceremonial death at the hands of a crazy old woman. It had taken a lot of luck, plus the training of my youth, but we hadn't walked away without any scrapes and bruises. Could it have really been that so little time had passed since that had all gone down? I thought through the last few days of training with the Hollows Group. Today was five days since I'd stopped the blood ceremony and saved Eric. Seemed like an eternity, though my body reminded me otherwise.

I took a breath and my back twinged, making me grimace.

"Eric is a good guy." I took out some eyeliner and leaned toward the mirror again as I attempted to outline my left eye. I ended up with a line that looked like a five-year-old had drawn it. "I don't know about meeting up with your lady. I'm still new to the Hollows Group, and it might not be a good idea for me to start crossing lines." The pencil dipped into my eye well, and my eye flooded with tears. "Damn it."

"Here, I said I would do it, let me do it." The fairy flew in front of my face and held out her hands. I gave her the eyeliner pencil, wondering if she could even handle the weight. It was about as long as she was high, but she grabbed it as if it weighed nothing. "Close your eyes."

I did as she said and the lightest brush of the pencil tip ran along the edge of my eyelid. "I'd ask your name, but I know that's probably out of bounds. So what should I call you?" I asked, trying not to breathe out too hard. I hadn't brushed my teeth yet, and I didn't want to kill the little critter.

"You can call me Kinkly. Friends call me Kink." She moved on to my other eyelid. "You have a lot of loose skin. Is that what happens to humans as they age? Or is something wrong with you?"

I gritted my teeth. "Are fairy critters always so subtle in their approach to insults?"

"I wasn't insulting you," she said as she ran the pencil along a lower lid. "If I'd wanted to insult you, I'd have mentioned the hovel you live in, the terribly made clothing you wear, or the obvious disdain you have for your appearance. Things you have the power to change. I wouldn't insult things you can't change, like your loose skin."

My mouth dropped open and I fought not to splutter—bad morning breath, remember? I snapped my mouth shut with a click.

"Open your eyes." She fluttered around my face as I blinked at her. "You have pretty green eyes, we need to highlight them. Are you in a mating ritual, is that why you are putting this stuff on? For the one with all the lube? He is very nice to look at. If he were smaller, I'd let him roll around on me in a bed of leaves."

I had to fight back a laugh. "No, not for Corb." Though that idea did have its merits. "I think I'll be running into my ex-husband later today. Kind of a face-off, if you will. He stole my gran's house from me, and now it's going up for auction. He'll be there, so I want to look good." Also there was a chance Crash could be there. He'd expressed interest in my gran's house. Maybe he'd want to buy it and give it to me because my makeup was on point? I snorted to myself, unable to take my own fantasy seriously.

"You mean you have a mate that is not a mate any longer?" She dropped onto the counter and scooped up a palette of colors. I held my hand out and she plunked it into my palm, then went for a softer brush. This was a perfect deal. One thing I'd never excelled at was the ability to highlight cheekbones, eyebrows, eyes, or lips. A swipe of mascara and maybe some lip gloss was pretty much the high end of my abilities.

"You are correct," I mumbled. "A mate that is a mate no longer."

"Hmm. Such a human thing. We kill our mates if they betray us. Close your eyes," she said, and I dutifully obeyed even as I smiled. Killing Himself would certainly bring me satisfaction. The brush flowed over my eyelids, tickling me a little. "Why would you trust me? You know that most people hate fairy folk. We have a deal, but even so, you are very relaxed. Other than when your heart rate accelerated upon seeing that lovely specimen earlier."

I sighed. She wasn't wrong about the heart rate business, or the fact that people didn't trust fairies. My gran had poured her wisdom into a book I'd been lucky enough to acquire, and in it, written in her own hand, was a warning not to trust any fairy. The fairy—or fae—were tricksters like no others. They cause trouble on a good day. On a bad day they'd hurt you just because they could and get away with it because they were so good at hiding their tracks. Which was probably why Eammon and the Hollows Group had turned down whatever job they'd been offered, regardless of the money.

So why had Kinkly asked me about trusting her? Her bringing up the trust issue was interesting. I dredged up a few more tidbits from my past schooling with my gran, my mind moving more quickly now that some of the cobwebs had been cleared. "We made a deal, and I understand you all take that seriously. Your wings were involved. Your own kind might have killed you for having been caught, correct?"

The brush strokes slowed. "You know more about us than I would have thought. The lady was right to ask for you. But the leprechaun said no. He judged us without knowing us or attempting to understand our problem. Would you do the same?"

Now that was interesting indeed. My mentor Eammon was, of course, the leprechaun in question.

"No," I mumbled. "Mostly, I'm done listening to the world and its opinions when it comes to people. By their standards I should not be friends with Eric because he's a bigfoot. Yet I would consider him a friend."

The strokes of the brush picked up speed again. "That is very wise."

15

I wanted to laugh at her. I knew buttering up when I heard it. Even if I hadn't realized what *Boy Butter* was based on the packaging.

"Nah, I'm just tired of jerks and assholes. I'd rather form my own opinions about the people I deal with than let someone else tell me they're a certain way because they are a fairy, or a bigfoot, or a werewolf." Or a blacksmith with magic hands.

She hummed a little as she worked on my face. "I like you. I didn't expect that."

A smile slid over my lips as she put something on them. "Two of my closest friends at the moment are a river maid and a walking skeleton. Why not a fairy too?" Kind of rounded out my current posse. My lips quirked up. "Besides, if Eric likes you, you can't be too bad."

The brush paused over my right eye and then picked up again. A few minutes later she stopped. "There, that is the best I can do given my canvas."

I opened my eyes and gave an experimental frown to see if said canvas wrinkled or not. "Pretty good, no crease lines, no red eyes." I nodded. "Good job, Kinkly." Really, more than a good job. My skin was smooth, eyes perfectly highlighted, lips just pouty enough to be enticing, not like I'd stuffed them into the business end of a vacuum.

She blushed and floated about until I held out the palm of my hand for her to land in. "May I come with you to see this ex-man of yours?" she asked. "He sounds horrible. I like to see horrible things. And maybe I can convince you to talk to the lady."

Subtle she was not, but I admired a determined woman.

My eyebrows shot up. "Why not? Maybe you can put a hex on him."

She flashed her super sharp teeth. "It would be my pleasure."

2

The auction for this diamond in the rough, partially furnished 1898 brick home, complete with its own resident ghost, will begin in under ten minutes! Seated right next to the infamous Sorrel-Weed House, you could turn this into an amazing Airbnb with a wait list a mile long!" The realtor's voice rang out over the small crowd gathered around the front porch of the home that I'd grown up in, the home my gran had lived in for as long as I could remember. "Created in a similar style to its more famous neighbor, this Greek revival house is classic and will never go out of style."

"What about the ghosts next door?" someone yelled from the crowd. "They really walk around at night looking for victims?"

Laughter rolled through the group, and Monica wagged a finger at the offending party. "Now, now. We here in Savannah love our history, and this place here"—she swept her hand backward to encompass Gran's house—"is as haunted as they come. You won't be disappointed! In fact, we already have a list of ghost hunters ready to come in and communicate with the dead!"

Savannah, Georgia was as notorious for its hauntings as it was for the sheen of wealth it had accumulated over the years, so a haunting wasn't unheard of. However, in a town that lived on tourism, a haunted house could become a money-maker for the right investor. Especially considering it sat next to one of the most investigated haunted houses in town.

Me? I was not the right investor—I was just a woman who wanted what rightfully belonged to her.

"Stupid people," I muttered as I watched their feet trample Gran's front lawn, which was really her front herb garden. Yes, it looked messy and unkempt, but she'd sworn up and down that was how the plants liked it, and they grew better when you didn't try to force them in a box. Kind of like people. The lavender bush by the wall was nearly shoulder height, its soft purple blooms dipping and bobbing in a soft breeze. Kinkly sat on my left shoulder, her legs using my boob for a footrest. The powers of a great push-up bra were all that made it possible.

"Yes," Kinkly said. "They do look stupid. Why are they stepping on all the good plants?"

19

My eyes swept over the people who'd shown up to bid, or maybe just to gawk, but I saw neither Himself—my ex-husband, for those not following along— nor anyone else I recognized, and my gaze came back to the person on the porch. The realtor, Monica, had on a too-tight pencil skirt and was cradling a clipboard in the crook of one arm as she flourished a pen in her other hand. Smiling magnanimously at the crowd as if she were a not-quite-as-pretty-Vanna White, she said, "This is very exciting. We've not had an auction on a house in our sweet little town in a very long time. I'll let you have one final look through, and then at noon on the dot, we will start the bidding at one hundred thousand dollars. The down payment, ten percent of the final amount, will be required immediately in the form of cash or a bank draft."

I didn't go into the house with the rest of the people, but instead waited on my spot in the middle of the only path in or out of the small fenced yard. Sweating for more reasons than the warm spring weather. Ten percent was a lot of any amount. I wouldn't be able to bid as high as I'd hoped.

As I waited, my thoughts circled around the house. I'd come to Savannah to reclaim it, although I'd initially intended to go a legal route. Himself was a divorce lawyer, though, and a good one, as demonstrated by the series of incomprehensible legal manipulations by which he'd both reclaimed my gran's house and left me with all our marital debt. Everything about the situation pissed me off, but nothing so much as losing Gran's house. It was about the only thing I'd wanted as our marriage fell apart.

And he'd damn well known it.

I let out a slow breath, fighting to push the anger away. Some people could use anger to propel them, but it had always exhausted me.

"Think positive," I whispered to myself.

"Positive what?" Kinkly asked.

"Happy thoughts," I mumbled, knowing the other humans in the yard would only see me talking to myself like a crazy woman.

"Oh, you want to fly?" Kinkly tugged on my ear, and I glanced at her and quickly shook my head. I wasn't sure if she was kidding, and the last thing I needed was to go floating over the yard and scaring all the people with what looked like a legit demon possession…wait. Maybe that was exactly what I needed!

"Yes! You can do that?" I clapped my hands together.

Kinkly tugged on my ear. "Then you have to agree to talk to my boss."

"Sure, talking I can do!" If I could scare away most if not all of the bidders, I'd be golden. Besides, talking never hurt anyone. Right?

Right.

Excitement and hope flared as Kinkly fluttered up to the top of my head and did a tap dance on my skull.

I was going to pull a Peter Pan and scare the ever-loving bejesus out of these people, and the only word I could come up with was epic. This was going to be epic.

A fuzzy tingle rolled from my skull down my limbs, and my hands floated up above my head, followed by my left leg, which left me standing on a single foot, like a really awkward ballerina. The pull on my limbs was uncomfortable for a moment, my body dangling from my arms and my left leg, but whatever gravity had held me down finally let go and I popped off the ground.

"It's cursed, this place is cursed! Demons! Gawd in heaven, I'm possessed!" I yelled and let out a strangled growl as I threw my head back. I wouldn't usually make a spectacle of myself to get what I wanted (at least not intentionally). But this was Gran's house. A little spectacle was worth it. Really, who was I trying to impress? No one, that's who.

The potential buyers came running back down the steps, flashes of horror on one face after another, and then the shrieking began. I got a glimpse of Monica's seething face as I spun in the air, moved by a force outside of myself. Because while it was one thing to want a haunted house, it was another to see someone floating around your potential yard all snarling and growling. Most people were all bluster and no bite when it came to this kind of thing.

I turned again, not meaning to. "Kinkly?"

"Sorry, you're bigger than I thought. I couldn't lighten all of you up."

I grimaced. "Whatever. You'll be able to get me down?"

"Um."

"UM?" I twisted around in the air. "Are you kidding me?"

Monica stomped down the front steps. "This is ridiculous! It's a stunt!"

She touched my dangling foot as if she'd pull me down, but instead she lifted off the ground with a squeal that would make a particular farm animal proud.

"She sounds like a pig!" Kinkly giggled, not one for subtlety. "I didn't think I could send my magic over her!"

"Contagious," I muttered as I tried to wiggle my foot loose of Monica's hands.

Kinkly fluttered around. "I'm trying, I'm trying! I'm not as experienced as some!"

I did my best to relax, but I was floating upside down, Monica hanging from one limb. On the bright side, all the humans from the area had left. My plan had worked. There would be no other bidders, and I'd have the house in no time.

Gran would be so happy! Hell, I knew I was grinning like a fool.

My thoughts must have summoned her, as a gray-haired woman in swirling skirts and a loose blouse stepped down the stairs, her body fading a little in the bright sunlight as she drew closer. I mean that literally, she did not have a solid body and I could see through her to the porch stairs.

Monica let out one last shriek and went quiet.

"Did she pass out?" I asked, though no one answered me.

I shook my foot and Monica's body flopped a little like a fish on the line, her fingers digging into me out of sheer self-perseveration despite the fact that she was out cold. Well damn. Score one for good instincts.

I pitched my voice low as I spoke to my grandmother, just in case Monica wasn't fully out. "Gran, I didn't know you could come out here. I thought you had to stay inside."

She didn't seem terribly troubled by the sight of me hovering in the air, but then again, she was dead. She was the *resident ghost* mentioned by Monica the realtor.

Gran spread her hands wide and brushed her fingers over the top of a plant I think was some sort of mint. It went right through her fingers, of course, but I did note that the leaves seemed to green up under her touch. Interesting. "The garden was my home as much as my house, and all those people were out here touching my things. I didn't like it, Breena. I truly didn't. When they came inside, I considered tipping the mirror on them, but that mirror has been in the family for too long to waste it on a few peasants tromping through my house." Her voice gained a measure of irritation, which told me she was truly angry.

A Southern belle in her own time, Gran didn't think it was passing pretty to show your anger. My lips twitched as I waited for the line…

"Bless their hearts, they have no idea what they are messing with, do they?"

Translation: What a bunch of idiots, I can't help it if they're so stupid they're going to hurt themselves.

I sighed. "I'm trying to get the house, Gran, I am. I came with money. And now I've scared a bunch of them off." Kinkly bobbed beside me. Could she see Gran? Not everyone could.

"Hey, I helped," Kinkly said.

Gran's eyes shot to her, but she shrugged off her presence and waved a hand at me. "Honey girl, don't fret. Things will work out. None of those yahoos will have my house, I'm sure of it."

If I hadn't gotten rid of all the people, she'd have been dead wrong—no pun intended. The only reason I had any money for the down payment was because Eric had rewarded me generously for saving his life. The other members of the Hollows Group had written him off as a paranoid kook, so they'd given me, a trainee, the task of protecting him. Too bad someone *had* been stalking him—a bunch of nut jobs who'd wanted to use him as a sacrifice for a bit of black magic.

Grave magic, as it were.

Although I'd prevented the black magic folks from hurting Eric, they'd held a different ceremony at a second location. My boss still hadn't told me what had happened with that, probably because the members of the Hollows Group weren't really the sharing type.

Not that I should talk.

I swallowed hard and shot a glance at my gran. I hadn't told her yet that one of her best friends,

Hattie, had been at the center of the plot to kill Eric and use his blood in a grave magic ceremony. We knew Hattie had intended to open some sort of gateway to call through a major demon, but why? What could she have possibly wanted? I didn't know, and that in itself was concerning. But there was no way to question her now—she'd been killed to stop the ceremony, by yours truly. I'm not sure I'd fully processed that yet either. You don't kill someone and feel nothing unless you are a true-blue psycho, and despite what Himself would say of me, I didn't think that term fit me.

"What's got you fussed?" Gran looked up at me, her wizened faced wrinkling up even further. She really was like a female Yoda, other than the ears and the green skin. Even her diminutive height added to the Yoda impression as she blinked up at me.

"Worried about the auction," I said, which was both true and not true. "I have enough for a down payment if the price doesn't go too high, but I might not be able to get a mortgage because of what Alan did to my credit. I'm banking on them not being able to check right away."

A quick glance around proved no one else had shown up for the auction, but that didn't solve my problem of dangling in the air. It would only take one or two tourists to notice my predicament, and I'd have a whole new slew of issues. I shook my foot and Monica's hand slid off, but she still floated just below me. "Kinkly, can you get us down?"

"I'm going to try," she said as she tapped my head again. Try.

"I'm not going to talk to your lady if you can't get me down," I said.

She let out a squeak and the tapping on my skull increased in intensity, but I didn't lower to the ground. I tried not to think about being stuck in the air for the rest of…well, for however long.

I wrapped my hand around the strap of my bag, reassuring myself that I still had the money. That was something, even if Monica and I had to make our transaction mid-air. The leather was soft and supple under my palm, and better yet, the bag held more than it should and actually lessened the weight of its contents. It currently contained my gran's thousand-page leather-bound book, a change of clothes made completely of leather, a stack of money, and the two knives that I normally kept strapped to my thighs, yet the whole package felt like it weighed less than a pound. Pretty nifty. The bag every girl dreams of, if you ask me.

Of course, that stash of cash had been winnowed down quite a bit. Eric had paid me fifty thousand dollars for saving his life. Sounds like a lot until you take the PayPal fees and taxes off. Kidding, he'd paid me in cash. I'd nearly peed myself when he'd handed it over. Shock doesn't even begin to describe the emotions that had coursed through me with the weight of the money.

But the Hollows Group had taken fifty percent, part of our agreement, and I'd also had to pay Crash.

Just thinking of Crash had me smelling his cologne. The blacksmith was a master at making weapons, and I'd taken a pair of knives from him with the caveat that I would give him ten percent of my first bounty.

I'd tried to give the knives back.

He'd refused.

I'd been forced to hand over the money. Not that another five thousand would have made much of a difference. I'd be able to go to two hundred thousand, but hopefully it wouldn't come to that.

The smell of Crash's cologne grew stronger as a huge hand wrapped around my unencumbered ankle. The magic Kinkly had poured over me was burned off in a flash of heat. Monica hit the ground in a crumple, and I would have been right there beside her if someone hadn't caught me.

Fire and flame, that's what Crash was made of, and his heat surrounded me in a toe-curling way. I somehow managed to keep my legs under me as he set me on the ground. My gran was looking past me, her eyes flashing with recognition. "Did you know him?" I asked, not caring that he could hear me.

She nodded and a smile whispered across her lips. "I remember him, but not what he is. That one is dangerous, though. Especially to you." Her eyes narrowed and then she was gone, having completely disappeared. I sighed. Kinkly, who'd managed to stay on my shoulder, scrambled around to peer back at Crash. She gave a squeak and flew away from my shoulder, out into the garden.

Monica groaned and wobbled to her feet. "Oh, the heat just takes the stuffing out of you, doesn't it?" Crash agreed, put a hand under her arm and helped her up to the porch, where she sat on a step. Yes, I did notice how his pants tightened as he bent over. Yes, I did look.

Heat flared through me again, and I tried desperately to school myself as he turned around and walked back my way, placing himself right behind me, where he'd been before. Damn him in all his chivalry and hotness.

"What are you doing here, Crash?" I didn't turn around and I didn't run away like Kinkly, although part of me thought I probably should. The man behind me was all kinds of stunning, from his rock-hard abs and bulging arm muscles to the lovely dark, silver-kissed hair tucked behind his ears and those blue eyes flecked impossibly with gold. All of that made me cross my legs and want to have a long, hot shower by myself. Trust me, I wasn't kidding about my libido having gone bananas.

Crash did not help that particular side of me, so it was best if I didn't even look at him.

"There's a house auction today, I hear," he said, his voice rumbling over my skin as if he were touching me. "And I'm here to bid on it."

I spun and glared at him, my resolution to keep him out of sight having given way to a blitz of anger that had burned away most of my raging libido. "Don't you dare! I just got rid of all the other bidders!" I was purposely not thanking him for getting me down from floating across the yard.

His eyebrows shot up in what could only be mock innocence. "Why wouldn't I bid? It's a beautiful house with great curb appeal, and as an investment, I don't think I could go wrong."

My eyebrows lowered in perfect contrast to his going up. To spite me. That's why he was here. We'd not parted on great terms, what with me trying to return the knives and him accusing me of reneging on a deal. All I'd wanted was to cut ties with him.

You see, he'd forged the demon-steel knife that had nearly been used to kill Eric. Worse, he'd given it back to Hattie after I'd stolen it from him. It had been a matter of sheer luck—with a sprinkle of good timing—that I'd managed to keep Eric safe.

I glared at him, anger stealing my voice. The best I could do was turn my back on him with a big huff and hope that he didn't want the house too badly. Though if what he was saying was only a little true, he wanted it badly enough.

Of course, that was when things went from bad to worse.

You see, my gran had had two besties. The one I'd liked, Hattie, had turned out to be a grave-magic-dabbling psycho. The other, Missy, I'd never liked. She'd always been cruel to me, and to others. I'd seen her do things behind Gran's back that would curl your hair, but she was careful not to leave marks.

Gran had never believed me. It was the one thing that hung between us. I'd never understood why she'd stood up for Missy.

But if the nice friend had been a nut, what did that suggest about Missy?

I needed to figure out fast, because she was strolling up the street, using her wicked cane to support herself. She paused at the small gate, as if to create a maximum amount of suspense. I didn't want to let her escape my vision, which meant I had to look around Crash in order to see her. A wave of cool air washed forward as she finally stepped onto the garden path, a wind that was impossible in the Georgia heat. I couldn't help it. I reached out and grabbed Crash's forearm.

That saying about the devil you know being better than the one you didn't? Well, I guess it didn't apply since I knew both of them, but for the moment he seemed like the lesser of two evils.

"Now we're friends again?" he murmured, and I looked up to see his eyes were locked on where I held his arm. I tugged him forward a few steps, away from Missy and closer to the opposite side of the yard. With Crash somewhat blocking me from her line of sight, I felt safer, but she was so focused on the house, a hungry look in her eyes, that she hadn't even glanced our way yet. You see, the thing is, I knew my gran had left me treasures hidden within the walls. But no one other than the person whose name was on the deed would be able to unlock Gran's secrets. So said Gran's book.

I was starting to think I wasn't the only one who knew that.

"She can't have Gran's house." I growled the words and Crash's arm flexed under my fingers.

"She's banana pants crazy and mean as a snake with a toothache in one of her fangs." No, as far as I knew she didn't actually have fangs, but at the rate I was going, who knew?

Missy stood near the far side of the garden, right up against the side butting up to the Sorrel-Weed house, which put a good amount of space between us. I wasn't sure it mattered, though. Her eyes hadn't left the house once in all the time I'd been watching her.

Crash turned his body so that he completely blocked my view of Missy and vice versa. "You think she'd hurt you?"

I looked up at him and saw something in his eyes that I wasn't sure I liked. Genuine concern. "Don't make me like you again, Crash. I'm still angry about the demon knife. That and not letting me return the two knives for credit. You're the bad guy, remember?"

He snorted, and his lips twitched. "Wait until you get a bounty that requires you to bend the rules, Breena, then we'll discuss those knives and what it means to be a bad guy."

I got up on my tiptoes, mostly so he wasn't looking so far down on me. I wasn't short at five-foot-eight, but these last few weeks had carved a good deal of my extra pounds off—pounds I'd used to my advantage in the past to throw my weight around.

"Right is right, wrong is wrong." That came out of my mouth as clearly as if my gran had whispered it in my ear. "But let's set that aside for now. Missy *cannot* have this house."

"Why?" He lowered his voice, his eyes flicking over my face as if he couldn't help himself. Softening just a bit as they dipped low to my lips. Score one for Kinkly's makeup help. "You afraid she'll sell the china?"

I blew out an exaggerated puff of air as Monica the realtor stepped back out onto the porch, a little wobbly, but moving around now as if nothing had happened. I frowned as she shook her head and clutched her clipboard to her chest.

She opened her mouth, closed it, and tried again. "It's like she's pretending she didn't just float across the yard like a balloon," I said.

"The human mind shuts things out," Crash said. "Fairy magic in particular tends to do strange things to humans."

I wanted to look at him, to see what his face was saying more than his words, but I found myself staring at Monica. She tapped the wooden porch with her foot to get our attention, using three hard knocks that reverberated harder than they should have in my experience. The sound vibrated through me, and I couldn't help but tighten my hold on Crash's arm.

"Interesting," he said.

Interesting? That wasn't the word I'd use. Was Monica with the shadow world? It felt like there was some intention behind those knocks, but intention to do what? Not just to get people's attention, but something else. She was human, so why the hell had she done that?

An intention to wake something.

That was my knee-jerk guess, and my guesses had a tendency to be pretty damn good. That meant someone had told her to do it, but not why, because I'd bet my last dollar she really was blind to the shadow world.

A few people drifted out of the house and into the overgrown front garden, as if all they'd heard was a simple knock.

Crap! So they hadn't all left? I pinched the bridge of my nose for a moment. I should have waited to pull my stunt show.

"Let's begin, shall we?" Monica's voice was not wobbly at all, though she'd locked her knees together.

"Wait," called out a voice that made my skin crawl. Any anger I felt toward Missy was burned up by the fury that *this one's* voice lit in me. It felt like a ticking time bomb.

"Um, Breena," Crash breathed out my name. "I can't believe I'm saying this, but you're hurting me. Ease off."

I barely heard him as he peeled my fingers off his arm, my hands settling into fists at my sides, finger-tips biting into my palms. My eyes were all for the lanky bastard who strode down the middle pathway toward the porch. His eyes were all for Monica, and he didn't once look my way. No, that's not entirely true. He glanced at me, but didn't seem to realize it was me. Ass.

Himself wore a three-piece suit and tie, a jaunty cap to hide his mostly bald head, and three days' worth of stubble. I suppose some people would think it made him look more approachable. I just wanted to kick him in the balls and be done with it. Okay, maybe I wanted to kick him in the balls, and then stomp on them when he went to the ground.

Of course, he swept the yard with his gaze as soon as he joined Monica on the porch, and he did a full-on double take when he saw me.

A look of satisfaction flashed across his features, then anger. He leaned into Monica and pointed me out, saying something as he did so. She glanced at me and frowned, and shook her head as if disagreeing with him. I thought I heard her say something about letting all bidders bid.

"That son of a…" I breathed out a number of my more creative curse words, several that my phone liked to autocorrect to duck. Ducking limp dick. Mother ducker. Jaw ticking, I stood my ground.

"He's not going to let you bid, is he?" Crash asked quietly.

My entire body shook with a hot rage that built with each passing second, and I couldn't answer him with anything but a shake of my head. I barely noticed that Crash had stepped away from me at first, and when I did, my anger only redoubled. He was acting as if I were contagious. Of course, he wanted the house for his own reasons—he wouldn't want an association with me to ruin his chances.

Monica beamed his way, and even winked at the crowd or, more specifically, Crash.

"Let's begin, shall we?"

3

Monica the realtor held her hand up, and started the bidding at one hundred thousand for my gran's house, the house that was supposed to be mine. I lifted my hand in answer, but her gaze swept right over me, and she pointed at someone to my right.

My jaw ticked and I tried again at one hundred fifty thousand. Again and again, her eyes and hand swept over me. I forced myself to look at Himself at her side, and he had the nerve, the ducking nerve!, to give me a smug smile that didn't reach his eyes. His hands were at his sides and he spread them a little, palms facing me as if to say *what did you expect?* Of course, he might also be getting back at me for the little display Corb and I put on for him.

Rat bastard indeed.

I had twenty thousand in my bag as a down payment, but I wouldn't be able to use it if I couldn't get a bid in. Not that it looked like it was going to matter—the auction was already above my pay grade.

Gran appeared in the doorway, and her eyes flicked to my far right, her left. I followed her gaze to Crash, who was bidding, but she shook her head, so I moved it further to the right. Missy stood there, silently bidding with just a flick of her cane when it was her turn.

Monica called out, "Four hundred thousand."

Missy lifted her hand. The house was now far out of my league.

I blew out a breath I'd sucked in as Crash nodded in response to Monica's query for more money. They were the only two left in the auction; the rest of the group was just watching now to see the outcome.

What was I going to do?

Think girl, think! I heard my gran's voice say, although this was my inner gran, not her ghost. *You aren't some inexperienced woman. You've got years of life experience under your belt, and years of working at a law firm too. You've got to do something or you're going to lose any chance you have at getting the house.*

If I could distract Missy long enough…maybe Crash would get the house. If he didn't have to pay as much, then maybe he'd be grateful? What his gratitude would do for me I didn't know, but something told me Missy was more dangerous. For now, anyway. For all I knew, she'd been in on Hattie's plan. I didn't want her to increase her strength with what-ever Gran had hidden for me in the house. All of that flashed through my brain in milliseconds and I came to a quick decision.

I strode across the garden, pushing several tall stalks of herbs out of my way to get to where Missy stood. She was so intent on her bidding war with Crash that she didn't notice. Kinkly floated down from a tree branch to land on my right shoulder, light as a feather. "Careful," she warned.

When I stood right behind Missy, I whispered, "I have her book."

Missy whipped around and stared hard at me. "What?"

A chance was all I was going to get. I didn't take my eyes off her as I flipped open the bag on my hip and pulled out the red leather-bound book, cra-dling it in my arm. I knew she'd recognize it. The front cover, hand etched with a crescent moon and a spattering of stars, was one of a kind, much like the handwritten pages inside. "This is what you're look-ing for, isn't it?" I stared down at the book, stroking the cover. "Written in her hand."

"Give it to me," she hissed, reaching for it. I jerked it away from her hands. "Celia left that book for me, and someone stole it from the house."

"Going once."

I shrugged. "I bought it fair and square. It doesn't bother me none that you had it first."

Her eyes about bugged out, which was not a good look on her. "Bought it? From who?"

"I don't think that really matters, now does it? I mean, I paid for it, and it's in my possession. I have the letter of the law—both human and shadow world—on my side." I smiled suddenly. "You wouldn't want to go against the council, would you?" The council being the thirteen supernaturals who oversaw the shadow world in Savannah. From what I understood, there was a mishmash of supernaturals on the council, from witches to necromancers, from shifters to leprechauns.

It was probably an idle threat. I didn't have much clout, plus I'd only met one of the council members, Darv, and he was a pretentious little prick who thought he was smarter than anyone else because he had a pair of balls dangling between his legs.

"Going twice."

I stared hard at Missy as her head started to turn toward Monica. "You won't believe what I found in here." I tapped the book and her eyes whipped back toward me, narrowing so rapidly I thought for a moment that she'd closed them.

A muttered word and her left hand began to glow. "Give it to me now, and I won't hurt you." Kinkly let out a squeak and Missy's eyes shot to the fairy. "Filthy vermin." Her hand lifted as if she intended to toss a spell at Kinkly. I'd seen her do it before. Zap fairies, that is, or really any supernatural creature she thought unworthy of air.

I grabbed her hand and her magic crawled over my arm, stealing my breath. The urge to bend my knee and my head under the pain was so sharp I couldn't breathe around it. Instead, I threw her hand to the side and sucked in a big gulp of air.

I tucked the book into my bag and took a step back, drawing her with me, fighting to keep my voice even. "I will never give it to you. It was my gran's magic that gave you and Hattie the strength to be far more than you ever could have been on your own. And Kink is a friend, and under my protection." I was guessing here, based on a few partially forgotten conversations from my teen years, but by the way her face began to purple at the edges, my shot in the dark had hit home. My gran had led the three of them in spell casting, mostly protective spells from what I could remember. Keeping the spirits of Savannah from rising up and attacking its citizens—you know, the usual. Not that I'd been any good at it, no matter how many times they'd tried to teach me. I just didn't have my gran's knack for spells. "Now that Hattie's gone, you don't even have her to draw off. You should have tried harder to keep her alive."

White-hot rage leached the color from her face. I'd seen her like that before. Basically any time my gran disagreed with her. Which had happened, although not often.

Here's to pissing off old ladies who could kill you in your sleep. That was one thing it seemed I *did* have a knack for.

Which made me think about Hattie, and how we still didn't know why she'd wanted to call that demon.

My distraction cost me.

A mumbled string of words flowed off the tip of Missy's tongue and her hand flicked at me, just an outward snap of her fingers, before I could so much as step sideways. The spell, or more likely it was a curse, sent sizzling sparkles toward me. They hit me right in the chest and sunk through my shirt in a flash. I could feel them brushing over me, but only for a moment before the necklace talisman my gran had sent me heated up against my skin, giving off a flare of light under my shirt. Missy stumbled back as her magic rebounded off that talisman.

Go Gran!

"Miss-ssy." I growled her name, as if she were a bad dog. She glared at me, then slowly her glare slid into a smirk.

"You have no idea what you've stepped into," Missy stepped close and whisper-hissed at me, then shook one knobby finger right at the tip of my nose. "You aren't your gran. Not by a long shot. You will regret ever—"

"Sold!" The word rang out above everything else and I slumped where I stood. I'd kept Missy from buying my gran's house, but I hadn't been able to bid on it either.

Missy shook her head at me. "You are still the foolish little girl who ran off all those years ago. You have no idea what you've done." She spun on her heel, sending her long skirts out in a flared circle that knocked a few patches of lavender down as she made her exit. She paused at the gate and looked back, as if seeing Crash for the first time. She swung her cane

41

and pointed it at him. "You dabble in things you'd best stay out of, boy."

Crash stared hard at her. "Missy, take your useless spells and go bother someone else."

Oh, snap! Her face closed down and she huffed her way out of the gate. Okay, now seriously, he'd been hot enough *before* he'd stared down my nemesis and sent her on her way. Damn. Why did the bad boys have to be so ducking good at comebacks?

The other bidders left rapidly, but one stayed behind. Crash. Of course he was the one who'd actually made the purchase.

He stood speaking with Monica, who alternately beamed up at him and glared at me. Of course, I'd distracted the other bidder, which meant the price hadn't gone up as high as it could have. I hoped that Crash appreciated my contribution.

Himself, who stood to the left of Monica the realtor, didn't bother to hide his distaste. His eyes all but shot laser beams at me. "I want to do another auction," he said, loud enough that I could hear.

I made myself move closer, if for no other reason than to piss off my ex.

Monica barely glanced at Alan as she took the paperwork from Crash, his signature clearly on it. Though his name wasn't Crash. I leaned in to get a better look, but all I saw was a fancy G before Monica folded the papers. "Well, no, that's not how this works. You see, everyone who placed a bid signed a contract agreeing the sale would be final if they won. We can't have another auction—you've sold the house."

Well damn, I didn't even get that piece of paper! There had been no chance for me then, even if the price had been right.

"Not for what it was worth!" Himself snapped. "It didn't go over half a million, and you promised me it would! She distracted one of the bidders on purpose!"

I tucked my hands into my pockets and closed the distance between the small group and me. "Well, I suppose it could have gone over that, if you'd allowed everyone to bid. But you didn't, did you?" I made one of those fake pouty faces, scrunching my lips up. "Pity you were so short-sighted. I would have paid double what he did." I tipped my head at Crash.

Monica's eyes bugged out, no doubt thinking about the commission she would have had, and if I'd thought Himself couldn't glare any harder, he was proving me wrong.

"You don't have any money," Himself said.

I opened my bag and pulled out the wad of bills. No, twenty grand wouldn't have gotten me far, but it looked good in my hands. "You're right, I'm totally broke." And then I stuffed the money back in my bag.

Monica's face slowly went red as she turned on Himself. "You said we needed to exclude her from the bidding because she didn't have any money!"

Oh yeah, get him, Monica!

I smiled and turned to Crash, my smile slipping. "Congratulations. Maybe I can swing by to...have tea sometime." I didn't want to say to see my gran, but he nodded like he understood.

"Actually, I have to discuss a business proposition with you," he said. "Will you come inside?"

Monica was right up in Himself's face now, all Southern hospitality gone as she ripped a verbal strip off him for costing her so much commission. Of course, she'd made her sale, and she was probably grateful she no longer had to walk in glass slippers with him.

Listening to someone else berate him was like music to my ears. A symphony I would replay over and over in the wee hours of the night.

I left Monica to it, following Crash up the stairs into Gran's house—I would never think of it as Crash's—and then into the kitchen. He turned to face me as he reached the butcher block counter. I slowed in the doorway and just breathed in the smell that still lingered from Gran—herbs, for the most part, but there was also a hint of her perfume.

"I have to go on a trip," Crash said. "I'm leaving Feish behind and I don't want her to be alone."

"Afraid your slave will escape?" I bit the words out, still not for one second happy about my friend's situation.

Yeah, see, I hadn't forgotten that bit about Crash. Feish—a river maid who rather resembled a fish—was, for all intents and purposes, a slave to Crash. Something I was not impressed with in the least, even if he seemed to treat her well.

44

Crash didn't so much as crack a smile. "No. She gets lonely and scared on her own. I want to know if you'll stay here with her while I'm gone."

"Here? As in my gran's house? This is your new hideout? I thought it would be an investment. You know, swindle the tourists and all that jazz."

He looked to the ceiling as if seeking inspiration from above. "Hardly a hideout. The place on Factors Row is done for a lot of reasons and the original owners want it back. The basement here will be my new shop."

I didn't know what to say. At first I wanted to jump on the countertop and shout *yes* to the rooftops. Living here would get me out of Corb's loft, and judging by his cupboard of lube, he was counting the days till I left. He was a young guy who wanted to party it up with the ladies, and despite the kiss we'd shared, I was most certainly not on his list.

But Crash was still one of the bad guys, or bad-guy adjacent, and I was wary of deepening our connection. An image of stealing a couple of Corb's extra lubes just in case Crash decided I was more than a pain in the ass flashed through my mind, a little more enticing than any scenario involving *Boy Butter* should have been. "I don't know if that's a good idea."

His eyes shot to Kinkly sitting on my shoulder, and she cringed as if he'd taken a swing at her. "Hanging with the fairies now? That's dangerous for a human."

I shrugged, and Kinkly gave a nervous giggle with the roll of my shoulders. "I laugh in the face of

45

danger. HA!" I smiled up at him. "I got gum out of her wings with some of Corb's extra-slick lube, and she did my makeup. It was a good deal. Nothing more." I was not about to tell him I'd agreed to speak to her lady friend.

His face was a careful blank, his tone just as careful. "Extra-slick lube?"

"No olive oil." I shrugged again, also keeping my face blank. Let him think what he wanted. "That man has about thirty buckets of the slick stuff in his bathroom."

Now Crash's lips did twitch. "No he doesn't."

Kinkly stood up and shook a tiny finger at him. "I saw them, he does. I don't know what bacon has to do with sex, but there was a lot of it…"

I laughed and put a hand over my eyes. "Blinded! I'm blinded, I tell you."

Yeah, the more I thought about it, the more I knew I needed to get out of the loft. I'd never be able to use that bathroom without thinking of the stockpile of lube. "How long would you need me to stay?"

"I'll be gone a few weeks, maybe two months at the outside," he said. I should've been happy I'd have Gran's house for that long, and I was, but I also felt a little sad that I wouldn't see him for a while. Or maybe I just missed the sight of his body wrapped up in a sheet—my usual view of him given my habit of visiting while he was asleep.

"So two months." I wiggled my lips, thinking. "And then when you get back?"

"You go to wherever you go. I don't share my home with anyone but Feish."

I could get my own place. Already my mind was racing ahead, trying to figure out where I'd be in two months.

If I took the job from the lady Kinkly wanted me to see…maybe it would pay enough for me to get out on my own again. Well, to be fair, the money in my bag was enough, but the longer I could save it the better. As of right now it was off the books, and the creditors Himself had set on me didn't know about it—even if he did. Damn it, I suddenly wished I hadn't flashed the money at him. Because if it was up to me, the creditors wouldn't. I needed to find a way to foist the debt back onto him, that's what I needed.

I looked around the kitchen. Would two months be long enough for me to find whatever Gran had hidden? It would have to be because there was no way I could afford this place, and now that Crash had it, there was no way he'd sell it to me. Would he?

"You want to sell me the house?" I had to try.

"No." His lips twitched as he leaned forward, closing the distance between us. Kinkly squeaked and flew away, perching on top of the oven range hood. I held my ground even as the air between us heated up in a most pleasant and uncomfortable way.

His eyes dipped to my lips, and I couldn't help the way my breathing hitched. "Don't," I said.

"Don't what?" The smile curving his mouth said he knew exactly what I was talking about.

I leaned into him. "Don't think I'd give you my body for the house."

His eyes popped wide and I barked a laugh as the words kept coming, my filter broken and my ducks no longer in a row but quacking away like mad. "Kidding. I'm kidding. I'd totally do you for the house."

Crash stared at me, his eyes crinkling at the edges as if he were fighting back a smile. "I don't know what to make of you."

"There's a club for that, monthly fees, and a T-shirt if they have any left." I smiled, a tiny wave of nefarious giggles threatening to break free. Broken filters were fun, especially around those who didn't realize you were done caring what anyone else thought. I mean, it wasn't like I could impress him either way. So why not just have fun with it?

He didn't step back, and he seemed to be at a loss for words. I sighed.

"Deal. I'll stay here for two months."

He held out his hand and we shook on it, which in the shadow world was as binding as any contract.

The problem? Part of me feared I'd jumped into poop creek without a paddle or a life preserver.

4

"Please, please come to see the lady now?" Kinkly whispered as she flew around my head while I walked away from Gran's house. The heat of the day was coming on strong, and the weight of the pollen in the air was a palpable thing.

I weighed my options. The job might be a bad one, but I had promised Kinkly I'd at least talk to *the lady*, plus I still had hours left before I was supposed to show up for training with Eammon and the other mentors at the Hollows Group.

"Where is she?" I asked.

"Follow me!" Kinkly shot out ahead of me, and I did as she asked. She was easy to spot amongst the tourists and locals who ambled along the streets. No one was in a hurry, and no one so much as looked at her. Well, that wasn't entirely true. Someone took a swing at her as they yelped "big ass bugs," and then she was gone in a burst of orange light, fluttering near a tree. She was leading me south through downtown Savannah, a meandering route that took us past a few of the squares, plus the infamous Hanging Tree. The demon that lived there had caused enough problems for the human world to take notice.

"Don't get too close," she whispered, zipping back to me to sit on my shoulder. "He's a right prick."

I skirted the large tree as a tour group paused in front of it, the guide explaining how it had earned its reputation. Picking up my pace, I hurried past the twisted up Hanging Tree, caught a glimpse of eyes watching me from the branches above and then jerked my gaze away. From the book of Gran:

Do not make eye contact with a demon. They can pull your deepest desires from you.

I didn't dare run—that was another no-no—but I kept my pace brisk and took note when Kinkly left my shoulder. "Why did you take us that way if you don't like the tree?"

She twisted around in the air in front of me. "What?"

My eyes narrowed with irritation as I caught on to what she was doing. See, that's the thing. I'd lived with a master manipulator for years, and Himself was a lawyer, so he knew how to screw someone over and make it legal. I could pick up when people were testing me. "Wait, you wanted to see how I'd react to a demon?"

Her wings picked up speed. "Come on, we need to be there when the sun is highest in the sky. Hurry please!"

I refused to do more than a fast walk if that was how she was going to be, dragging me around past demon-possessed trees!

"Why? What are you worried about?" I said, slowing even further.

"I…" She tipped her head from side to side, agitation clear on her tiny features. "The lady wanted to make sure you are not attached to a demon. We heard a rumor that you killed one. If that were true, it could have meant that you were in fact working with another one. Killing demons is no small thing, and you're just a human."

She wasn't wrong about that last piece. I crinkled up my nose and wiped a bit of sweat off my forehead. "Fine. I get it, you don't want to trust my word. I know that's how the shadow world works." Didn't mean I had to like it. I swiped at my brow again.

Spring it might be, but warm it certainly was… only…I glanced up at the sky as the light around us suddenly dimmed. Well, damn it. The air tightened around us, the deepening humidity a sign of an oncoming storm that I hadn't anticipated. When I picked up the pace after all, Kinkly smirked at me. But it was too late—as I followed her on a merry chase, running much more adeptly than I would have a few weeks ago, the sky opened up before

51

we reached our destination. Tourists scattered, but I kept running, the rain soaking me through in a matter of seconds. I might as well have walked into a waterfall. I shaded my face with one hand. "Kinkly, how much further?"

The fairy zipped this way and that and I realized she was dodging the drops of water as they fell from the sky. "The fountain!"

I blinked through the water streaming over my eyes. She'd led me to Forsyth Park. The most stunning of all the Savannah squares, it was full of flowers nearly year round, perfectly groomed with a massive fountain not quite in the middle of it. A fountain that was the draw for every person who went to the park. Which meant I must have heard her wrong. "What?"

"Into the fountain, the way will open!" She zipped forward through the rain, diving under the first swell of water that rushed over the fountain, and then she was gone, completely out of sight.

Standing at the edge of the fountain, I looked over the rim to the water. The piece itself was two-tiered, with a large statue on top. The water that poured over it was heavier than usual with the addition of the rain, making a perfect curtain, not unlike that waterfall I was considering earlier.

Sighing, I hopped over the black wrought iron fence, and let myself down into the pool of water at the base of the fountain.

I hissed as the cold water filled my shoes and slid up my legs to mid-calf. Sloshing forward, I headed straight for the base of the fountain, which I couldn't see anymore under the torrent of water.

The smell of honey and fresh bread wrapped around me and tugged me forward the last couple of steps. The water parted around me rather than soaking me, and I blinked as I stepped into a place that could not possibly exist. It just couldn't.

A meadow spilled out in front of me, extending literally as far as I could see, with soft rolling green hills dotted with a myriad of wildflowers. Warm air rolled over me, and my clothing and hair instantly dried. A few smaller animals bounded and played among the long grass and flowers, but I saw nothing larger than a few bunnies and some songbirds dipping through the air, calling to one another. I did a slow turn and saw a fountain identical to the one I'd left behind. "That's the in and out?" I asked.

According to Gran's book, there was always a doorway in and out of Faerie—or what the average person would call fairy land. Looked like the fountain was the way station for this place. Of course it was, I was being an idiot and getting stuck on the in and out because I was having a hard time believing I wasn't asleep and having a seriously wild dream.

A flutter of wings turned me forward again.

Kinkly motioned at me with both hands. "Come on, this way. Lady Karissa waits for you at the seeing pool."

I took a step, then stopped and frowned, recognizing the name but not placing it. "Lady Karissa?"

"Yes, that's her!" Kinkly smiled and flew away before I could ask her another question. I strode after her, parting the long grass with ease, the stalks reaching to my elbows and the seed heads tickling me. As we walked, I took note that the landscape didn't change much. The wind was warm, the air sweet, the scenery beautiful, but it felt...empty. Even the smaller critters were gone now.

A glance to the left showed a glittering sea, the waves beckoning, but there was no accompanying sound of crashing water. It felt like I was looking at a painting, like the waves weren't even moving. I shook my head.

"Enough to drive one crazy." My gaze shifted forward again, and I took two more steps and stumbled to a stop. A ring of trees lay ahead of me, clustered tightly together except for a narrow opening. That hadn't been there when I'd stopped to look at the glittering but lifeless sea. I found myself touching the bag on my hip, feeling for the knives that I always carried with me. They had gotten me out of a scrape or two already. I really hoped I didn't have to pull them out here.

The waist-high grass around me parted as I walked toward the ring of trees. Kinkly didn't hesitate but shot ahead into the middle of the space and landed on a tree branch on the right-hand side. I stood at the entrance for a moment and took stock of what I was really looking at.

The seeing pool was a circular ring of metal about four feet around just set on the ground with what looked like a mirror nestled within it. So not water at all. I took a couple of steps in, wanting a better look, and the trees behind me groaned and closed off my escape route. Across from me, a shadow dipped away through the far trees, but I couldn't make out if the person was even male or female. Or a person. But whoever or whatever it was, it was slinking, definitely slinking.

"Kinkly, did you lead me into a trap?" I asked as I slid my bag strap off my shoulder and reached in carefully for my knives.

"No, but if I did I'd say no too, so maybe? No. I don't think so?" She seemed uncertain by the end, which did not bode well. "I hope not."

Yeah, that did not bode well at all. What had I gotten myself into this time?

I should have paid more attention to my gran's book. I knew better, but here I was following a fairy into the middle of a literal nowhere.

The far side of the ring of trees, right where that slinking shadow had dipped out of view, parted, the trees bending, almost bowing before the woman who stepped out of the shadows. A woman I recognized. "Karissa from *Vic's on the River*'s bathroom?"

Yeah, not exactly the classiest of greetings, or meetings for that matter.

Her hair was coiled up onto her head in an intricate crown braid, a weave of colors ranging from darkest black to a golden hue so bright it would rival actual gold. On top of the braid was a legit crown, though it was small, delicate, and very much an understated piece if you ignored the massive diamond in the middle of it the size of an orange. She'd been pretty at the restaurant, but my mind had forgotten the details of her, which meant some sort of fae magic had probably kept me from being able to identify her. Clever.

She wore that same lovely pantsuit and refined top that I *had* taken note of. Rather elegant, and understated like the crown. She clasped her hands in front of her, nails filed to perfect points and painted a deep red, closer to black than red. I took all the details in, the nails somehow keeping my attention more than anything else.

Her smile was soft, nothing like those nails. "Yes, we met quite by chance. I'd like to think it was fate bringing us together. Did the makeup help your confidence that day?"

I blinked a couple of times, reaching up to touch my face. Sure, it was dry, but no doubt the rain had washed all of Kinkly's hard work away. Hopefully it hadn't also left makeup stained all over my face. "Actually, I forgot that I was wearing it. Constant issue with me."

Her lips curled upward. "Excellent. I don't need a doddering old fool, or a woman obsessed with how she looks. I need help, Breena O'Rylee, and I do believe you are the only one who can actually help me."

I mimicked her stance, clasping my hands in front of my body. Like I said before with Kinkly, I knew manipulation when I saw it. Or, more accurately, when I felt it. Himself had taught me that much. "So what you mean is, Eammon turned you down." I suspected *he* was the doddering old fool, though I wasn't sure who the woman obsessed with her looks would be. Could it be Suzy? It was possible.

The frown that flashed across her face made me think of a lightning strike. There and gone before I was even sure I'd seen it, but the afterimage was burned into my mind.

Power. That was what she held, and she had it in spades.

If I weren't careful, I'd be on the receiving end of one of those lightning strikes.

"He did." She gave a slow nod. "In fact, every single one of the mentors turned me down."

"Why?" I looked her straight in the eye. "I assume you offered a good payment?"

"I did."

"So why would they turn you down? I get the sense they could use the money."

Her jaw twitched. "I need someone to watch over a fairy ring for me. Starting now, and running for as long as ten days."

So she didn't want to tell me why Eammon had turned her down? Interesting. I'd have to circle back to it.

"Ten days. During what time periods, or are you looking for solid surveillance?"

"Ten days, specifically between three a.m. and noon. When you finish your training tonight, you will go straight there." Her eyes, I realized, were many colors, shifting with the light around us. At that moment they were soft gray, like clouds.

"And what exactly would I be surveying?" I unclasped my hands. "Something dangerous?"

"No, a fairy ring is full of fairies." Karissa walked around the metal ring toward me. "They are doing important work, and I need to ensure they are not disturbed. I cannot be there at all times."

I doubted she was telling me everything, or even a fraction of the truth. The urge to grab Gran's book and do a quick read-up on fairies was strong. Later, I'd look later. "Okay, so you can't be there at all times, and you want me to watch over them. So who exactly is going to bother them?"

Her face paled and then tensed and then went back to being pale. "This is where I'm not sure. The Unseelie have been active lately, far more active than I have ever seen them. I fear that they will make a bid for my throne."

Pursing my lips, I nodded as if I knew what the hell she was talking about. Unseelie, the word tugged at my mind, but I couldn't place what an Unseelie was, so I went for the bluff.

"How exactly would they do that?" I raised both eyebrows. "I mean, would it be an insurrection, or is there some sort of object they'd need to steal, like your crown?"

Her lips tightened and I swear she rolled her eyes. "The crown is just a symbol. The relic the fairies are searching for is far more powerful and important. If the Unseelie get their hands on it, then it would mean war between the humans and the fae. That is the Unseelie goal, and trust me, you do not want that. No one—except the Unseelie—wants that." Her words had power and bite to them, but I let them roll off me. I wasn't going to be pushed into a job that Eammon and the rest of the Hollows had said no to.

"Is there a specific Unseelie you are worried about?" I really needed her to spell this out for me. "Could you give me a description so I at least know who to look for?"

Kinkly flew up to my right. "All Unseelie have a mark on them, a mark here." She spun and lifted up her hair, showing off the back of her neck. "A mark of the crescent moon showing that they walk in the darkness."

I stared at her. "So I'm supposed to ask anyone who shows up to lift their hair?"

"You can assume any who disturb the fairy ring are there to cause harm. They are either Unseelie or friends to the Unseelie." Karissa's voice was soft. "I realize this is a great task, and so the payment is accordingly high. I offer you one gemstone for every successful day that you watch over the fairy ring."

From her pantsuit pocket she pulled out a handful of stones. Precious gemstones. Very large gemstones that I knew would fetch some serious money. My friend Mavis had inherited a ruby ring from her grandfather—whom she quite rightly hated, but that's another story—and she'd sold it. That ring had been worth over twenty thousand dollars, and it was half the size of the gems I was looking at, and some of these were diamonds.

This was a two-hundred-thousand-dollar payday, on the low end, if the Hollows didn't get their cut. Maybe enough to convince Crash to sell me back my gran's house? No, I didn't think so either, but it would be a good start.

Still, I knew better than to be hasty. No amount of money could give me back my life if I was killed in the line of duty. And I wasn't a hundred percent sure that I wouldn't have to give the Hollows a cut regardless of their lack of involvement. I'd signed a contract with them. I'd have to look it over, see if there was a non-compete clause.

"What is the item?" I asked.

Her hands clenched. "It is a valuable artifact that holds the power to control all of Faerie. It has been found by the Unseelie. I must gain hold of it as soon as possible so I can hide it once more."

I pursed my lips, mulling her words over and looking for loopholes. "And you can't get it yourself, why? Because I can feel the power rolling off you. Shouldn't you be able to just pop on in there and grab it?"

She smiled and dipped her head. "You are perceptive; that is what I need in the one who watches over the fairy ring." Karissa paused and held out her hand, a ball of purple energy lifting above her palm. "Yes, I am powerful, but the spells laid over the fairy ring and the item in question are old, and a direct approach is not possible. Only a select few can break through the layers of protection." She snapped her fingers and the purple energy slid away.

"And who are these select few?" I found myself more than passing curious as to what could be more powerful than her.

She shook her head. "I have told you far more than I had thought to as it is. That is enough. The spells will be weakened as the fairies cut through the layers of protection. When the layers are thin, then you must tell me immediately."

That made little sense, but I supposed the situation would be clearer to me once I saw what was actually going on. "I have one more question."

"You are full of questions," she said. "Curiosity killed the cat."

"But satisfaction brought it back." I smiled at her. "Satisfy my last question. This sounds like an easy job, easy money. Tell me why Eammon and the others wouldn't work for you—the truth now—and I'll consider the job."

See? Circling back.

Her eyes flashed and above us the sky rumbled. Yeah, lightning was definitely in her toolkit. The hair along my arms and the back of my neck prickled upward with the pull of the electricity in the air.

"They do not like my first husband, that is part of it." Her eyes kept on flashing as every muscle in her seemed to tense. "To be fair, I don't like him much either. This one is my preference." She snapped her fingers, and a slim figure stepped out of the trees to my left, startling me. Pale blond hair braided back from his head, bright blue eyes, a sharp jaw, and soft lips were paired with a body that was still to my mind somewhat underdeveloped. He reminded me of that elf from the *Lord of the Rings* movie (don't ask me his name, I can't remember those wild fantasy names with more vowels than consonants. The cute elf, you know who I mean!).

"Pretty boy." I spat the two words out before my filter kicked in. Karissa laughed as she smoothed her hands against his bare chest.

"Yes, he is a pretty boy, and so obedient. I don't like men who can't be brought to heel. This one is eager to please, never argues, never causes me grief, and does all he can to make me happy."

I couldn't resist. "Did you kill the first one?"

Her laughter rang through the trees. "No, he is far too strong, though I would if I could. I cut all ties with him, but he is…hard to untangle oneself from. I am still connected to him as all women are connected to their ex-spouses. An offensive thought." She wasn't wrong. "My ex…he is a blacksmith, of all things."

I nodded, but my brain was working in overdrive.

Remember what I said about my ability to guess things? About my brain putting pieces together until sudden understanding would hit me like a ton of bricks tossed by a strongman? Yeah. That was usually a good thing.

Except this time I could all too easily see the shadowy character slipping away through the trees right before Karissa stepped out. There'd been something familiar about the figure—or at least its slinking. If I'd looked closer, would I have seen the broad shoulders of a man who'd entangled himself in my life too? I mean, how many supernatural black-smiths were there?

My mouth hung open, flapping as I tried to find the words. "Crap. Is your ex-husband Crash?"

5

"Get moving!" Eammon yelled. "What the hell, you bunch are the slowest recruits we've had in years!"

I tried to pick up speed, I really did. But running a two-mile lap around a graveyard in the remarkably high heat that spring brings in Savannah was no easy thing. Not dressed in work wear, which in my case was leather pants, a tank top, and the waist/thigh strap and sheath system that held my knives.

"Holster," I muttered to myself as the proper word for what I wore finally came to my oxygen-deprived brain. I had knife holsters on my thighs.

The other part of my brain kept on stuttering over what I'd learned that afternoon. Crash had an ex-wife. I don't know why that was surprising. I mean, he was gorgeous, and all full of manly alpha vibes that had my panties in a twist, so it wasn't exactly shocking that someone had wanted to lock that down. But damn it…did she have to be a fairy queen? A stunning, powerful, beautiful fairy queen? One that I kind of liked?

My feet slowed as I went over her request again. Watch over a fairy ring, get paid a giant ducking gemstone for every eight-hour shift. The thing was, I wasn't nineteen anymore, and while I was pretty sure I could pull one all-nighter, could I do ten or more in a row? With like four hours of sleep a day? I wasn't sure I could do it. Not that I'd agreed to. I'd left Karissa with the promise that I would answer her by the end of the night, before what would be my first shift.

I worried at my lower lip, thinking. I'd never had kids—not for lack of trying—but that meant I'd had little experience with the sleep deprivation camp that children put their mothers through. Sure, sure, dads too, but let's be real. Whose boob are they latched on to? Not daddy-o's.

A shake of my head freed me from the whole breastfeeding thought spiral. Crash had an ex-wife and she wanted me to work for her. I was living in a house that he owned. My mentor, Eammon, hated Crash because of a business deal gone sideways. I wiped sweat off my eyes before it could sting.

The job would bring in a heck-a-lot of money.

A job I didn't have to tell Eammon about, according to my contract. In my paperwork with the Hollows group, it said I was free to take on any additional work so long as it didn't interfere with the training and the Hollows group had already passed on the job. In fact, the wording was perfect to the point of being suspicious. The hours working for Karissa wouldn't overlap with my training, so I was technically in the clear.

Temptation called to me, and while I tried to tell myself I hadn't decided yet, I knew I had. I was going to take the job.

Kinkly was supposed to swing by after training to get my answer, and lead me to the fairy ring if my answer was yes. A grin curled my lips. Hell, yes, I was going to get Gran's house back one way or another. A couple more jobs like this, and I should have more than enough money to convince Crash to sell.

The other recruits were well ahead of me, hell, they'd lapped me already. To be fair, we weren't that far into our twelve-week training program. But I was the oldest of the group by nearly twenty years, and it showed when it came to the physical part of the training. At least I knew how to roll with the shadow world. Most of the others still freaked out regularly when exposed to an aspect of their new reality.

Poor Luke was the worst. He passed out from shock on a regular basis. Not good considering he was the resident young werewolf.

"You really are slow, you should go faster. Move your legs more. Like this." Kinkly's voice pulled my eyes to one side. She floated above a tombstone that had partially crumbled, her wings fluttering madly as if that would help me run faster.

"What are you doing here? I thought you were supposed to come by at the end of the training?" I'd left her behind at Forsyth Park and hurried back to Corb's place. He hadn't been there, which was good because I wasn't sure I wanted to hear his spluttering explanation about all the lube in the bathroom.

"Came early to watch you in action. Don't worry, the mentors won't see me, and if they do, they won't know about your visit with the queen."

I flapped a hand at her, rather frantically, to shut her up.

Werewolves had better hearing than most, and I was jogging toward Sarge, who stood next to the tombstone marking the entrance to the Hollows. As I drew closer, I realized his head was hanging low and he just looked...sad. Kinkly had ducked around behind the angel tombstone, so I said, or rather huffed, "Hey, Sarge, come run with me. Keep me company."

He lifted his eyes and slowly broke into a jog next to me. I'd say he was making fun of me, only I really wasn't moving that fast. Running is not my forte unless I'm running for my life, in which case I'm not half bad at it. I mean, I'd still die, but I'd give whatever was chasing me a good twenty-foot sprint.

"You look blue," I said as we jogged side by side. "What's got you down?"

"Unrequited love," he said with enough seriousness that it made me bite back a kneejerk quip.

I blinked up at him, not sure if he was joking. He was in his mid-thirties, built like a brick house—muscle for days—had lovely amber eyes, a great sense of humor, and was for the most part pretty sweet. "Seriously? Who wouldn't want you?"

Oops, I'm not sure I was supposed to blurt that out. I'm going to blame it on the lack of blood flowing to my brain as it fought to keep my body moving. He, like Corb, was a hot potato that my raging hormones would love to wrap their greedy little hands around. Sure, he was a werewolf, but I liked dogs just fine.

Woof, woof.

He barked a low laugh. "Thanks, Bree. I think that…no, never mind. I'm used to it, and I'll get over it. How did it go at the auction today?"

Ah, so he knew about that then, did he? "Well, I didn't get the house." I didn't slow to a walk, but my jogging was so slow I might as well have been walking. "They didn't even let me bid. Himself made sure of it."

"Himself?"

"Yeah, it's what I call my ex. He thinks so highly of himself, and I hate saying his name, so it seemed to fit. It just popped out of me one day, and after that it stuck." I paused and then went through what had happened at the auction, including the parts where I'd kept Missy from bidding so Crash could get the house.

"You should try to separate yourself from Crash," he said, but it felt like he was saying the words by rote, like maybe he didn't really believe them. I frowned up at him.

"You know, we might not have known each other all that long, but I can tell when you're saying something you don't believe. Why should I stay away from him?" I asked. "I mean, don't get me wrong, I'm trying to keep my distance, but I want my gran's house back, and he's in the way."

His unusual amber eyes met and held my gaze. "It's what I'm supposed to say. I'm a mentor, I shouldn't be encouraging you to be involved with, or hang around, characters who have been deemed shady by the council."

Huh. So this wasn't just about Eammon's beef. Crash had pissed off everyone. I had a feeling *deemed shady* was worse than it sounded. Tack that on to him being the fairy queen's ex…

He really was a bad boy.

I didn't like the shiver that thought sent through my body.

We jogged past three tombstones before I spoke again, choosing my words carefully. "So—hypothetically, of course—if I told you that Crash had offered to let me stay in my gran's house for two months, to help keep Feish from being lonely, you'd tell me not to do it. Right?"

Sarge startled, and for just a moment, I could have sworn he'd brightened up. "Hypothetically answering, I'd be obligated to tell you it's a bad idea. But I do think Corb could use some space. He's mentioned to me more than once that he wishes you weren't underfoot. And if Crash isn't there, you should be fine."

I thought again about the buckets of lube under the sink and the fact that I'd interrupted Corb's carnal activities the night I'd arrived in Savannah. Tried not to think about the panty-melting kiss he'd given me just a few short days ago. That was just...that was nothing. I cleared my throat. "Yeah, I agree. I think he needs to get laid."

Sarge grinned then, bright as the sun, more his normal jovial self. "You'd better believe it. But who'll do the dirty work?"

I laughed as his eyes swept over me, and again I had to banish a curl of heat from my body. "Don't look at me, I won't be the one doing the laying. I'm the *old lady*, remember? Besides, he probably couldn't keep up with me in that department. He's well past his prime in his thirties, and I"—I touched a hand between my breasts—"am just swinging into my best years of a libido that will not die."

Sarge's eyes went wide, a slow look of what could only be called horror flicking across his face. As if his mother had started talking about orgasms. Multiple, mind-blowing orgasms.

I laughed at him as we both slowed to a walk. "Please, you're telling me that you didn't know that women sexually peak in their late thirties?"

He cleared his throat. "I try not to think about women in their late thirties and sex in the same mental space."

70

My jaw dropped. Oh, snap. I mentally scratched him off my Hot List. That kind of mentality was not attractive, not in the least. I scrunched up my face and bent at the waist with a hand to my back. "Oh, me aching back, it hurts me fierce, young lad! Nothing like the big O to make it better. Would you be helping me out?"

The look of horror he'd given me before was nothing compared to his current grimace. "Are you speaking like a pirate again?"

I straightened up. "Whatever. I was going for old."

"Terrible. On so many levels." That last bit was whispered and I was probably not supposed to hear him, but I did. Yeah, he was off the Hot List. In fact, he was officially on the Not List. Even if he begged like the wolf he was, he would not be upgraded.

Nothing like acting like a jackass to kill whatever good looks God blessed you with.

He rubbed his hands over his face as if he could wipe away the image of me having sex. Yeah, total jerk. "Look, I'll back you up if you want to take that room at your gran's. That would give Corb some space I think he desperately needs, which will in turn make him less cranky—and thus easier to work with. All of that to say, I think you can handle Crash, especially since he won't be there, and the risk is worth it in my opinion."

Part of me wanted to say thank you, the other part wanted to be offended that he clearly thought so little of me and my fellow forty-plus women. Plus, he made it sound like I was a horrible roommate. Corb hadn't seemed all that cranky to me, but then I didn't work with him like Sarge did. I settled for a nod. "Thanks. I think."

He clapped me on the back, sent me stumbling off to the side with the blow, then peeled off to go run with his trainee, Luke, swatting him on the ass when he got close. "Men," I muttered at the locker room behavior. I considered trying to keep up with them, but they took off like a pair of sprinters, laughing and chasing each other.

Of all the trainees, I was fondest of Luke. He'd gone into this whole thing so he could pay down his dying mother's medical debt, but he wasn't getting out. Sarge had bitten him, and now he would become a werewolf. Or maybe he already was? I'd have to look it up in Gran's book.

"Go easy on the kid, Sarge," I whispered. Sarge turned back to look at me, just a fleeting glance, and gave me a nod. Because of course he'd heard me, damn werewolf ears. I glanced at where Kinkly had flown and saw her perched on the angel's shoulder. She lifted both hands above her head, a raise the roof move. I gave her two thumbs up.

I made myself walk at a brisk pace, jogging where I could. My muscles felt like water and there was enough sweat flowing from my skin that I could have watered a garden in the Sahara Desert. I swiped a hand across my face, under my eyes—again. The graves around me were mostly unkempt, stones in disrepair, and names so old that they could no longer be read. From the corner of my eye, I caught the swaying of an all-too-familiar figure.

"Robert, I haven't seen you for a few days." I slowed to a stop and Robert made his way to me. He was not your typical friend, not by any means, but he was loyal and had saved my bacon more than once.

Robert was a skeleton with long dark hair that covered his face and head. I'd never fully seen his face, but I knew he had teeth in there somewhere. He swayed as he walked, his clothing a tattered mess on his narrow frame. With his clothes on, you couldn't really tell he was a skeleton. The rags hid the worst of the bones, but here and there I saw bits of white.

I patted my bag. "I brought you something."

His swaying slowed as I pulled a flask from the leather bag hanging against my hip. He'd asked for whiskey, and after all the help he'd given me on my last job, he'd more than earned it. I'd only put two shots of whiskey in the flask, not knowing how it would affect him, and also because it was Corb's bottle.

I held out the flask, which he took carefully, almost, dare I say, reverently. "Friend," he whispered.

I wasn't sure if he was labelling me or the whiskey his friend. Maybe both. "Cheers, Robert. And thanks again for all your help."

He tipped his head back to down the whiskey, which gave me a look at the vertebrae that held his head on. The whiskey slid through his mouth and trickled down his body, following the line of yel-lowy-white bones until it dribbled onto the ground below him in a puddle that would have looked more than suspicious under anyone else.

He handed the flask back to me and I tucked it into my bag.

Then he hiccupped and whispered, "Friends," which was quickly followed by a wobble of his feet and a weird-sounding giggle. He toppled to the ground, wrapped himself around one of the tombstones, and started snoring.

"What the hell?" I put a toe against one of his cloth-covered feet. I could tell from the resistance against my boot, or lack thereof, that there were only bones under the material. "Robert?"

I crouched by the tombstone, using it for balance even as I cursed my tight hamstrings. My backside and thighs screamed at me, but I lowered myself close enough to poke at him again. "Robert, are you okay?" I didn't think I could kill an already dead skeleton, per se, but I didn't want anything to happen to him. Robert was, if nothing else, super protective of me. In the shadow world it was a good thing to have friends with some oomph in their bite.

Voices caught my attention, cutting through the early evening air. I stayed where I was and looked over my right shoulder to check out the newcomers. Two figures walked toward the entrance to the Hollows Group training facility, more specifically toward the tomb with the broken-winged angel. Fluttering at the top was Kinkly, frantically motioning for me to stay down, which I did.

I froze in my crouch as the figures both did a quick sweep of the area and the shorter of the two pointed at the group of running trainees at the far end of the graveyard. Where I should have been.

"The newbs are out there, we have time," the one figure said. Male, with a nondescript voice that I didn't recognize. Middling height, frame, nothing unusual stood out about him.

"Good, I heard that one of their trainees ruined the ceremony. We were able to salvage something, but…trouble." I knew this guy's voice. I just couldn't place it. But bless his heart, he was talking about little old me! I pressed my fingers against my temples, trying to figure out just where I'd heard his voice before.

When it hit me, I literally staggered and ended up on my knees behind the tombstone. This was the guy who'd threatened my life. How could I have forgotten him? On my first visit to Crash to procure blades, this douche canoe had shown up and demanded that Crash make him a special crucible. Crash had agreed, but told DC (douche canoe, stay with me) that making it would take time. Said DC had then threatened my life if the crucible wasn't made on his timeline. With all that had been going on, that particular death threat had slipped my mind.

So just what the hell was he doing here? Not to make good on his death threat, or at least I didn't think that was the case.

I watched from around the corner of the tombstone as the two men, who were apparently oblivious to me, went down the long curving stairs that would take them into the Hollows.

I waited about five seconds before I pulled myself to my feet, cursed at the tingling in my lower legs, and then sprinted as fast as I could to cover the distance between me and the angel tomb. Hands on the gray-veined marble, I slid around the edge until I could peer down the stairwell.

Once more, voices floated up to me.

In for a penny, in for a pound or ten.

I took the first step, then paused to make sure there was no one coming up the stairs in a hurry. The Hollows was wrapped up in some sort of magic that I was still trying to fully grasp, but one of its eccentricities was that the stairs always stayed pitch black. Good for me, because I was going further down to listen to what was going on from the darkness of the stairwell.

At least that was my plan.

Of course, my plans had a habit of not going as, well, planned.

MOON | 18

6

Standing there in the darkness of the stairwell of a tomb in the graveyard that I was supposed to be running around, it struck me that this might have been one risk too many.

I mean, the one dude had threatened my life, and if they were potential customers, Eammon wouldn't want me to mess things up with my eavesdropping. Still, I lowered myself onto one of the steps to listen in. Because let's be honest, if they were working with Crash, then they likely were not working with the Hollows Group.

"Grave consequences," Tom said, his voice rumbling up to me. "Grave indeed." He was one of the

Hollows mentors—the calm one of the bunch, as far as I could tell.

Louis was up next, his French accent heavier than usual. "What exactly do you expect us to do about it? You can't imagine we will—"

"There will be jobs offered to you. Do not take them if you value the lives of your trainees." There, that was Douche Canoe throwing his weight around again. He was threatening our lives to get his way, just like he'd done with Crash. Of course, Crash probably didn't care too much about the threat, but I wasn't terribly worried for my safety. He was a *do the job no matter what the cost* kind of guy. He wouldn't make the crucible to save me—he'd make it to get paid. From what I could tell, a job was a job to him. I sighed. What a waste of a hunk of handsome man. Maybe that was why Karissa had booted him to the curb. Too much forging of weapons, not enough nooky at home.

I shook myself, and realized I'd missed part of the conversation I was supposed to be listening to.

"You'd best keep it in mind, Eammon," Douche Canoe growled.

"Get out," Eammon snapped. "Your kind are not welcome here."

Get him, Eammon! I wanted to cheer my mentor on, but I held my tongue. Good thing, too, since the next thing I heard was a number of footsteps headed my way. My heartrate spiked and I bolted up the stairs, scrambling to keep my feet quiet but faster than the approaching pair of men.

Ninja I was not, and I knew that there was at least one loud clatter as I ricocheted off the sidewall of the stairs. Hopefully their ears weren't any better than mine. I burst out of the stairwell, grabbed the edge of the angel tombstone, and pulled myself around it before dropping to the ground. The exceptionally large mosquito buzzing in my ear had me cringing. I couldn't even swing at it.

Worse yet, the mosquito landed on my shoulder and whispered, "Are they still in there?"

"Shush!" I hissed at Kinkly as I pressed my back against the tombstone, crouching down as far as I could get.

"Are the trainees out there?" Douche Canoe asked.

"I count them all."

"Good. I want you to keep track of them. As I told Eammon, I will not be thwarted. Our plans will move forward one way or another, no matter the cost."

I wanted to laugh, I really did. Because I was the 'oldie' of this group, and even I thought his manner of speech was ridiculously old school. Yes, I know in theory that forty-one isn't that old, but when you're hanging with a bunch of early twenty-year-olds, you *are* the oldie.

And for those who want to disagree with me about how a forty-one-year-old thinks and feels, you can stuff it. Not everyone rocks their forties, and not everyone suffers through them. I, Breena O'Rylee, sit solidly in the middle. When I'm feeling bummed, I feel ancient, and when I'm feeling saucy, I forget my age and can hang with the best of them. I think.

But I digress.

As I crouched there breathing in the humid air and thinking that they were pretty stupid if they figured Sarge for one of the trainees, a thump rippled through the air and sent me sprawling sideways.

On my hands and knees, I pushed slowly up to peer over the bottom lip of the grave, between the angel's feet, at the two figures.

"You're good at this," Kinkly whispered with more than a little awe in her voice. "They didn't even look your way. It's like you're invisible."

"Forty-one-year-old woman," I whispered, as if that would explain it all. The rest of what I might have said slid away from me as I stared out across the graveyard. What could only be called a wave of magic rushed out across the training grounds, a swirl of darkness like a living mist, and before I could so much as draw a breath it slammed into the other trainees and Sarge. They all went down, one right after the other, like dominos.

I had to clap a hand over my mouth to keep the flow of curses contained. If I was discovered now, I had no doubt that I'd be next in the domino line, and that would leave no one to help. Triage at its worst. The two men, Douche Canoe and his friend, strolled down the path toward the exit. Partway to the gates, the air in front of them shimmered and they stepped through that shimmer and just disappeared. Gone.

Holy crap on Christmas toast!

"Eammon!" I yelled for him as I scrambled to my feet and got running as fast as I could toward where Sarge and the other trainees had gone down. I hadn't known I could run that far, that fast. Crazy what some adrenaline could do for even me. I slid to a stop at the first body, which was Suzy, her blond hair spread out around her head like a halo. I bent and put two fingers to her neck and found a steady pulse. "Kink, help me check the others!"

"Okay." She seemed uncertain, but she flew around to Luke. "He is breathing."

I checked the others quickly and stopped at Sarge, who was in his wolf form sprawled out flat on his belly, snoring softly.

I did a slow turn to see if there was any other damage to the area, but it didn't look like the wave of magic had done anything besides knock them over. No, that wasn't right. They hadn't been clubbed unconscious—they were all sound asleep.

Eammon didn't come huffing and puffing up to me, and a chill swept down my spine. I really didn't want to run back to the Hollows tomb, but for Eammon not to have heard me meant...well, what did it mean? That they had been knocked out too? Or worse?

"Kink"—I pointed at the trainees passed out on the ground—"stay here with them. Come get me if someone is in distress."

"Um, I don't know."

"I'll owe you," I said and tried not to grimace as the words came out of my mouth. Something in my dusty memory banks tried to tell me that owing a fae—even a small one like Kinkly—could go badly. But I didn't have time to give it more thought.

I had to stumble-jog back to the tomb. The burst of adrenaline was totally gone, and my body was not-so-graciously reminding me that I was not in shape for this. Sure, I was in better shape than I'd been, but exercise hadn't magically made me younger. My body was going to grump at me come morning. Tomorrow was going to hurt.

I made it back to the tomb, breathing hard. Hands on the walls of the stairwell, I guided my way down through the dark, listening to the heaving of my own breath.

Running was not my friend.

"Eammon?" I tried his name first and got a groan in reply. At least that meant he was alive, right?

I stumbled on the last step, going from dark into the light. "Eammon, you okay?"

"Ah, lass," he groaned, his voice turning me to the left. He sat next to the tall barstool he used for lectures. Over the past few weeks, it had occurred to me more than once that he might be tempting fate, what with his short legs, shorter frame, and roundish physique.

"They knocked you out too?" I crouched next to him.

He blinked up at me. "You saw them?"

I shrugged, not sure how much to tell him. It wasn't that I didn't trust him, but Eammon and the other mentors had made it clear that they didn't approve of my alliances. Particularly my interactions with Crash. Which meant I had to be careful. What would they do if they found out Douche Canoe had already threatened me because he'd found me in Crash's bed? Wait, that makes it sound like we were *together*-together. Yes, I'd been pretty much naked under the covers, but it wasn't like that. Honest.

I'd be bragging if I'd managed that.

Regardless. If I ever wanted to buy my gran's house back, I needed this job. Karissa's gig would pay well, sure, but it was a one-off thing, and I knew in my heart that Crash was going to make me pay through the nose and jump through some hoops while I was at it to get the house in my name.

Eammon prompted me. "Breena? You saw them?"

I nodded. "I watched them leave, so I only got a look at them from behind. I was sitting down taking a…break." Which wasn't entirely untrue. "They blasted magic across the graveyard and hit all the trainees and Sarge too. They're okay, I think, but they're all sound asleep."

Eammon rubbed his head. "Check on the other mentors here, lass."

I did as he asked, going to Tom first. His breathing was shallower than the rest I'd checked, and his dark skin had an awful ashen tone. I found a blanket in the spare gear room and covered him up. "Tom is in shock."

"That will be the magic." Louis sat up with a low groan. "It will have hit him the hardest, draining him."

Tom wasn't the only one who had been hit hard. Louis's pale skin was even whiter than usual, and the dark rings under his eyes made it look like someone had punched him. Twice.

I offered him a blanket that he shook off.

The last in the room was Corb. I put my hand against his neck and found a pulse, then laid the blanket over him. He muttered something in his magic-induced sleep, and his hand slid over mine, holding me tightly enough that I stayed with him rather than attempting to pull away.

I looked over at Eammon. "Everyone is alive. Could they have killed us?"

The look on Eammon's face said it all, but he answered anyway. "Yes. They are unhappy with our meddling in the ceremony, and the fact that Sarge and Corb were double agents, as it were. We're lucky they didn't kill the two of them."

My hand tightened on Corb's. He could have died. A wee part of my brain wondered why he hadn't. Eammon was right—shouldn't they have targeted the two mentors who'd tricked them? Not that I wanted anything bad to happen to Corb or Sarge, not in the least. But it didn't make sense, which left my skin down my back itching with the weirdness of it.

"You going to tell me who they are?" I asked. "So we can keep an eye on them maybe?"

Eammon opened his mouth and croaked like a frog, so sudden and sharp that everyone in the room jumped.

I giggled, my nerves getting the better of me. "Excuse you?"

"I don't think I can speak their names," he grumbled. I looked at Louis, who opened his mouth and let out a massive, "Heeee-hawwwww!"

Silence fell on the room as the donkey bray faded. With all that energy, all that fear bubbling up in my gut, I swear I couldn't help it—I burst out laughing, bent at the waist because the noise was so ridiculous. Funnier than that though was the look on Louis's face. He wasn't angry.

He was *offended*.

"Of all the creatures I could be forced to sound like, a donkey is not the one I would have chosen." He sniffed and put a finger to his nose.

I put my free hand to my lips. "I'm sorry, Louis. I wish you could have seen your face."

He glared at me, though there was a slight twinkle in his eyes, as if a part of him wanted to laugh too. "I'm glad you find this so amusing when we are dealing with heeee-hawwwww!" The bray flew out of him in a spray that had me pressing my face on Corb's chest as I shook with a new round of laughter.

Louis's face was a careful blank as I tried to pull myself together. I kept my hand on my mouth and my knees clamped because I had to pee like crazy, and the more I laughed the more I struggled to keep from wetting my pants.

Eammon cleared his throat. "It seems," he said carefully, "that we cannot speak their names, or what they are up to." A tiny "ribbit" slipped out of his mouth.

"But to make you sound like animals? Is that because they have a sense of humor?" I asked.

Eammon stared at me as he pulled himself up off the floor and wobbled to standing. "No, they did it to humiliate us. We couldn't protect our trainees or even ourselves, and this is their way of showing us that we're worthless. We are the animals, they are the ribbittt."

"You describe them, then, if you are so smart," Louis said softly, more than a bit of venom in his voice. No doubt he wanted to see what I would sound like.

I shrugged, settling my hip against Corb's because his hand still clung to mine. "Douche Canoe—the leader of the two—would be in his later sixties, judging by the creping of his pale skin and the sagging around his neck. Never mind the fact that he was definitely wearing a toupee of some sort to hide a massive bald patch. Poorly done, if you ask me. The other I would guess is his son? Similar build, not as old obviously, but the features of his nose and eyes were very much the same. White boys, but they've been around here for some time, and there is something else kicking around in their background, although I bet they don't talk about it. Probably a family secret."

Louis's mouth flapped open. "How can you even describe them?"

I shrugged. "The magic didn't go over me. I was behind them, behind the angel tomb."

"They miscounted," Eammon breathed out softly. "They counted Sarge as one of the trainees, thinking that they had everyone here." He rubbed his hands together and then smoothed them over his face. "Not that it matters. Even without the spell I wouldn't take on another bounty that would involve ribbbittttt!"

Corb's hand tightened on mine as Eammon's croak rippled through the air. "What's happening? Where the hell did meow-meow go?"

His eyes blinked up at me and fell back down to our hands, still linked. He let go. "Oh my GAWD, they made you into a pussy…cat!" Yes, I added that second word because, well, because he wasn't a pussy. He was kind of a badass and I can admit to crushing on him, but that's what made it all that much better.

Funnier. The funniest.

Corb sat up too fast and swayed. I grabbed his shoulder and helped steady him, sitting him back down, even as I snickered. "Dude, you freaking meowed!" I whispered at him. "That is not going to help you in the lady department unless she's a crazy cat lady!"

He blinked up at me. "I meowed." And then he spewed a massive amount of curses. I took a step back. Not because his language bothered me, but because he'd jerked to his feet in the middle of the swear tirade and slammed a fist into the punching bag anchored above his head, snapping it off where it was connected to its hanger. My eyebrows went up.

"As always, that is a most helpful answer, smashing shit," I said. "So these guys who did this spell, you can't speak their names, or what you think they are up to, but we know that they have something to do with the ceremony Hattie tried to perform?"

There was a chorus of hee-haw, ribbit, meow, plus a tweet-tweet from a barely conscious Tom. I had to close my eyes, fighting to keep my face straight and my words smooth. I was having a dream, I had to be. This was insane in the weirdest way possible. It would also be kind of awesome if not for Douche Canoe's threat. "I assume that's a yes."

Eammon lifted his hand. "We are going to get back to training. That's what we are going to do. You are a trainee. This does not concern you. We will not interfere with anything. Ribbit-ribbit is stronger than all of us. The council will have to deal with this."

Except that it did concern us, or at least me. Douche Canoe had threatened my life. He'd spelled all the trainees and the mentors, which meant that no one could so much as discuss the situation.

And he'd done it because I'd stopped Hattie before she could sacrifice Eric.

"Are you sure? I mean, if they are up to something bad—I mean, that is totes obvious"—look at me being hip!—"shouldn't we be trying to stop them?"

"No." Eammon gave me a hard stare. "We are taking the warning."

The question of the day was, who did Douche Canoe want us to stay away from? Eric? Shoot, what if the bigfoot shifter was in trouble again? I put it on my list to check on Eric as soon as I could. That wouldn't be stepping in things.

I tipped my head at Eammon so he thought I agreed with him. The thing was, I knew when to hold my cards and when to fold them.

Actually that's not true, I've never played poker and have no idea how either hand would apply to this situation. But in that moment, I was content to sit back and watch. There was no point in going off half-cocked and shooting myself in the foot. Yes, that's a much better analogy.

7

After the laughing fits and the hee-haws, meows, and ribbits of the mentors within the Hollows training grounds (and a seriously needed pee break for me with all that laughter) the other trainees were brought in. As groggy and disoriented as if they'd been day drinking since dawn, they sat down on the stools provided. Eammon led the charge in explaining the situation—or not, as it were.

"Tonight you face another one of our challenges. When you're hit by a magical spell of unknown origin, you must be prepared to fight through the feelings it causes and attempt to determine just what damage it is doing."

I stared hard at him and he studiously ignored me. Eammon was going to lie to the trainees so he could sweep this mind-boggling situation under the rug? Of course, they wouldn't start barking like dogs because they didn't know anything about Douche Canoe and his friend. But what if the spell had other side effects? Because they'd thought that I—a.k.a. the person who'd screwed up the whole Hattie thing for them—was out there running with the other trainees. Maybe they didn't know which trainee had caused the problem with Hattie, so they'd gone after everyone to cover Douche Canoe's bases.

Of course, telling them they'd been attacked with an unknown spell that could have unforeseen side effects would just scare the ever-loving spit out of them. Besides, Eammon wouldn't even be able to explain the situation because of the animal-sound issue. I slowly gave him a nod—I might not like his decision, but I understood it—and his shoulders loosened as he gave me the subtlest of acknowledgments that he'd caught what I'd thrown down.

Louis stepped up in front of Eammon and raised his hands above his head to call all the attention to him.

"We're going to work on spells tonight, finding them, identifying them, and diffusing them," Louis intoned. "This is important in our work because there are many other uses of spells, including defense, apprehension, and sowing confusion. We will start with a simple spell used to alert the user that someone is near."

He pulled a thin vial from his belt and poured the contents into one palm as he swirled the fingers of his other hand around and around. Like a miniature tornado, the spinning pulled specks of blue sparkling dust into the air. Next he blew on the dust, spreading it out in a line that lowered and settled into the stone floor, disappearing as if it were never there.

I took a few steps back, the sparkling dust reminding me that Kinkly was probably still waiting for me topside. "I'll be right back." I didn't wait as Corb barked at me to stay where I was, instead hustling up the stairs and out into the now fully dark night. "Kink, you okay?"

A flutter of wings pulled me around. "I am here. You came to check on me?"

"I don't know if you can come in the Hollows—"

"I don't want to. It's dank and cold in the tombs of the Hollows." She spoke softly. "I'll wait here until you're done." She tucked into the crook of the angel's neck, wrapping her wings around her tiny body.

I gave her a thumbs-up and turned as a hand grabbed my elbow. Startled, I stumbled backward, and would have fallen if not for Corb grabbing both my arms and holding me upright. "Are you really okay?" he asked.

"Jaysus, lawd! Not if you scare me like that. You could have stopped my age-ed heart." I winked at him to soften the words. Because we both knew he'd been a dick when I'd first come to Savannah, but it was hard to forget that kiss.

I mean, I didn't see myself settling down, or making a go of it with him, but maybe a tangle in the sheets? Sure, I'd be game. The thing was, while he was very different than Himself, they *were* related and that freaked me out more than a little. Never mind our age difference. Corb was more than a handful of years younger than me, but that I could handle. I think.

"The"—he paused as if testing out the word in his mind—"thing that happened didn't hurt you?"

I shook my head. "Nope. I think Eammon was right, they miscounted."

He hadn't let go of my arms. I looked up at him. "Are *you* okay? Do you all need to take the night off? I wouldn't argue. A hot bath and a couple shots of that Jameson you've 'hidden' from me would not go amiss."

His lips twitched. "We have to keep the trainees training. And that Jameson is tucked at the back of the cupboard where you shouldn't be able to see it."

I made as if to step back, but he followed me until I bumped up against the base of the angel's tombstone. "I got a chair and snooped." I paused. "Corb, you sure you're okay?" I tipped my head to one side as if that would help me see him better. "You seem off."

He swept me into a crushing hug before I knew what was happening. I hugged him back, sighing a little as I breathed in his cologne. *Night*, I think it was called. I could see why he had no problem with the ladies. I patted his well-muscled back, something you had to feel to fully appreciate. "I didn't think something like that would bother you so much."

He pulled back enough that he could press his head against mine. "Corb?"

"Just let me hang onto you for a minute." He said it with more sweetness than our reluctant rooming agreement should warrant.

His fingers pressed hard against my back in a not-unpleasant way. Warm. Safe. "You have a good meow," I said, because I'm an idiot sometimes and awkward is something I can pull off no matter what the occasion. He loosened his hold so he could look me in the eye.

My comment got a smile out of him, but he didn't pull away. Nope, those eyes of his were locked on mine, and the tension was building because I couldn't look away. I stared up at him, and we were just too damn close for this to be anything but serious sexual tension.

And I wasn't sure if that was good or not.

He started to lean in—holy crap, he was going to kiss me again!—until someone cleared their throat.

Corb didn't startle, but I jumped as if an electric cattle prod had been smacked against my plentiful cheeks. I turned to see Sarge standing there with a pretty good glare on his face. I grinned at him. "Phew, I thought it was going to be Eammon coming up to yell at me."

Sarge's face didn't change. "She got an offer to take care of Crash's new place that he bought. She already agreed to do it."

My jaw dropped. That was *not* how I'd wanted to tell him, and if my reaction time had been any quicker, I'd have strangled Sarge. As much as I told myself Corb's opinion of my plan didn't matter, it kind of did, at least to me. Corb's hands slid off my arms, and I felt the loss of his touch a worrying amount. Maybe it was the loss of adrenaline. Maybe it was the loss of the heat from his hands. I shrugged as if Sarge's words were nothing. "You could go back to your life. I feel like I'm...interrupting things all the time." I thought about all the lube in the bathroom and forced my feet to move. Forced my face to smile. "Look, you're well stocked to have a great time as soon as I'm out of your way, and that's great. Good."

He frowned. "What are you talking about? You aren't in my way."

I shook my head as my hands found the edge of the tomb. I didn't feel like reminding him that I'd seen his collection of *Boy Butter*, amongst other things. "I'll get my stuff out tomorrow. It's all good."

And just like that, I was sliding, limping really, back down the stairwell. As I climbed down, a few snarled words caught my ears, but I kept going. I didn't need to hear them fight—I'd done enough spying for one day. I just hoped it wasn't because of me. I'd had about enough of Sarge's 'help,' and I didn't want Crash angry with me. I liked him too much. I froze on the bottom step when I realized my mental faux pas. Not Crash, Corb. I didn't want Corb angry with me.

95

"Oh, you are in too deep, girl," I whispered to myself.

The mentors continued our lessons as if nothing had happened, but my mind kept returning to Douche Canoe and his buddy. Or son.

"This way, to the graveyard for the rest of the spell chasing," Louis said as I reached the bottom stair. He led the way back up and I groaned out loud.

"Damn stairs." I waited for everyone else to go up ahead of me so they wouldn't have to see me struggle. Maybe it was my knees, maybe it was my tired legs, but the stairs and I were not on speaking terms.

Topside for like the fourth time, I watched as Louis set out a variety of spells. "Go out, find them, tell me what they are, and then shut them down."

The other trainees didn't move. I cleared my throat. "How?"

"You have not been reading your training manual then?" Louis looked down his nose at me. I lifted both brows at him and fumbled around in my bag for the thin manual we'd been given.

"You mean this ten-page stack of paper that you stapled together by hand?" I flopped it in his face, dropped it, and pulled out my gran's book. Suzy let out a gasp.

"Now that's a freaking manual!"

"You cannot use that," Louis snapped.

I didn't even look up at him. "Watch me." I skimmed the pages until I found the one on detecting spells. I knew I'd seen it in there somewhere.

"Most spells, with the exception of the most powerful, throw off a different and distinct taste. Generally speaking, the more pleasant it is, the worse the spell," I read aloud. "For example, a spell that is made for keeping others away will taste similar to soured milk. There are a few exceptions, and you must learn to recognize those." Gross. I really didn't want to be putting random spells into my mouth. Lord only knew where they'd been.

Louis made a grab for Gran's book, but I jerked it away from him. "No touching." I turned my back on him and read the final bit about breaking the spells out loud for the other recruits. "Breaking the spells requires concentration and a push of your own energy through it." Though maybe that was just for spell casters? This was, after all, Gran's book. I'd never been particularly good with the spell-casting side of her training.

"I've got one!" Luke yelled from the far right side. He flexed his hand and shoved it through the air ahead of him. A shower of green sparkles went up into the air as he broke the spell. "Tasted like sour milk, totally!"

Suzy was next. She found a spell and busted through it like it was nothing.

And me?

I tried to find the spells that Louis put out for us to find in the graveyard. Got zapped three times, tripped twice, and got frozen in place more times than I wanted to admit. By the time the training for the night was done, I was exhausted in body and spirit. Everyone else had done well, though, and that brought me a measure of satisfaction. I wasn't sure if I'd failed to find them because my intuition was off, or because I was too busy thinking about everything else that had happened.

And I still needed to check out the fairy ring for Karissa. Poop, this was going to be a long night.

Hopefully, Kinkly had some special way to magic me there, because I usually got a ride from Sarge or Corb, and both had already left for the night. I scrubbed a hand over my eyes, which were so tired they stung and tingled, and waited by the angel tomb as everyone left. Eammon was the last to go and he paused to look me over. "What do you be doing, girly?"

"Just taking in the night air." I yawned wide, my jaw cracking.

Eammon's eyes narrowed. "You're always the first one gone. What's up tonight?"

I leaned back against the angel tomb, the stone cool under my hands. "Stretching myself and my stamina, Eammon. Important, don't you think?"

He pursed his lips. "So I see you've still got that book of your gran's?"

This was not the direction I'd expected our conversation to go. "Yes."

"I suggest you look up the inherent dangers of fairy rings." He looked down at his nails as if considering the need for a trim. "I'd also look up making deals with fairies. You know, if you were looking for some added reading." He slowly lifted his eyes, as green as a spring meadow, complete understanding in them. "I'd also say that of anyone here, I'd trust you to handle something like that."

For the second time that night, my jaw dropped. "Speechless, I have no words. I am without words." How the hell did he know? It was my turn to narrow my eyes.

Eammon didn't quite smile, but it was close. "I think you need a more reliable mode of transportation, especially with all the travel you'll be doing. Tom and Louis suggested you ask your friend Robert if he can help you out with that."

With that, he turned on his heel and walked away, whistling a tune to himself. I just stood there a moment, waiting for him to be a distance away before I turned up to see Kinkly still waiting there on the angel's shoulder.

"Did you tell him?"

She shook her head rapidly, sending her hair flying every which way. "No, not a word, I swear. But we have to go. And he's right, it's a distance."

I worried at the inside of my mouth. "Robert, you around?" He'd passed out from the whiskey so it was possible that he was out for the night. A swaying figure stepped out from around a tombstone, long hair hanging low.

"Friend," he whispered. "Good whiskey."

I laughed. "I'm glad. Listen, I'm going to have to do a lot of running around, and I don't have a car. Eammon seems to think you can help me with that. Can you? Or is he full of leprechaun shit?"

What in the world an animated skeleton was supposed to do to help me, I had no idea. I mean, I was still reeling a bit from what Eammon had said. Not only did he know that I'd taken the job from Karissa, but he was quietly helping me.

After all of the other mentors had turned her down.

After Eammon himself had turned her down.

Color me suspicious, but what do you want to bet that he'd purposefully sent her my way? If I recalled, leprechauns were connected to the fae, but I couldn't remember any details. My thoughts scattered as Robert began to move.

He held out a hand, bones showing, and snapped his fingers. The click-clack of bone on bone was shockingly loud, and I took a step back, my legs feeling like jelly. It reminded me of the realtor's stomping at Gran's house—it felt as if he'd summoned something powerful with that one snap of his fingers.

Nope, nope that was not jelly legs, that was the ground heaving around and under us. "Robert, what is going on?"

"New friend." He swayed as he shuffled to the side, and something burst upward out of the ground where he'd been standing only a moment before. My brain couldn't quite make sense of what I was seeing.

A long bony limb—no, two long bony limbs—came out of the ground, pulling the rest of a body out of the dirt. Round nose, long face, hooves.

"Lawdy, Robert, is that a horse?" I stumbled back further as the big animal finished yanking itself out of the ground. Lying there a moment, it seemed to catch its breath—and considering it was dead, that was something—before it heaved itself to its feet. Although not as skeletal as Robert, it was still missing a few chunks of hide and bits of muscle. The tail was ragged, not long at all, and the mane hanging from its neck was super stringy, wrapped into dreads in places. The undead horse gave a long, low snort, blowing chunks of...something out of its nostrils.

Kinkly landed on the horse's rump. "This is rather gross, but it will work. The undead can go unseen by many creatures, and the fae are included in that list."

I gave her a look. "You can see them."

She smiled. "Yes, but I am with you. That's why."

Her answer made no real sense. I mean, why did being with me give her the ability to see the undead critters?

Why could I see them anyway?

I did a slow circle around to the side of the horse. I'd ridden a living horse before, but that had been years ago, and I'd only tried because I'd figured it would be a good idea to work with a larger animal than a dog. What it came down to was that I liked horses, I just didn't know much about them.

"Do I just...get on?" I looked around the horse at Robert.

He swayed as he shuffled to my side. "Friend. Ride."

At least it still had a saddle, something that could only be explained by magic. I reached up and grabbed a handful of the stringy mane, stuck my foot in a stirrup, and tried to hop up. I didn't quite make it, and I found myself hanging from the side of the saddle in mid-air, my nose pressed against the older than dirt leather.

Yelping, I slid down off the horse's side, one foot still lodged in the stirrup—far higher than was comfortable to stretch. The horse stepped sideways, taking me with it. "Wait, not yet!" I yelled as I hopped along with it, trying to find the right balance and momentum to swing my butt up into the saddle.

"Here, I'll help, you need it." Kinkly fluttered behind me, and the next thing I knew, she was pulling my shirt up, baring my middle as the neckline strangled me.

"Gah!" I gurgled and gave one last hop as Kinkly pulled me from above and Robert shoved me from behind. Another blink and Robert climbed up over the horse's hind end and sat behind me.

"Okay, so…" I looked at the horse and realized there were no reins. Even my rudimentary knowledge of horses told me I needed some way to steer it. As it stood, there was no way for me to control the beast. "How do I make this work?"

Kinkly flew in tiny circles out in front of the horse. "Maybe just tell it to follow me?"

That was as logical as anything else. I mean, only a few short weeks ago I'd have been losing my mind over this whole night. Look at me go, embracing the madness of the shadow world! Gran would be proud. Himself would poop himself. That made me smile.

"Follow Kinkly," I said, then added, "please."

Kinkly didn't wait for any other encouragement. She shot ahead of us, a spray of glitter leaving a trail behind her. The undead horse lunged forward, which threw me backward against Robert, who pushed me back into the saddle.

"What the hell?" I screamed the words into the wind as I flopped up and down and sideways on the back of an undead horse, an animated skeleton holding me in my seat as we raced after a fairy who did nothing but laugh at me.

That sentence should have only applied if I'd been eating magic mushrooms.

The wind ripped around my face, lashing my hair against my eyeballs, but I didn't close my eyes. Nope, I knew the general direction we were headed, and I didn't like what was coming.

"River, that is the river!" I yelped as the horse slid down the cobblestones, hooves spookily silent, muscles bunching, headed for the bottom of the road. But I might as well not have said anything because it *ducking* leapt into the river. I did close my eyes then, and my mouth to help hold my breath.

I wish I could say that the horse ran across the water, but it sunk down as soon as it landed, going in almost over its head. A squeak escaped me as the river rose around my body, right up to my chin.

I lifted my head up, ready to leap off the horse, but my legs seemed strapped to it still, feet still in the stirrups. Slowly I realized that the undead horse was rising, at least until its head and part of its back was above the water. "Seriously?" I twisted around as we swam across the river.

Kinkly stayed just ahead of us and, other than Robert, I had no one to exclaim to that this was the weirdest shit yet. That I had no idea how it could get weirder. "Robert, this is weird. It can't get weirder, right?"

"Friend," he whispered.

I really shouldn't have wondered. By then, I should have just accepted that there was always going to be a weirder moment.

8

The ride from weird town ended in a rush, and far faster than I would have thought. After the swim through the Savannah River, almost getting mowed down by one of the oversized shipping ships (don't judge me, I can't find the right words, I'm still reeling), Kinkly led us out through the same forest that Eric lived in, which was part of the wildlife reserve.

In fact, we passed his house at break-neck speed. Not that I think he saw me. It had quickly become apparent that *no one* saw me on the back of the undead horse. Not one person so much as blinked at us. Sure, it was almost three in the morning and we were moving surprisingly fast, but there was more to it than that.

Whatever magic kept Robert animated and, for most people, unnoticed also affected the horse. And as the horse's rider, I apparently fell under its magical umbrella.

For all intents and purposes, I was invisible. I mean, a forty-year-old woman often was, but this was taking it to a whole new level.

"Here. We stop here." Kinkly shot back toward us, and the horse put on the brakes so hard that I flipped forward, flying over its head. The sudden twisting of the world meant that I got to look up at the night sky and the tree branches thick with Spanish moss draping off each branch before I landed flat on my back.

A whoosh of air flew from my mouth and I lay there, feeling the desperation to draw air and the inability to do so. I couldn't do anything but lie there and wait. What felt like hours but was only seconds later, I finally drew a ragged breath, gasped, and drew another.

"You okay?" Kinkly bobbed above me, her sparkling dust falling all over my face. I waved her away.

"Peachy keen." I rolled to my knees, the soft ground giving way under me. I pushed up to my feet and wobbled a little. Adrenaline pounded through me, making my head a bit light. A quick body check, and I knew I was okay, if a bit embarrassed.

"Come on, come on." Kinkly beckoned for me to follow her. "This way to the fairy ring."

I did a half turn to take in the undead horse and Robert still sitting up on it, my manners kicking in. "Thanks for the ride."

Robert slid off the horse and I got a glimpse of spindly bone legs. You'd think it would bother me, but honestly, it barely registered on my radar of weird anymore. The horse snorted, tucked its legs underneath itself, and then slowly sunk into the ground, the soft dirt washing over it until it was gone.

"Now that is bananas," I said, more to myself than anyone else.

"Horse," Robert answered, correcting me.

"Okay, so that is technically correct." I laughed, and Robert nodded.

Kinkly flapped her wings in my face. "Come on!"

I followed Kinkly and Robert followed me and we were off through the forest. It was quiet but for the sounds of bugs and night birds, and the distant slosh of water against a shoreline. I tried to stretch my senses the way my gran had taught me, to be aware of everything all at once. Tried to hear beyond all the night noises, but got nothing but my own heartbeat. Bleh.

Kinkly swept back to me and tugged on a stray strand of hair that had escaped my ponytail.

"Ouch!"

"Quiet now, you need to get down," she whispered. "We can't let them see us. They're not supposed to know we are here."

Get down. Crap, she was going to make me army crawl through the bush? I closed my eyes and reminded myself that this was for Gran's house. Or a chance at Gran's house.

Crash would sell at a certain point. Right? From what I'd heard, he moved his office somewhat frequently. He'd been on Factors Row only a year, and before that he'd stayed in the previous place for six months.

I dropped to my belly, the ground under me still damp, though not as bad as where we'd first stopped. Grasses tickled my face as I pushed my way along the path, cursing Kinkly for making me do it and cursing my body for not being in shape despite the last two weeks of hard work. Let's be honest, don't we all want to achieve our perfect weight after one workout, and then get offended when it doesn't happen?

Yeah, me too.

With the dark of the night, it was difficult to see exactly where I was going. Up and over a big root I went, and from there I slid down into a hollow between two trees.

My skin tingled, like buzzing ants were crawling up and down my arms and along my spine. Ahead of me was a cluster of massive oak trees, planted tightly together. Each trunk was pressed against its neighbor, as though they were trying to block out the world. I'd never seen a cluster of oak trees grown like that. Their branches hung low, thick with Spanish moss, and acted like an additional curtain to block them from sight.

I twisted to ask Kinkly a question, but she was gone.

The buzzing sensation against my skin increased, and I crouched down in the hollow, barely breathing as a series of fairies, dressed mostly in black with only a yellow accent on their chests, swept around the grouping of oak trees before landing on the one closest to me. I counted fifteen of the little critters, all male.

They pulled from their backs little tools that flashed bright in the moonlight. Silver was my first thought. Iron was something that bothered the fae, so any tools would be silver.

As a team working three at a time, they began to worry at the tree closest to me, driving their weapons into the oak's trunk, digging out the wood one sliver at a time. I squinted at the spot they were chopping at and realized this was not the first time they'd been at it. But the tree was healing even as they worked.

Which explained why Karissa thought this would take another ten days before they dug all the way through to the center where the artifact was stowed away. I frowned, tapping my fingers against the tree root I leaned forward against. There were a lot of questions rolling through my mind.

Like why exactly didn't Karissa just take the artifact herself? She'd evaded the question earlier, but she seemed pretty powerful. Much more so than a bunch of tiny fairies with what amounted to needles. And why exactly didn't Kinkly want me to be seen by these fairies? I thought back to my conversation with Karissa, going over the words in my head. And then I realized she'd never said *her* fairies were doing the digging here. Just *the* fairies.

Duck me, what if these fairies belonged to the Unseelie she'd mentioned? What if I was watching the bad guys, waiting for them to slip up?

I settled down into the hollow, finding a position that was pretty comfortable. I patted the ground beside me and Robert slid down to sit, swaying only a little as he did.

I didn't say anything as I slid my gran's book out of my bag and laid it on my lap. Turning the pages slowly, I didn't dare turn on my flashlight for fear of being noticed, which meant I did a lot of pulling the book right to my nose in order to read in the super dim light.

Nearing dawn, the light shifted enough that I could really get reading between checking in on the workers.

My fingers stilled on a page marked *Unseelie*.

My gran's familiar handwriting filled the page beneath it.

Unseelie are not inherently evil, as some would believe, however they are known for their trickster nature—they will not always give the truth when asked, or they may give half-truths in order to manipulate. The division between light and dark fae is not so certain, and there are some who believe there is a third fae power—the Dark Fae, who derive their power from death and destruction. I have not seen this power, but I have encountered Seelie—the fae of the sun—and Unseelie—the fae of the moon—and both carry inherent power and dangers.

Any dealings with them must be made in contract form, their names signed by their own hand, or there is no certainty that they will follow through. (I made a mental note to try and get said paper signed by Karissa.) *The power of the Seelie is at its height between noon and sundown, and the Unseelie are most powerful between three in the morning and noon. They can, of course, be awake at other times, just not as strong as when their deity calls to them.*

I peeked up over the roots and looked at the fairy men, who were still going strong, working at the tree with great fervor. Watching them, I was willing to bet that they were Unseelie, working while their power was at its strongest.

I held the book tight to me as my mind raced, trying hard to put the pieces together. Karissa wanted to protect the item, but the Unseelie were after it. So why had she hired me to watch their attempts to steal it?

The answer dawned on me. She wanted me here so I could let her know when they were close. This way they'd do all the digging, and she could swoop in and take the item with little effort. Clever, very clever. I found myself smiling. I liked her style, it was crazy smart, and very much using what she had on hand to make it work.

Day fully broke above us and brought with it a fresh wave of heat. It wasn't long before I found myself wondering how close we were to noon. My belly grumbled hard, reminding me that I had not eaten in a long time. My gran's book had kept me busy, and between that and the fairy men, I'd not noticed my hunger or my fatigue. A yawn cracked my jaw and I struggled to keep my eyes open for the first time that night.

Moments later, the fifteen small fairy men dispersed, flying away in a V-formation, straight up through the trees and off to wherever it was they slept. Which meant it was time for me to go too.

And maybe that's where my thoughts would have stayed if not for the person who stepped into my line of sight.

There was no mistaking those broad shoulders, the dark hair touched with silver at the temples, or the blue eyes ringed with gold. Not that I could see the nuances of his eyes from where I sat, but I'd had some up close and personal looks into them. And then there was his body, built from hard work over a forge making knives and whatever else he made.

My temperature rose as he strode around the tree, the small fairies buzzing around him. I couldn't hear what they were saying, but he was nodding. They were saluting him and then they sped off, leaving the tree and Crash.

He slid his hands over the smooth trunk of the tree, and damn it, the heat burning through me cranked up a notch. He had nice hands. Big hands, probably rough with work. I swiped a hand over my face, fully expecting it to come away soaked with sweat.

Nope, no sweat, just a rush of heat as though I'd spiked a fever.

Crap, what if he looked my way? What if he saw me there? I didn't know if he was good, bad, or somewhere in between. But I did know he was Karissa's ex-husband. And he was inspecting the work of what I suspected were Unseelie fae.

Time to go.

I slid backward, pulling myself out of my little hollow, keeping my eyes on Crash's back. If he turned around, there was no way he'd miss me.

The dark and my hollow hideaway had kept me from the fairies. I doubted Crash would be so easily fooled. Robert had disappeared, as was his habit, but I wasn't worried—he always resurfaced when I needed him.

Up and over the little ridge I'd first climbed down, I slid down the other side, the crack of a branch breaking under my foot as loud as if I'd shot off a gun.

Crap! Just my ducking luck!

I moved as fast and quietly as I could, driven by the need to put distance between me and the fairy ring that I was pretty sure was being run by the Unseelie. Which probably meant Crash was one of them, something that made my mind stutter. I tried to lock on to the sound of water, to get to the river, but there wasn't even a whisper of it this far into the forest, which left me running and taking turn after turn without any real idea of where the hell I was going.

I spun and crashed into…well, Crash.

"Ooof!" I yelled as his hands locked onto my arms, keeping me from falling flat on my face. Yes, those hands of his were worn, I could feel the calluses on them.

"Are you okay?" His hands were ridiculously gentle, and all I could think was that I'd never been jealous of a tree before that moment.

"Sorry, I'm just totally turned around." I was breathing hard, which meant my boobs were bobbing up and down as I heaved for air.

He smiled down at me, which made my stomach do some serious flip-flops. "I can see that. What are you doing out here? Not on a job for the Hollows, I hope?"

Double-dipped poop on my shoe, this was bad. Douche Canoe had hired Crash to make a crucible. If Crash told him, even in passing, that I was out here working on something, what do you want to bet Douche Canoe and his son would be back to hurt everyone attached to the Hollows? They'd made it clear they did not want anyone in the Hollows near this job. I found myself shaking my head in denial as I tried to come up with a reason for my presence in the middle of the woods.

"No, no job. I'm…just trying to find Eric's. I told him I'd come visit, but finding his place again is proving…difficult." I smiled back at Crash, hating how my body reacted to him. Because damn it, he was all kinds of bad boy hot.

He slid my hand over his arm, right into the crook of his elbow, and tugged me along. "Come on, I'll make sure you don't get turned around again."

The heat off his skin soaked into my fingers, and I found my hand curling around a bicep that was ridiculously muscular. Like we were on a stroll together. A date.

Nope, that was a ton of nope. I was not going down that path, no matter how hot he was. Crash was not a good guy. And I was done with assholes. And I was working for his ex-wife, who seemed intent on grabbing that artifact out from under him, and it would be all kinds of awkward if that little tidbit got out.

"So, what are you doing out here? Seeing as you left me with Feish because you were going away, right?" I said with all the innocence I could muster.

He didn't even glance at me as he brushed some exceptionally long Spanish moss out of the way. "Checking on a few things."

"Well, that's not suspicious at all," I said.

He shot me a look. "And you're just out here visiting the bigfoot?"

"Want to make sure nobody is trying to stick him with a demon knife again," I shot back, without a single hint of venom. Go me.

Crash shook his head. "You don't understand, Bree."

Oh, screw that. "Then enlighten me. Don't tell me I don't understand and then deliberately leave me in the dark. That's a dick move." I tried to yank my hand from his arm. "Guys pull that all the time, you know. *You don't understand*, but then no follow-up! Why don't you help me understand then? I am capable of thought."

His jaw flexed. "No."

"Oh well, at least we've got that out of the way." I squirmed until my hand was free. But he grabbed it again, locking our fingers together. I glared up at him, my anger rising faster than the water during a hurricane.

He lowered his face to mine so we were nose to nose. "Savannah isn't safe, Bree. It hasn't been for a long time, but it's getting more dangerous. I am doing what I can to stop some of this from happening. Though I doubt your friends would see it that way."

I glared right back at him. "Some of what exactly? You think killing Eric would have helped? I doubt that very much."

His eyes narrowed, and I could feel the anger pulsing between us, both his and mine. "Stubborn. Just like your gran."

"Highest compliment ever." I tipped my chin up, just a half degree, enough so that I was looking down my nose at him.

Blue and gold eyes raked over me, dipping to my mouth. Oh…donkey balls.

Before I could back-pedal, before I could so much as tell him nope, not today, no matter how hot you be, his lips were on mine.

There was nothing tentative about his kiss, nothing that made me think he was worried about hurting me.

No, this kiss was fire and passion, steel sheathed in silk as his arms wrapped around my middle, tugging me against the length of him. Should I have pushed him away?

116

Should have, could have, didn't.

Because I was kissing him back. I wove my arms around his neck and let the fire from his mouth, the heat of his touch rip through me without thought. Wildfire, the fire of a need that I hadn't felt in…how long? Never.

The answer was never. No kiss had ever burned through me like this, leaving me fighting to get more of it, to feel more of him against more of me.

Why the hell did someone so wrong for me have to feel so ducking right?

His hands slid under the back of my shirt, pressing against my bare skin, and I groaned against his mouth, unable to stop myself. One hand came around between us, took mine and slid it down, over his belly to—

"Excuse me, hate to interrupt."

We both froze, tangled together, our lips still touching, my hand precariously close to parts I had seen and admired but hadn't thought I'd ever be touching.

Crash looked behind me as he slowly let me go, as if completely unembarrassed to have been caught. I was glad for the delay, as my knees and thighs were shaking with lusty adrenaline.

"Bigfoot," Crash rumbled, his voice thick with darkness and that same fire he'd been kissing me with, and the sound shot straight to my nether regions. I had the ridiculous urge to cross my legs and count to twenty in an attempt to get the feeling to pass.

Eric cleared his throat, and I could imagine him pushing his glasses up on his nose.

I turned to catch the tail end of that very move. His bowtie bobbed with his Adam's apple and he clasped his hands in front of him. Dressed like a professor, right down to his tweed jacket, the overly tall man looked just like a man. Bigfoot was the shape he could shift into, which left him looking vaguely like a wookie. Not scary at all, and one of the gentlest people I knew.

"Eric," I said. "I came out to see you. And I got lost."

"In his mouth?" Eric tipped his head to one side, his words delivered without a trace of sarcasm, as if getting lost in Crash's mouth were totally possible. Damn.

Maybe even a year before that would have made me blush. Not anymore.

Remember? No more ducks to give.

I shrugged. "What can I say? He's hotter than sin and a great kisser. Doesn't negate what he did. I'm still not happy with him about that."

Crash grunted as if I'd jabbed my elbow into his middle. I looked over my shoulder at him. "Thanks for seeing me to Eric."

And I walked away from him, slipped my arm through Eric's and tugged him down what I hoped was the right path.

The thing was, I let myself look over my shoulder at Crash.

Hands on his hips, his eyes locked on mine as he winked and blew me a kiss, which sent the heat unfurling through me once more. So that was the game, was it? I smiled back at him, even as I slid my arm around Eric's middle.

Take that, Crash.

His laughter followed Eric and me through the forest. And I couldn't help but smile. Damn it, he threw all the conventions of a stereotypical male out the window.

The problem with that was I liked it a little too much.

9

Eric led me through the swampy forest, not saying much as we put distance between us and Crash. I didn't realize just how tense I was until I saw his little house waiting for us through a stand of trees and let out a sigh of relief I couldn't hold back.

"Did you really come out here to see me?" Eric asked, and the hopeful tone in his voice dug at my conscience.

"Yes, I've been planning to come out and thank you for the extra money. That was a shocker." I glanced up at him and he beamed. Freaking beamed with an ear-to-ear smile.

"Were you able to get Celia's house?"

My own smile slipped. I quickly told him about the auction, then found myself telling him about Kinkly and Karissa too. And about Douche Canoe and his lackey at the Hollows the night before.

He let me into his house and bustled about the small space. "Let me make some tea and get you something to eat, then we can discuss this. It seems like a lot happened in a very short period of time. Not really that unusual for the shadow world, as you've seen, but still it can be overwhelming."

I slumped into a straight-backed chair and looked around the room, taking in the changes. The windows were bigger—he'd had them expanded to let in more light since I was here last. The change was so new, the molding around them was a bright, fresh white. The fireplace wasn't raging, and there was an overstuffed couch with a hand-knit blanket on the back of it that was calling my name. He'd made a fast turnaround from the freaked-out shut-in I'd met such a short time ago.

The adrenaline, the lust, the fear—it all left my body in a rush and I slumped in my seat. "Eric, I am too old for this shit."

"No, I was wrong about that," he said as he pushed a cup of tea into my hands and sat down across from me, "I'd wager you are just the right age. Old enough to have life experience in dealing with people, young enough to still make things happen. Perfect." He clinked his tea cup against mine, and damn it, my eyeballs started swimming. I dashed away the tears.

"Thanks, Eric."

"You showed me that," he said softly. "I used to hate being judged but I did it to you. Then you showed me that I was wrong, so very wrong. You saved my life. No amount of money can ever repay that. But I hope you'll accept a lifelong friend."

Yup, swimming eyeballs again. I reached over and squeezed his hand and nodded, then took a sip of tea, the warmth sliding through me. I put the cup down, knowing I should head back to Corb's to sleep, or even Gran's. But I didn't think I'd make it. A thought came to me.

"Could I stay here for the next few…mornings? I'm doing a job out here, and it takes all night." I paused. "I can pay you."

He flopped his big hands at me. "I wouldn't hear of it. But given what you said about Karissa and Kinkly, I'm guessing this has something to do with the fairy-crossed land?"

My eyebrows shot up. "Fairy-crossed land?"

He leaned back in his chair and stretched his legs. "There are chunks of land in our world that still belong to the fae. They are holy to them, and the fae protect what's theirs. It's said these places are guarded by magic so old no one knows how or even who created the spells. It's said the land not far from here protects a very powerful item that could give the bearer great and terrible gifts." He paused and took another sip of his tea. "The fairy queen has been making the rounds the last few days, but Crash chased her off."

"Can I trust the queen?" I asked. "I mean, thinking back to my last conversation with her, I'm sure she didn't tell me everything."

Eric stared into his tea as if the answer would be found there. "Honestly? The fae, as you know, are all slippery. Take a look at Crash. He helped Hattie. But then he helped you too. So I would say that depending on the day, and what you bring to the table, the answer is maybe. Maybe trust her."

I downed the last of my tea and Eric pushed a plate of pastries toward me. They were stuffed with jam, and I didn't know what they were, but they filled my mouth and my belly as he continued to talk.

"If you're dealing with the fae, be careful. The queen is…difficult at best. And Crash is Crash. He'll use whatever means necessary to get his way. Even seduction isn't below him."

The pastry in my mouth turned to concrete and I struggled to swallow it down. "Right. Because he's fae?"

Holy crap, Crash was fae?

Eric wrinkled his nose up and wrapped his big hands around the tea cup, completely engulfing it. "Yes, but he's one of very few who can live in both our world and the fae realm. The rest need to go back and forth regularly to keep their beauty and power strong. Not him."

My tongue stuck to the roof of my mouth. "I thought the fae didn't like steel, I thought it burned them. I know he can touch it, he makes weapons."

Eric smiled. "Crash isn't his first name. It's the one he's taken. He's the Smith, Bree. He's the fae king."

And I'd kissed him. Jaysus lord in heaven. I closed my eyes and leaned in my chair, and that was about as far as I could go.

"You need to sleep. We can talk more when you wake up."

I'm not sure if he picked me up, or if I wandered over to that overstuffed couch, but a moment later I was lying down, the soft blanket over my body and tucked around my face as I snuggled deep into the cushions.

Sleep slammed into me, yes, slammed. I was out cold, and yet as deep as it was, I still dreamed.

Of Crash and Corb. Of Eric, and of Feish wringing her hands. Robert was there too—*everyone* was there. Eammon and the other mentors all looked sad. So sad.

I blinked and walked around them, trying to get their attention only to realize I couldn't, which was when I realized why.

In the dream, I was dead.

Wake up. Now.

I jerked awake, sweat rolling down my face as I sat up and tried to figure out where I was.

Eric sat at his table, bent over a piece of paper, a few books splayed open around him. The sound of his pen scratching across the paper was the noise that I could say might have woken me up. But those words shifted inside my head.

Danger.

"Eric. We have to go." I flipped off the blanket, struggled to get my legs moving as the cramping and tightness from all the running and training caught up to me. Advil, I needed an Advil, maybe a whole bottle. But whatever was pushing me was full on shoving me now, the feeling of danger riding me hard.

An instinct that was trying so very hard to keep me alive.

As if reading my mind, Eric shoved two pills at me. "We aren't going anywhere until you take these. You moan in your sleep. You should have taken them before you passed out."

I grabbed the pills, dry swallowed them, and then took his hand. "We have to go!"

"It's fine, it was just a dream," he said, but then he went still and cocked his head to the side.

I don't know what it was, but whatever instinct I had said to *get down.* I yanked his hand hard and pulled him to the ground as the boom of several guns ripped through the air.

Something stung my left calf and I yelped and reached for the meat of my leg. Warmth oozed out around my fingers and I realized I'd been shot.

I'd been shot!

The gunfire eased off, and along with it, the feeling of danger slid out of the room. I lay there on the floor staring at Eric. "You think that was for you or for me?"

He blinked at me, and his round-rimmed glasses only adding to his resemblance to a startled owl. "That's a good question."

I held my free hand up, stopping him. The danger had eased, but there was the sound of footsteps running toward us. How the hell I could hear that over the pounding of my own heart I don't know.

But I rolled onto my back, facing the only door of the house, and pulled my two knives as the door was kicked open. My left blade flew from my hand before I registered that the person in the doorway was not one I wanted to stick with my knife.

A flash of bright steel, end over end. Crash caught the blade handle, a mere inch from his face. "Good throw."

"Better catch," I breathed out, horror quickly replacing the adrenaline. Anyone else, I had no doubt, would have ended up with a blade in their face. "Are they still there?"

Crash shook his head. "Not that I could see."

I sat up. "Eric, you got some wraps?"

"Oh, yes, of course, I have a first aid kit."

Crash let himself the rest of the way in and crouched beside me. He handed my knife back and I put it away, thinking that everyone was acting very calm for the current situation. Nobody was running off half-cocked or flapping their hands in hysterics. Then again, everyone here was over forty.

Go middle-agers!

I pulled my pant leg up over my knee, hissing as it slid over the bullet hole. "Damn, at least it went right through."

Crash's hands slid around my leg, the heat from them increasing second by second. "Yes, a clean wound is the best outcome here."

Eric knelt on the other side of me and pulled out a needle and thread. "Here, we can stitch this up."

"I can fix it," Crash said.

"And then she'll owe you," Eric said softly. "That needs to be her decision."

Crash's jaw ticked and then he slowly nodded. "You are correct. The law stands no matter what the circumstances."

His words were strangely formal, but something else stood out to me more: he was holding my gaze in a way that made me think he didn't want me to take him up on his offer. Weird, but I didn't need to owe him anything else.

"I'll take the stitches," I said. Crash moved to leave and I grabbed his hand. "Yeah, you need to give me something to hang onto while he sticks me with the needle."

His fingers wrapped around mine and I closed my eyes as Eric pushed the needle in through the screaming tender flesh around the bullet hole. Because the bullet had gone right through, he had to stitch both sides.

"Why are you here, Crash?" I asked. "Seems a little convenient that you show up and the shooter stops."

"Terrible idea accusing him," Eric whispered. But I opened my eyes and stared straight into Crash's gaze.

"Well?"

Crash didn't smile, his face was neutral. "I could ask you why you are sleeping out here with the bigfoot."

"Guns first," I said. I noticed he didn't rush to explain himself. I mean, I could guess that he was still out there trying to get through to the item protected by the oak trees. But I wanted him to say it.

I wanted him to be honest with me about something.

Crash's hand wrapped a little tighter around mine. "It smelled like a shifter to me. And moved like one too, but it felt...off. That's the only word for it. As if there were magic involved. And then he was gone before I could get a read on what type of shifter he was."

I snorted and then hissed as Eric pushed the needle through another layer of flesh. "Right, well, it seems that's a given, magic being involved, that is."

Crash's lips twitched upward. "I mean that the shifter felt as though he'd been spelled hard."

I didn't quite understand what Crash meant by that, but the pain suddenly ratcheted up and my teeth clamped shut.

"Almost there," Eric mumbled.

"I'm impressed," I said through gritted teeth. "You've got big hands, but you are pretty quick with a needle."

Eric smiled and blushed. "Thank you."

Crash didn't let go of me, his hand locking fingers with mine in a gesture that I couldn't deny left me feeling a little breathless.

Stitched, with a brand new wrap around my leg and my pant leg back in place, I stood up, testing the leg.

There would be very little running for me tonight.

"I'll take you back to my place," Crash said, helping me stand.

"You think that's a good idea?" Eric asked.

"I think you should come with her," Crash said. "You don't know who they were after."

"I'd like to know who they were," I pointed out as I hobbled to the door and peeked out. There was no sign of anyone, certainly no guns pointing at me, or at least none that I could see or sense. "And I can't go home. I have training."

Crash grunted. "You can barely walk."

"Training isn't all physical, you know that, right? If you're stupid, all the running in the world won't save you." I attempted my eyebrow arch, still thinking that one day I'd manage the move. But that day was not today. Both eyebrows rose high.

I folded my arms. "Eric can come with me to the Hollows. He'll be as safe there as anywhere." As soon as the words left my mouth, I regretted them. Because it was a lie and I was no liar.

Crash's eyes narrowed. "Something happened at the Hollows?"

I clasped my hands behind my back. "I'll tell you on the way, how about that?"

At this point, did it matter who knew about Douche Canoe and his friend? I wasn't sure. Eric knew, but Eric I could trust. And if Crash was working for Douche Canoe and his pasty little friend, what then? I mean, I knew he was making the crucible, but that didn't necessarily mean they were his best buddies. But he might be obligated to say something to them. I couldn't risk that.

Crash didn't let go of me, but instead scooped me up into his arms and strode out the door, Eric trailing behind us.

"I can walk," I said, though I'll be honest, the whole being carried around thing was nice.

I wrapped my arms around his neck, bringing us even closer.

"You could hobble at best, and you are already going to be late for your training. I can drop you off at the river, and Eric can help you get to the Hollows from there." Crash's voice rumbled not only in my ears but through my body, pressed to his chest as I was. "Unless it's not safe at the Hollows?"

The urge to lock my legs around him rushed over me, and I closed my eyes as I fought off a wave of lust and libido that threatened to overwhelm me.

"Too tight," Crash whispered, and I realized I'd tightened my hold on his neck.

"Sorry, sorry!" I shook my head. "And yes, it is safe at the Hollows. Just fine and dandy as always."

The day was bright, the sun high, the birds singing, and yet I'd been shot. Eric and I were probably supposed to be dead. I looked back at him. He was a good guy, no matter that he was a shifter—a halfman, as my gran would have said. He smiled at me and hurried a few steps, his long legs eating the distance between us.

"So what happened at the Hollows?" he asked softly.

130

Crash slowed a little and I sighed. Damn it. In for a penny, in for a pound. "Two mages came by last night. They spelled all the mentors and the trainees. Because we interfered with Hattie's ceremony, saving you."

Eric's face fell. "There is something I should tell you about that."

Crash slowed further, stopped and turned toward Eric. "What happened?"

Eric touched his bowtie and lowered his head, and when he spoke again, pain filled his voice. "There was another ceremony, a third one. They were truly prepared. My cousin was killed in New Orleans that same night."

"Eric, I'm so sorry," I reached a hand out to him and he took it, his palm engulfing mine. "I'm so sorry. If we'd known…"

"I know. I tried to warn him, but he thought I was being ridiculous. He said I was being paranoid." He shook his head.

Crash put a hand on Eric's shoulder, but said nothing. A very manly move—no words, just a hand on the shoulder.

Eric patted his hand, again no words.

"We need to hurry." Crash slid his hand around my back again and picked up speed. "You two have to get to the Hollows."

"But what about the mages? They put a spell on all the mentors and trainees so no one can speak about them, and they made it pretty clear they'd punish any one who interferes." I bounced the words out because Crash was jogging, moving at a good clip. "What if one of those guys shot at us?"

That slowed Crash. "You were just out there visiting a friend. Why would they come after you? I don't know who shot at you, but I'm sure it wasn't a mage."

I shrugged, as if I hadn't been out there on a job, working for his ex-wife. "They could be angry that I interfered before. They seem pissy in general, like they wear their underwear two sizes too small and it pulls on their pubes with every step they take."

Crash's face went carefully blank, and then he let out a chuckle. "You...you're right, they are generally pissy." As if he knew.

I swallowed hard, deciding to take a chance. "One of them was the guy you're working for, Crash. The one who wanted you to make the crucible."

That slowed him down. His eyes closed for just a moment. "That is...not good."

"You know who they are?"

"I do. But I can't speak their names either," he said.

He slowed further and his hands loosened their hold on me. The second my foot hit the ground I grimaced. For some reason, the wound had been at the back of my mind as Crash carried me. Even now, it was bad, but not as bad as before.

He took my hand and led me out to a boat—Feish's boat, with Feish in it. Her eyes widened when she saw me and Eric. "My friends, what are they doing out here?"

"Getting into trouble," Crash said.

132

"Hey, I resemble that!" I said as I stepped around him, taking Feish's webbed hand as she helped me into the boat.

Eric followed, but Crash did not.

"Wait, where are you going?" I leaned over the edge of the boat, splashing water at Crash as Feish backed us away from the shoreline.

He gave me a wink. "I don't like people shooting at my friends. I'm going to see if I can track the shifter."

Eric rocked the boat as he settled into his seat and I tightened my grip on the edge. "Crash, don't get hurt."

Gah, I hated how that sounded. Like I cared. I mean, I did. But I wasn't supposed to care. Another wink was all I got, and then he turned away and jogged back the way we'd come.

I slumped in my seat and put a hand to the wound in my leg. It was definitely better healed than it should have been.

Was that Crash? Had he healed my leg even after I'd asked him not to? Did he want me to owe him a favor, after all? Ducking men and their ducking games. The memory of his kiss reminded me why we girls put up with them. Hotness factor one thousand, that was why.

Feish looked me over. "Are you okay?"

I sighed. "Maybe. I don't know." And I really didn't.

As the boat scooted down the river, headed toward the boundary line of the Hollows, a fluttering set of wings caught up to us.

"Kinkly!" I yelled as she shot toward my hand. Her wings were tattered and she looked like she'd been pulled backward through a knothole. "Hey, what happened?"

"Fight with the B-boys." She slumped as she landed in my upturned palm. "I was coming to check on you, and they caught me as they were leaving."

I pulled her close and whispered, "The yellow and black fairies?"

"Yes. Pricks," she mumbled. "They roughed me up, but I'm faster than them. What did you see?"

I gave her a quick report, down to the fact that Crash had almost caught me but still didn't know what I was doing because I'd used Eric as an alibi. Kinkly looked at Eric. "Hi, Eric. How are you doing?"

"Kinkly. I'm well." He was being strangely formal. I realized then that she was showing a lot of leg and he was blushing like crazy while trying not to stare. Oh, lordy, that was not a match made in heaven. The size difference alone was staggering.

Kinkly nodded at him, then pointed at my leg. "What happened? Did Crash shoot you?"

I shook my head. "No, someone else."

She sighed and lifted above my hand. "I'll check in with you after I report back to my queen."

Just at the periphery of my vision, Feish stiffened up. Of course, she would understand what I'd gotten myself into more than anyone else. Karissa was Crash's ex. Feish would of course side with him. "Okay, sounds good. Be safe, Kink."

She blinked at me, what I think might have been tears. "Okay. You too. Don't get shot again." She paused. "Bye Eric." And then she was gone in a flash.

"Goodbye," he whispered, sounding like a love-sick puppy.

I leaned back against the edge of the boat. The sun was on its downward slide already. I was going to be late for training if we went the usual route to River Street then across Savannah's downtown district to get to the Hollows. "Feish, how long before we are there?"

"Ten minutes, if we go all the way by boat," she said. "You be a little late, but not too late."

True to her word, we pulled up not nine minutes later to the riverside edge of the graveyard the Hollows called home. I might have brought a couple of uninvited guests, but at least I was on time.

Eric held out his hand, but I didn't need any help. My leg felt almost like new.

Crash had definitely pulled a fast one on me and healed me. There was no other way I'd be doing this well after being shot like that. I rubbed at my leg, a tingle running down it. Yes, definitely something magic.

"Son of a bitch," I muttered. Feish threw me the rope and I tied the boat up to a small tree. From there, the three of us hurried up the slope to the back side of the graveyard. The sound of training reached my ears before we crested the last of the rise. Meaning the sounds of running, grunting, and an oof or two.

Luke was the first one to see us, his young face an open book as he grinned my way. "Hey, Bree, you brought friends!"

I grinned back. "Yes. I. Did."

He and Suzy came over and fist bumped me. See, I could be cool when I wanted.

However, others were not so cool. Sarge stalked over to us, a strange smell wafting along with him. "What the hell is this? You can't bring them here."

My jaw dropped. "Wait, what?"

"Feish works for Crash. She can duck right off." No, he did not say duck, but my autocorrect fixed it for me.

"Have you lost your marbles along with your sense of humor?" I snapped. "Go chew on a bone, you oversized poodle."

Sarge strode up to me. "You're out."

I blinked up at him. "What the duck?"

His eyes narrowed, his whole body vibrated, and his hands clenched like he was trying to keep from strangling me. This was not the Sarge I knew. And yet I was staring at him as he said words I couldn't believe. "You brought enemies here, to the Hollows. That is strictly forbidden. You're out."

My fists shot to my hips as my own temper flared. "Are you crazy? Eric was a client. Feish is my friend. And I just got—"

"Get out. I don't care if you got shot," he growled the two words, his mouth elongating as he began to shift to his wolf form. "As a mentor, if I believe there is a cause, I can remove you from the training program immediately. There is a cause. You are bring-ing harm to the Hollows."

A wash of power seemed to flow off him and push me back, and even though I didn't understand, I had no doubt he'd somehow just cut my ties to the Hollows.

"Sarge, have you lost your mind?" I couldn't lose this job. I needed to keep training, to keep learning. More than that, I liked most of the people here, they were becoming friends.

Suzy cleared her throat. "I think you're being harsh, Sarge. Eric is fine I'm sure, and Feish is not going to—"

"You can go too then." Sarge wheeled on her, and that same push of power curled around her. She gasped and stumbled backward as if he'd struck her.

He'd lost his mind, that was the only way I could make sense of it. This was not the lighthearted, sweet guy I'd met. His body kept on shifting, kept on changing until he was the massive werewolf I'd tackled on that first night in the cemetery.

I didn't take a step back as he bared his teeth and growled at me. I was between him and Feish and Eric. "Sarge, don't make me stab you again. 'Cause this time I'll cut your balls off to make sure we deal with the obvious overload of testosterone that is fry-ing your brain."

His ears flattened against his head, but he didn't come at me.

He didn't back down either.

Eric touched my shoulder, his big hand engulfing it. "We should go. Before this gets any uglier than a werewolf being territorial."

He wasn't wrong, but damn it, I hated to leave as if I were the one who should have my tail tucked between my legs.

I put my hand on top of his, and gave it a pat. "You go with Feish, take the boat. I'll meet you at my gran's house."

Sarge snarled, snapping his teeth in my direction, and my hand shot out and smashed him right in the nose. He dropped to his belly, eyes shut tight. "You are being a total shit. I don't know why, and I don't care at this point," I said.

Eric and Feish hurried back down the slope. I didn't want to leave either of them alone, so it was best that they went together. I watched them go to the boat and get in before I turned my back on them.

Suzy, though, would be alone if I left now. And if I remembered right, she had a car.

I walked over to her and touched her arm, feeling the clamminess of her skin. "Come on. I can drive if you want."

When I directed her toward the gate, she went willingly enough. I realized that no other mentor had witnessed what had gone down. I wanted to go find Eammon, but I didn't dare. Because I had a feeling that Sarge would do more than snap his teeth if I pushed this right now. "I'm sorry you got sucked into that," I said.

"Not your fault. He's lost his mind. But I need this job, I can barely pay my rent right now," she whispered.

"Let's go get a drink," I said. "We can discuss our options."

And that is how I ended up in Suzy's battered old car—dusty blue if you didn't count the rust spots as orange—which barely had room for two in it because of all the stuff jammed into the backseat. I twisted around to try and identify the items that were taking up all the room and ended up shaking my head. There was too much of it, contained in boxes and bags, and it smelled a little funky. "Are you living in your car?" Was this what she'd meant about her rent being too high?

"No." She flopped in the driver's seat and turned the key. The engine turned over surprisingly well for what the car looked like. "I just don't trust my landlord, so I keep some of my stuff in here."

"Paranoid much?"

"Oh, totally." She bobbed her head and grinned, but the grin slid off her face. "Life is much better if you think everyone is out to get you. That way, you're never surprised when the knife finally comes swinging your way."

I rolled my eyes. "That sounds like something Corb would say."

"He is my trainer, or I guess he was." She tried to smile at me again, but the edges of her lips trembled. "And he had his reasons for picking me. One of them is that we think alike." Her eyes swept over me.

"What was his other reason?" I smiled back at her so she wouldn't think I was being a bitch. Apparently it didn't work. She glared at me, and tears pooled at the corners of her eyes.

"It's not like that. I mean, yes, he's hot but… he's not interested in me, he made that clear," she snapped.

I held up both hands in mock surrender. "I wasn't being a jerk. I was just wondering if you had a connection to the shadow world. Eammon picked me for my family connections and previous training." At least, that was what I assumed. I'd never told Eammon who I was, but I had to admit it was too much of a coincidence for him to have randomly approached me.

"Oh," she said, all the ire going out of her. "I think it's because my mother is half siren."

I stared hard at her. "Seriously? Like you could sing a man to his death and…"

"And make him enjoy it while he died? In theory, yes. But the truth is my blood is too diluted. So the siren in me calls men, but I can't kill them unless I use a weapon. Corb was immune to my call, and I liked that." She seemed a little too sad about that for my liking.

I cleared my throat. "So are you dating anyone right now?"

She glanced at me. "Are you hitting on me?"

I rolled my eyes. "You know what, just because you are young and beautiful does not mean that everyone wants to sleep with you."

"Sure it does."

"No, it doesn't. I am just trying to get to know you since we both got kicked out of the Hollows. Also, you need to get used to the idea that at some point you won't be the young one anymore. You'll be just like me, fighting to prove yourself." And apparently losing that fight because one stupid werewolf got his tail in a twist.

I bit back the rest of the words that wanted to pour out of me. How it was hard to get anyone to take you seriously if you were a middle-aged, divorced woman starting a new career. How I was finding it all beyond exasperating. Irritating as duck.

She giggled at me. Freaking giggled. "I will *never* be you."

I gritted my teeth and stared out the window. "One day, you'll understand, and by then you'll have wasted your youth thinking it would last forever."

"No, seriously, I won't age. That's the perk of siren blood. I'm over fifty already."

I might have strangled her right then and there if not for the fact that she'd tried to stick up for me back there with Sarge. She was older than me, but had none of the side effects of age. I settled for twisting around to stare hard at her. She shrugged and turned the car onto River Street. "Look, I don't age like a real human. I really am still like a teenager in a siren's lifetime."

Yes, I could see that with my own eyes—she didn't look a hair over nineteen. "Great."

"It's not my fault. People don't see me either, you know. They see a young blond white chick, and they think I'm an idiot. That I couldn't possibly have a brain in my head, or muscles in my body. Because I'm pretty."

"Heartbreaking," I drawled.

"It really is," she whispered.

I twisted in my seat. "I have a friend who is a woman of color, her name is Mavis. If you want to talk about being treated cruelly for no reason, taken for granted, and walked all over as if you are nothing, then you can talk to her. *She* has a shit deal. But don't complain to me because you have perfect skin, teeth, and hair, and there are some things in life you have to actually work for. Do you expect that everything should just be handed to you? Get over yourself."

She sucked in a sharp breath. "That was mean."

I was angry now, and whatever compassion I might have had for her because of the Hollows situation was gone. "That was honest. Pity no one has told you that you have a leg up that most women would kill for."

And yes, maybe that was harder than the situation warranted—again, she'd just lost a job. Damn it, we both had. What the hell was I going to do now? I rubbed my hands over my face and let out a deep sigh. "Look, I'm sorry if that was harsher than it needed to be."

"Doesn't make it not true." Suzy tapped her fingers on the steering wheel. "We're both in the same spot now. Stuck." We were both quiet until she parked the car a few minutes later.

She turned to me. "Whenever I'm stuck, I get my cards read and it helps me figure out what to do next. I can't think of a better time for that than right now, after I lost a chance at a job that I loved. I'm going to a tarot reader, do you want to come?"

I got out of the car. "You sure you want more of my pithy, hard-ass truths?"

"Maybe." She shrugged. "It's been a long time since anyone has been anything but afraid of me. Even my mother."

My eyebrows shot up. "Seriously? I give you a smack down after you got fired for sticking up for me, and you still want to be friends?"

She shut her car door with a loud slam that bounced through the night air. Just after dinner for most people, there was still a lot of movement along the river's edge. Lots of people out walking hand in hand.

"I think honesty is a great foundation for a friendship, even if it is with an old lady." She grinned at me and I glared at her.

"That's rich coming from the half-century chick. And just so you know, I think I see a wrinkle," I shot back.

Her hands flew to her face. "Really?"

"Left eye," I said.

She gasped and bent to look in her side mirror. "I don't see it."

Suzy kept on talking, muttering about derma-planing, laser therapy, and a spell that her mother had given her on her deathbed. But my eyes were drawn to the river flowing in front of us. River Street was named because—you guessed it—it ran along the Savannah River. The river was wide and deep and dark, flowing out to the Atlantic Ocean. I'd spent my childhood looking at it, and yet that night it seemed entirely different. Maybe it was the quiet of the night, or the clear sky above that allowed the stars to reflect in the water, but the river called to me. It felt like more than just a river.

I was at the top of a set of stairs that led down to the actual river when Suzy caught up to me. "Did you really see a wrinkle?"

"Must have been my mirror," I murmured. "Does the water seem different to you?"

She paused and looked out over the river. Her breathing slowed and then hitched. "Yes. It's alive tonight. It happens at certain times of the year. It is full of the dead, you know."

I jerked around to look at her. "What?"

Her eyes were misty as she stared into the water. "The dead of the ships that went down, of course, but also the supernaturals who scared the locals. They don't talk about that in the history books, or even in the tours. Dead people suspected of being supernatural were stuffed into coffins full of rocks, wrapped in chains, and sunk out in the river. It's deep enough they could do that."

There was a moment, just a split second, where I thought I could see the past, see the panic on people's faces as another sweep of plague ravaged their city.

They'd been desperate, the kind of desperate where they'd do anything to stop it. The vision changed, and I watched as the panicked humans stuffed *living* people into coffins, wrapped the death traps in chains, and rowed them out to the middle of the river. Some fought back, and a few of them had fangs that drew blood, something that only emboldened the humans and filled them with righteous certainty. I blinked as the images faded to nothing.

I bit my lower lip. "The ones they sunk, were they from the shadow world? Some of them were vampires."

"Yes," she said. "They were the ones who worked with the humans, trying to help them. And in the end it got them killed. My mother said it was a big part of why the shadow world keeps to itself, even now. But the vampires made it worse. They drew a lot of heat for it, which is why they were wiped out by the rest of the shadow world after that." She paused and the air grew heavy with the weight of her words. "I think," she said, "there are a lot of people who would want to meet us now, but the past has shown us that humans aren't capable of sharing. We are too frightening for them."

I gave a slow nod. "Yes, I can see that. Similar to what my gran told me. She always told me it was safer this way. That the best way to look after those in the light was by staying in the shadows."

Suzy was very still as we stood there staring out over the river, the past flowing around us as surely as the water before us. I shook myself and the spell—if it was even that—broke. "Let's go see that tarot card reader."

She blinked a few times and then nodded. "Yeah, let's do it."

10

Suzy led the way down the stairs on River Street to the actual water's edge of the Savannah River. The water lapped at the banks below the walkway, splashing up here and there. She was clearly bringing me to a different tarot reader than the one Sarge had brought me to at the start of training. Then again, there had to be hundreds of tarot readers in Savannah. To the left of us was someone else walking down River Street, enjoying the cool air no doubt. But unlike us, they disappeared over the edge of the street toward the river itself.

"Where is this tarot reader?" I asked. I mean, what if she was leading me to my death? Completely possible seeing as a) she had lost her job defending me and then b) I had basically kicked her ass in a verbal spar that was nothing but hard truths.

"He's in one of the old slave's quarters. A very old man, but good at what he does," she said, picking her way along the path.

I frowned. "Enslaved."

"Right," she said. "He dabbles in darker magic, and the blood and death here work for him."

My feet stuttered and it wasn't because I'd stumbled or had a muscle cramp. "Why are we not going to Annie from before?"

"Because she won't tell you shit. She gives you a card and then says nothing. She's not going to deliver any bad news like a real tarot reader. We need to figure out what we're doing, you know? The Hollows is out, so we need to find new paths."

I frowned. "Maybe I don't want bad news. I've had a lot of that lately." Besides, I had a habit of picking death cards, and that was the last thing I needed just now.

"If you don't know what's coming, how do you stop it?" She looked over her shoulder and raised a perfect eyebrow in an enviable arch. Damn it. I didn't try to out-arch her—I knew when I was beat. Besides, she had a point. Maybe knowing what was coming, good or bad, was not a bad thing.

Maybe I'd be able to use whatever the tarot reader said to figure out who was shooting at me? Or maybe why they were shooting at me.

"The tide is out, which is going to make this easier." She jogged ahead of me down the path. Of course she didn't know about the whole gunshot thing. The second I tried to break into a jog, the still somewhat wounded calf cramped up and I yelped. She looked back at me. "You need to hurry. If the tide comes in while we are still with him, we'll be trapped."

I forced my aching legs to move, wincing with each step of my wounded leg, limping along behind her, feeling every bounce of my hips and even a ripple under my bra strap along my back. Back fat is a real bitch, let me tell you.

Suzy ducked suddenly to her right, as if stepping directly into the seawall, but of course it was an opening into one of the old enslaved quarters. Water dripped from the ceiling, and the only light came from sputtering candles placed here and there to lead us further into the depths. I couldn't help but notice not only the shackle bolts that still hung from the ceilings and walls, but how shiny they were. As if they were still in use.

Jaysus lord, this was maybe not the best idea.

My guts twisted as we went further into the tunnel, far deeper than was prudent given that we might need to scoot back out quick.

"Ah, Suzanne, lovely to see you. And you brought a friend." The tarot card reader's voice tugged at my dusty memory banks. Okay, I wasn't that old, but it felt like it at the moment. I was tired, sore, sweating, and tired (yes, I meant to write tired twice). I wanted to go home, and bury my face in a bowl of ice cream chased with a good dose of whiskey, and yet here I was tagging along with Suzy as if I could keep up with her.

Suzy slowed. "Where is Dracus?"

I glanced at her and tried to get a look at the speaker in the shadows. "Dracus is…otherwise occupied. I was just leaving."

I was guessing Dracus was the tarot card reader that Suzy had wanted to see, but if that was the case, then, "How did you know her name?" I asked. "If you aren't the tarot card reader?"

Suzy stiffened as if just realizing she didn't know this new dude.

Laughter rolled to us through the darkness. "I know many, many people. I make it my business to know them. Especially the talented ones that the Hollows Group bring in."

"Bree, I think we should go." Suzy took a step back, and in theory, I was right there with her, except that something stopped me. Instead of going back, I stepped up beside her and got my first good look at this guy who knew her name, but shouldn't.

There were candles stuffed into random nooks along the curved wall, held in place only by dripping trails of wax. The smell of fetid sea water and marijuana was strong, and if the plumes of smoke around his head were any indication, he was the source of the smoke. I made myself take the space in, trying to memorize it like Eammon had been instructing me. That was the best way to prepare oneself to fight, bargain, or run. Or so Eammon had said. I'd yet to put it into practice.

The man sat behind an old card table with green felt peeling at the edges, something that almost certainly was not his own. The legs were probably rusted, but I couldn't see them. At the four corners of the table stood long black taper candles that sputtered pale blue flames. I tried to look past him into the confines of the tunnel, but there was nothing but darkness.

"Not ominous at all," I muttered under my breath. Apparently not as quietly as I thought because Suzy shot me a look.

"I can read your cards for you. I am as good as Dracus, or perhaps even better." He spread his hands over the table, showing off a deck of tarot cards.

Suzy seemed drawn forward, her feet moving even as I tried to grab her arm and stop her.

There was no way she thought this was a good idea, or I was a monkey's uncle. My mind leapt back to our lesson from the day before, the recognizing and breaking of spells.

The problem? I was no good at either, but I still tried. The smell of weed was the only thing I could pick up on, and if I weren't careful, I'd be higher than a kite. Could that be covering the scent of the spell? Because I was sure that Suzy was under some sort of compulsion.

Suzy flopped a hundred-dollar bill onto that green felt table, and I shook my head. "Suze, this is a terrible idea. Take your money, let's go." I touched her and got a zing up my fingers. Yup, she was definitely under a spell.

Damn it, could I not get a single break?

The tarot reader turned his head my way. The way those candles lit the shadows instead of his face made me think that he was eyeless, and I didn't like that. Until those dark holes where his eyes should have been flashed a bright pink, of all colors. My lips twitched. "Okay, Pink Eye, that was weird but hardly terrifying. You can get drops for that, you know. Any pharmacy should carry them over the counter."

He snarled and Suzy hissed something at me that sounded like *shut the duck up.*

"You are insolent," he said.

And with that one word—*insolent*—I knew who he was. Or sort of knew who he was.

"Douche Canoe's friend," I whispered and took another step back. Suzy didn't move. I reached for her and tried to drag her toward the exit. How the hell had he come to be here? Had he somehow followed us? The figure on the top of the river's edge had been him, I was suddenly sure of it. Which meant he'd somehow known where to find us.

A tingle of apprehension curled through my feet, up my legs, and settled into the pit of my stomach.

"This is a bad idea. We need to go. Right now," I said.

"Would you be quiet? I like his voice," she said, but there was no heat in it. More like she was drugged. Or in this case, spelled.

I clamped my mouth shut, mostly because I realized right then how much danger we were in. Suzy had no idea, but I did. This fellow was one of the bad guys and had, only yesterday, put a spell on the entire Hollows Group, yours truly excepted, and threatened their lives. What if there had been more to that spell than keeping them all from talking? There could have been anything in it. Tracking. Compulsion. You name it.

"Pick your card, half-breed," he growled at Suzy.

She sucked in a sharp breath but still reached forward and took a card, sliding it across to him.

"It is the Fool," he all but purred. "That's rather fitting, don't you think?"

"I am not a fool!" she yelled, and the sound of her screech rebounded through the space. I took a step back and bumped into something...skeletal. I froze until I peeked over my shoulder to see Robert there, swaying side to side, his long hair hiding his face as always.

"What are you doing here?" I whispered the words, or more accurately mouthed them.

"Friend. Trouble."

Oh, that was not what I wanted to hear, but let's be honest, I was not surprised. I slowly turned back to the rickety table, and the man on the other side of it, who would probably kill me if he figured out I was the one who'd put the kibosh on the bigfoot sacrifice ceremony. Oh, and that I'd escaped his spell.

"Suzy, the fool doesn't mean that you're an idiot." I forced my feet forward to stand next to her. "I always get the death card, and I haven't died yet."

She turned her face to me, perfect blond hair swinging in its high ponytail. Her face was artfully streaked with tears that looked as if they'd been painted on. If I'd been that angry and crying, my face would have been splotched with red spots, streaked with snot and tears, and I'd struggle to speak clearly between hiccupping sobs. She, on the other hand, had no problem speaking.

"Oh. I didn't know that."

"The fool card means the start of a journey. Which is good considering what happened tonight, don't you think?" I said. There was probably more to it than that, but I wasn't going to get into it with her. Certainly not with this one in front of us.

"Now you are a tarot reader?" Pink Eye turned his gaze on me. I stared back.

"Nope, but I've seen enough readings to know the fool does not mean she's an idiot. Unless we're saying she's stupid to give you a hundred bucks for a single card pull." I put one hand on my hip. Sure, maybe it wasn't the most logical approach to take with a dangerous adversary, but the best way to fight fear was to counter attack. Be confident, don't let them see or smell your fear—that's the deal with dogs, and this dude was a dirty dog. "You're a scam artist."

"I am not. The power in me is strong."

Cripes, he sounded like the Emperor in *Star Wars*. That flash of pink in his eyes made me shake my head, though, and it dulled the fear a little. "Seriously, pink eye is contagious as all get out. Don't touch your face, Suzy, God only knows what he had on his hands when he touched the cards."

154

Suzy gasped and looked at her hands, then wiped them on her pants. Pink Eye stood up, and yeah, I had to admit power rolled off him, pushing me back a step and stealing a breath from me. "For you, I will draw for free. Because I see your fate is coming faster than you could possibly imagine, and I wish to watch you fail."

I shrugged as though his words and power meant nothing to me, even though my belly was rolling and the nausea that came with it was trying to ram its way up my throat.

"It'll probably be the death card. It shows up all the time with me." I hadn't planned on touching the cards at all, not least of all because I didn't want pink eye. More like we had to go before he did...whatever it was he wanted to do to us. I was betting he hadn't arranged this little meet-cute to invite us for tea and cookies.

But my hand seemed to have a life of its own as I reached out and let my palm hover over the spread of cards on the rickety table. Using my middle finger, I slid the cards around until one seemed to warm under my touch. "This one." I slid it out to the edge of the table, where Pink Eye took it and flipped it over.

"The moon card." He breathed slower, his words coming in an almost hypnotic trance. I stared at the card, at the big moon dominating the majority of it. It was not put together like most of the moon cards I'd seen over the years. A massive rotting wolf's head dominated the image, its mouth open and snarling, a huge yellow moon behind it. Great. "Hidden enemies await you, and your path is dark and fraught with danger, madness. You will go to a place where your mind will play tricks on you." He paused. "And I see passion, like a tornado ripping your world apart, but you seek it out despite the danger of it." He blinked those stupid pink eyes up at me while I struggled to breathe because his words were like nails being driven into my body with disturbing accuracy. Cold sweat broke out along my body, and my arms bumped up with gooseflesh in the cool of the tunnel.

Okay, he was good. Very, very good.

"Vaguebooking if you ask me," Suzy muttered, her voice cutting through the emotions raging in me. "Even I could have said something like that. Nothing about a new journey for you? You lost your job too."

She'd broken the spell between me and my buddy Pink Eye. He looked between us. "You are no longer with the Hollows Group?"

"No," Suzy said even as I said, "Yes."

Because call me crazy, but I had a feeling there was a certain protection that came from being with the Hollows Group, and this one would take advantage of the fact that we were no longer associated with them.

I took a step back and shook my head, bumping into Robert. I put a hand behind me and tried to get him to move in front of us, because I was done with this pink-eyed dude, done, done, done. He was bad news, and we had every reason to leave now. We'd both pulled a card. We could pretend that was good enough for us.

Suzy and Pink Eye didn't see Robert, as far as I could tell, and I didn't want them to either. He was my secret weapon, and despite the fact that he only showed up when I was in real trouble, I felt safer for having him there.

The water sloshed around our feet as I hurried out. "What the hell is his name?" I asked no one in particular.

"O'Sean," he said from behind us. "My name is Sean O'Sean."

I shouldn't have stopped, I really shouldn't have, but my sense of humor insisted otherwise. My feet stuttered to a stop as I spun around. "No."

"No, what? Sleep." He somehow stayed in the shadows even though we were right near the opening and the moonlight was illuminating the edge of the tunnel, Suzy's closed eyes, and…oh shit.

I blinked at Sean O'Sean and he blinked back at me. "Why are you not sleeping?" he murmured.

I obediently closed my eyes and did my best to slow my breathing to something reminiscent of sleep. Or in my case exhaustion. Because whatever spell he'd put on Suzy and the other trainees clearly allowed him to put them asleep at will, and if he realized he couldn't do that with me, I had no doubt there would be repercussions.

I could fake it, I had to. My chest tightened with a sudden fit of hysterical laughter that I barely managed to hold inside. How many times had I faked it with my ex? Himself had never figured it out. Surely I could out-fake Sean O'Sean. A snicker climbed up my throat as Sean O'Sean walked around the two of us. With my eyes closed I knew I was at a disadvantage, but I did have my weapons strapped to my thighs. I could fight back if he tried something.

Of course, that was where our fake tarot card reader stopped next, his hand sliding over my thigh, where one of my daggers rested in a sheath. "Interesting. These belong to the Smith. Yet you have them? Dangerous weapons for such an inexperienced woman."

Oh, lordy, I was in trouble. He tried to pull a knife, hissed, and snatched his hand away. "You've blooded them already, have you? And whose blood is it? Powerful, a witch…perhaps you are not the noodle-headed old lady you seem to be."

My eyes popped open into a perfect glare. "Who the hell are you calling an old lady?"

He stumbled back, then pointed a finger at me, pink eyes blazing in the darkness. "You were the one who stopped the ceremony."

Yeah, I was in trouble all right.

He lifted his hands, and for a moment his face was illuminated by a swirl of light cupped between his palms. His mouth worked on a spell, teeth flashing a little too sharp for my taste, eyes pink, and if I knew anything, it was that I couldn't take my time dithering about what to do.

"Robert!"

The skeleton lurched forward, features still hidden beneath his rags and long black hair, to tackle

Sean O'Sean to the ground. There was a burst of light, and Robert shrieked and was flung backward into a pile of bones and rags.

I pulled my two blades out, but Sean O'Sean was already on his feet and prepping another spell. "You won't be messing up anything else, old lady."

"We're back to *old lady*?" I feinted to the left and he followed, but I was already moving to the right and slashing the turquoise-handled blade at him, aiming between his hands. The spell he was making had pooled there, and I had to stop it. I had to or both Suzy and I were done.

A pulse of energy ran through me, from the ground all the way up my legs, torso, and into my hands in a flash, as if charging the blade in my palm.

"I thought she was the one," Sean growled as he threw a spell at me. I dropped and rolled, bumping against the wet wall of the tunnel. "I followed her to kill her. But I'll be happy to kill you both."

I didn't have to ask why. "Wrecking your plans, am I?"

"Bitch."

"Every inch of me." I grinned as I lunged forward, that energy still coursing through me from the ground as I managed to drive the blade between his hands.

A flash on the metal tugged at my eyes as the knife went through the edge of his spell. A moment of absolute quiet seemed to implode the world, and then a boom ripped through the air as the spell exploded, and both Sean O'Sean and I were flung backward. Him into the depths of the tunnel, and me out into the incoming tide of the ocean-fed river.

I hit the water and went under into complete darkness, my butt hitting the bottom quickly, which told me I wasn't very deep at least. The cool water eased the backlash of the spell, that and the salt water, which helped diffuse any lingering effects of the magic.

I pushed off the bottom and broke the surface, still gripping both knives. With a wobble, I found my feet and stood up in neck-deep water. I slid both knives into their sheaths and sloshed forward. Suzy looked over the edge, eyes blinking sleepily. "What happened?"

"Time to go," I said and held a hand up to her. She grabbed me around the wrist, grimaced, and helped haul me up and over the edge.

"You could stand to lose a few—"

"Shut it." I barely looked at her, my eyes locked on the back of the tunnel. "Come on, we'd better see…" What? If Sean O'Sean was going to come out after us? Probably. Also, there was Dracus, the actual tarot card reader. And Robert. I needed to see if he was okay. He'd blown apart into nothing but bones and rags.

Dripping briny water, I forced my wobbling legs forward. I wasn't sure if it was fear or not. Chose not to think about it too much.

"Maybe we should just go." Suzy tugged on my arm. "I don't want to go in there. I feel funny."

I swung a look at her. "This was your idea, but I gotta say I doubt you had this in mind."

"I brought us down here? No, I wouldn't have. It's scary," she whispered.

That did not sound like Suzy at all.

What in the hell had old Pink Eye done to her? Because without a doubt he'd put a spell on her.

Damn it, like I needed one more thing to fix.

11

I made myself go back into the tunnel that had once served as a prison for the enslaved. It felt even more ominous this time, but I had to know if Sean O'Sean was still in there. That, and I had to gather up what was left of poor Robert.

With a flashlight in hand (I never left home without at least one in my handy cross-body bag), I ventured inside. Robert was first. There were no rags or scattered bones to be found, just the single finger digit bone he'd given me before. I'd take that as a good sign. I scooped it up and slid it into my bag. "Hope you are okay, friend," I said quietly. Not that I was afraid or anything.

Who was I kidding? I was freaking terrified. I had to stop twice to clamp my legs together to keep from peeing myself, and even then I couldn't be sure I hadn't because I was already dripping so much water, what was one more trickle?

What if Sean O'Sean wasn't dead?

What if he was?

Flashlight in one hand, knife in the other, I made it to the green felted table before something touched me on the back. I screeched and leapt forward as Suzy screamed behind me. We did a weird dance that had the flashlight bobbing and my hand trying to fight the impulse to throw the knife at her. My reflexes were decent, but spotty. Kind of like Wi-Fi out in the country. Sometimes the signal was strong, but more often than not it was a spinning ball of death while I waited for something to jog my training memories.

"Jaysus!" I yelled. "What the hell are you trying to do? Stop my heart?"

"Sorry, I just didn't want you to go in by yourself." She was shaking hard in the light, but she was there. See, that was more like the Suzy I knew. Bold. Well, sort of bold right then.

I took a quarter turn so my light flashed over the table again. The moon card was still there, flipped up. I tucked it into my bag. I didn't know why I needed to have it, but I did. One of those gut feelings. "Stay close," I said.

Suzy took me at my word and all but hugged me as we crept further into the tunnel. The water was coming in now and each step we took splashed. The first body we found was not Sean O'Sean.

"That's Dracus," Suzy whispered. We stared down at the old man with no hair, a big gut, and his tongue sticking out of his mouth in a forever raspberry. There was no rope around his neck, but there were plenty of spells that could have strangled him. I made myself bend and touch his neck, just in case.

"Still warm, but no heartbeat," I whispered. He'd barely been dead when we'd walked in the tunnel. Nothing we could do now.

I stood and shuffled in a little further, sweeping the flashlight back and forth.

"What is that?" she whispered as we neared the back of the tunnel. There were no candles back here, but there was a large dark shape on the ground.

Face down.

In a puddle.

"I think you killed him," Suzy whispered. "Did you kill him?"

I made myself walk forward and bent to touch his neck too. The problem was his neck was crumpled at a weird angle. No need to touch that. "His neck is broken. I think he hit the wall when the explosion sent us flying apart."

"What do we do?" she whispered.

The water sloshed in around our ankles now, and we'd be in trouble ourselves if we stayed that deep in the tunnel. "We leave them both. The tide will pull them out."

"We'll get caught," she whispered.

"We didn't touch Dracus, and O'Sean's own magic threw his ass back here. Let the river of the dead have them," I said.

My words added a weighted chill to the air and the river sloshed in harder.

I backed up, grabbed Suzy's hand, and hauled ass as if I hadn't been shot earlier that day. We ran all the way back to her car, where I took the keys from her shaking hands, put them in the ignition, and peeled the tires to get out of there.

I'd just killed someone. A bad someone, but still someone. Sure, I hadn't really killed him. I mean, it was his own magic that had sent him flying. But still.

Second person in one week. This could not be good.

"Oh my God, you killed him! What are we going to do?" Suzy repeated her question.

"What do you mean what are *we* going to do? You didn't do anything. He spelled you," I said as I turned the wheel hard at the top of the incline in order to get us further away from the riverfront.

"He...are you sure he spelled me?"

"You don't feel different? Because you seem different. Like, before we went in there you were all full of confidence despite having just lost a job, but he put some kind of spell on you and now you're terrified with like zero confidence," I said, checking mirrors as I drove. Mostly to see if anyone was following us.

I had us back to Perry Street and Corb's loft in no time. There were no lights on inside, and I doubted that he was back yet. "You can stay here with me tonight. You aren't yourself. Maybe it's a good thing we both got canned." Because I wasn't sure how we could have kept this from the mentors. This was... this was bad.

Then again, there was a good chance Douche Canoe could track all of the mentors and trainees, and that he could also control them like Pink Eye had messed with Suzy. I should at least warn the mentors that I had an inkling of what the spell would do. I'd tell Corb, I decided, and he could do with the knowledge what was best for him and the others.

I parked the car and she let herself out, but she was not steady on her feet by any means. "Wait," I said, thinking of Robert. "I just have to do something quick."

I hurried across the street and over to the wrought iron fence that wrapped around Centennial Park Cemetery. A quick dig in my bag produced Robert's finger bone, and I put it through the fence so that he was in the cemetery. That felt right, like he would be able to recharge. "There you go. Hope that helps."

Backing away, I didn't bother to answer Suzy's pointed questions. "What was that about? What did you put in there? I thought I saw a skeleton, is that right?"

Interesting. I hadn't thought she'd seen him. "You had your eyes closed," I said as I let us into Corb's loft, "so you tell me how you saw a skeleton."

She walked next to me as we climbed the long flight of stairs to the main floor of the loft. "I don't know, I just did. It was when you were shoving me out of the cave, like seeing a ghost. He was there and then not."

"He's a friend. And he got hurt, so I had to put him back there for now," I said, not wanting to say much more than that. Not that I had much more to say. As far as I could tell, there was no real pattern to who could or couldn't see Robert. Louis, the Hollows's resident necromancer, couldn't see him, but Sarge could. But maybe that's because Robert had bitten off Sarge's ear?

I shook off the questions and headed straight for the liquor cupboard that Corb thought he was hiding because it was above my eye level. Time for some Jameson.

I snorted and pulled down a bottle of whiskey before turning to Suzy. "Pick your poison."

She startled and then eased onto one of the barstools at the kitchen island. "Rum and Coke."

I made her a drink with a double shot of rum, and an extra splash for good measure, and poured the same amount of whiskey for myself—straight up. I snapped mine back and the burn raced all the way to my belly, chasing away a coldness that I hadn't even realized was still there. Of course, I was dripping water all over Corb's original hardwood floors, which could explain the cold. I sighed and stripped right there in the kitchen, shoving my leather pants and loose tank top into the sink. Suzy arched a brow at me.

"You aren't my type."

"Not giving you a show," I said and blew out a breath. "Corb will not be happy if I wreck his floors."

She tapped her glass and I obliged, then did the same again for myself. I like my whiskey, but mostly I was prepping myself for the phone call I knew I was going to have to make.

"I need to tell Eammon what happened," I said. And maybe I could talk to him about being canned by that idiot Sarge.

"Gods, no!" Suzy spluttered rum and Coke across the counter and all over my bare skin. I looked down at the brown flecks, grabbed a dishrag and wiped them off.

"Okay, why wouldn't we tell him? There may be five people who lead the Hollows, but he's *in charge* in charge. And he needs to know what happened with Sarge too. And that the spell the O'Seans put on everyone is doing weird things to you. Making you less confident. Making you susceptible to them. Maybe it'll wear off, maybe it won't. We just don't know." Over the last few days, Eammon had taken the lead in cleaning up the mess that was Hattie's blood ceremony gone awry. I'd seen just how competent he was at managing not only the Hollows, but the shadow world at large.

"Because it's a bad idea. I don't want anyone to know." She frowned and rubbed at her head. "I don't feel so well."

I poured her another rum and Coke. "Drink up, then shower, then bed."

She did as she was told, which in and of itself was strange. Suzy had a stronger personality than this. I'd

168

seen it that first day we were brought into the Hollows. Not to mention every training day since. I was almost positive the spell was making her this way. But no one else had seemed more fearful than usual. I mean, look at Sarge losing his marbles.

Huh. That thought tried to take root, but it was extinguished by the drink in my hand.

It didn't take her long to get her drink down, and then I hustled her off to the shower. I found her a clean shirt and shorts, and set them on the back of the toilet while she showered. "You okay?"

"Wobbly."

"Please don't make me come in there with you," I muttered and stepped out of the bathroom. I liked her and all, but we weren't exactly friends. Maybe one day. The friends thing, not the shower thing.

A fluttering of wings pulled me toward my bedroom. Kinkly sat on the windowsill in there, peering at me in my bra and underwear. Her wings had been stitched back together, but I could still see where the tears had been. I put my hands on my hips. "You have something to say?"

"You're all wet. And kind of soft," she said. "What happened?"

I sighed. "We had some trouble down on the waterfront. Hang on, I want to show you something."

She squeaked as I turned around, and I looked over my shoulder. "What, is there something on my back?"

Kinkly shook her head, her rust-colored hair floating around her face from the fanning of her wings. "No, I thought you were going to strip."

169

Oh for duck's sake. I may or may not have muttered that under my breath, minus the autocorrect, as I strode out of the room and to the kitchen where I'd left my bag. I found the tarot card, pulled it out, and turned to go back to my bedroom. Only I bumped into a bare chest that was way too well defined to belong to anyone but Corb. I slowly looked up, found myself speechless.

And in nothing but my underwear and bra. Awesome.

"Hi. What are you doing here?" I asked. Stupid, stupid I know.

His eyebrows shot up over very sleepy eyes. "I live here."

"Right, what I meant was I thought you weren't here tonight. I thought you were out on a job."

He turned his head to the bathroom, where the water turned off. "You brought a friend home?" That voice turned more than a little gravelly.

Jealous? He was *jealous*? I'd heard of men like him who got possessive over potential lady friends, but I…he was jealous on *my* behalf? My brain couldn't quite keep up, so my mouth made up the difference.

"Well, I was out, we got all wet and dirty, so I knew we needed to clean up. I left my pants in the sink so they could drain."

His eyes shot to mine and there was so much heat in them I wasn't sure that I wouldn't just spontaneously combust. Or maybe that was a hot flash. Oh Jaysus in heaven, don't let me have my first real hot flash in front of Corb!

"Breena, I need help," Suzy called out, cutting the moment between Corb and me. He visibly relaxed when he heard her voice, even as I pushed past him.

"Just sit down," I said as I opened the bathroom door. Suzy sat obediently on the lid of the toilet seat, wrapped in a towel, shaking like a leaf. I helped her dry her hair and put it into a quick braid, then helped her dress and hustled her off to my bed.

"Here, I'll turn on the heating pad," I said as I covered her up and flicked on the electric hot pad I used for my aching muscles. I slipped it under the blankets, settling it on her belly. Her eyes were closed and her face was pale, but at least she wasn't shaking any longer. "There. In the morning, you'll feel better." At least I hoped she would. I hoped that whatever spell was affecting her would go away. I brushed my hand over her face, my hand warming against her skin. She snuggled deeper into the covers.

"You'd make a good mom," Suzy mumbled, and then she was out cold as if her words hadn't struck to the core of me. She hadn't known what they would do to me, or what I'd been through in my life only to be told I'd never be a mom.

I bit my bottom lip to keep my emotions in check and then slowly breathed through them like my counsellor back in Seattle had taught me. I brushed a hand over her forehead again. Even though I knew she was older than me, she looked like a teen. And I felt weirdly protective of her.

I gathered up clean underwear, a shirt, and shorts for sleeping in. Even though I was exhausted, and most likely in some sort of shock from what had happened with Sean O'Sean and poor Dracus, there were things I had to do. For one, I wasn't sure I could head back to the fairy ring tonight. Part of the problem was that I wasn't convinced I could stay up all night, but there was also the issue of Crash. I'd used Eric as my alibi for being in the woods, but Eric was now at Gran's with Feish. If Crash caught me out there again, he'd know I had a different reason for being there.

Speaking of, I needed to let Eric and Feish know where we were, and that Suzy and I would be staying here tonight. Because the shooter might still be looking for Eric or me, or both of us.

So many things. So little brain power left.

I stumbled forward, eyes closed, heading to the bathroom.

Corb stopped me in the hallway. "What happened tonight, Bree? Sarge…he said he fired you and Suzy for insubordination."

So they all knew then. I sighed. "Can it wait until I've showered?"

He gave me a quick nod, his eyes watching me closely. "Bad?"

"Worse than getting fired. And can you get a message to my gran's house? Tell Eric and Feish to lock it down. Lights out, and put Gran on duty." His eyes widened, but I didn't wait for him to respond—I just let myself into the bathroom and closed the door behind me. Kinkly was waiting for me on the shower rod, her lithe legs dangling as she swung them back and forth.

"What did you want to show me?" She leapt up and flew down to hover in front of my face. The tarot card rested on the bathroom counter. I must have left it there when I'd come in to take care of Suzy. I set my clean clothes down and tapped the card. "This. I know the moon card, and there are never any fairies on it, but in this one there is a shadow of a fairy in the corner."

I stripped off my bra and underwear and flicked on the shower, stepping into the stream of water before it was even really hot. I didn't care, I just wanted to wash the briny stickiness off my skin and put on fully dry clothes. The rose-scented shampoo seemed to wash away the smell of the tunnel as I worked it through my hair, and the knots started to relax across my shoulders.

"Kinkly," I prompted her as I turned off the water and grabbed a towel. "What do you think of the card?"

She was standing on it, really studying it. "You are in danger."

"No shit, I got shot tonight." I pointed at my calf, where the stitches Eric had put in were a stark contrast against my pale skin.

Her eyes widened. "I think that I will take this to the queen. It might affect whether she wants you to watch the ring tonight. I'll be back later."

With that, she rose from the sink, taking the card with her, and flew out the window. She ducked back in. "Be careful, Bree. I don't think you can be too careful right now. If I don't come back, then you don't go to the ring. Okay?"

"Yeah, I agree." No problem there. I felt dead on my feet.

I tugged a brush through my hair to untangle it, but didn't dawdle. I had no doubt that Corb was waiting up for me.

Once I was dressed, my hair up in the towel, I padded out to the kitchen to find Corb not there but in the living room. He had a glass of what I suspected was whiskey in his hands, and a mug of something steaming sat on the table next to him.

"Hot will do you more good than cold right now." He pointed at the mug. His eyes swept over me, lingering on the stitches in my calf. "What happened?"

I sat down next to him on the couch and wrapped my fingers around the mug, the heat sinking into my hands. I noticed the two Advil on the table and would have laughed except that I was out of energy. The wound in my leg was hurting again, even though it was mostly healed. "You know me too well. And that is my first bullet wound." I felt weirdly proud of it. Like it was a mark of honor.

I popped them into my mouth and dry swallowed them. At that moment I wasn't hurting too badly, but the shadow of the morning was headed my way. As soon as I stopped moving, I was going to start tightening up.

"Talk to me, Bree. What happened tonight? Who the hell shot you and why is it healed up?"

A sip of the hot liquid and I wanted to groan. I'd ask him later what it was, some sort of hot toddy that was sweet and spicy and had a most pleasant heat to it that loosened my tongue and fuzzed my brain a little further. Not in a bad way, though. "I was visiting Eric. Someone outside of the house shot at us, and I got hit. He stitched me up, not sure why it's healed so fast. Then I came to the Hollows with Eric and Feish. Sarge lost his marbles and told me that they were not allowed on the grounds. He said I'd broken a rule by bringing them there. When Suzy tried to defend me, he canned us both."

Corb swirled his drink as if he were calm, but I could feel the tension radiating off him. "He has that right to drop any of the trainees off the roster. We all do. But only under extreme circumstances."

I snorted and shifted so I sunk deeper into the couch. "Great. Well there was that. But it gets worse."

"How?"

Did I trust him? That was the question of the day. I *wanted* to trust him, but not at the cost of being a naïve fool. I looked up into his face, seeing the similarities and the differences between him and his asshole cousin.

"Bree. I'm not him." He reached over and brushed his fingers under my chin. "I'm not him."

I shifted and found myself leaning into his side. I didn't pull away. "You're right. So sure, here we go. Well, Suzy and I left the Hollows, and she decided it would be a good idea for us to go to a tarot reader for guidance. You know, since we'd both lost our jobs."

"Annie?" I could hear the frown in his voice. I clutched the mug to me and took another sip before answering.

"No, someone else. It turned out it was Pink Eye. Douche Canoe's friend."

Corb slid his arm over my shoulder and held me to his side. "Try again. Did he have a real name?"

"Sean O'Sean," I said.

"Meow," Corb breathed out.

I giggled, feeling the effects of the drinks I'd pounded down on an empty stomach. "Oh, right, so you can't even say anything about him when I say his name first? I saw him last when he and the other guy, Douche Canoe, who I assume is O'Sean senior, set the spell on everyone."

Corb meowed again and I patted his thigh. "Maybe you should just let me talk."

The story spilled out effortlessly until I got to the pink eye part.

"Wait," he said. "You're sure about the color?"

Apparently that didn't interfere with whatever spell he had on him. "Yes. Pink. I made fun of him."

"Of course you did." He laughed softly, the rumble of it a very nice sound through the fogginess of the booze. He'd obviously put more than I'd realized into the drink.

"Are you trying to get me drunk?" I tipped my head back to look up at him. He winked down at me. Winked. Flirty, cute, too-young-for-me bastard.

Not Crash. That thought floated through me. He was not Crash.

"No, I'm trying to make sure you sleep tonight." He shifted his seat on the couch, which meant that I slid further sideways so we were kind of smushed

176

together. Not that I minded. He was warm and a part of me knew that he would always try to protect me. A quality more men should have, in my humble opinion. He took the mug from my hands as I leaned my head against his shoulder, breathing him in. Yes, he did smell as good as he looked. The urge to bury my nose against his skin and just breathe him in was way too strong. I settled for a little sniff.

"He put Suzy under a spell, putting her to sleep, and I had to fake being under the same spell." I snickered. "I can fake it well, just ask Himself. Wait, no, he thinks it was all real." Oh, I hadn't meant to let that slip, but Corb's only reaction was to chuckle.

As nice as this all was, a part of me was trying to point out that he was acting super cozy with me. Like…something was off with Corb. The same way things were off with Suzy. And, in a different way, with Sarge.

"Keep going," he said.

"O'Sean realized I was the one who'd ducked up Hattie's ceremony." I yawned and closed my eyes. "He started to make a spell, and I yelled for Robert—"

"Who is Robert?" There it was again, that hint of jealousy. Interesting.

I smiled. "Robert is my friend. He's a skeleton. He bit Sarge's ear off at my interview."

Corb probably thought I was crazy, or maybe he thought I was making it up. I didn't care in that moment, not one bit.

"Anyhoo. Robert attacked him for me, distracting him, but he got blasted so I put his finger bone in Centennial Park when we got back." I could feel myself slipping deeper under the spell of the alcohol, plus the exhaustion that had been a constant state for me since I'd moved back to Savannah. "Sean O'Sean was going to fling a spell at me, but I cut through it with a knife and it blasted us both backward. Me into the drink, him into the back wall of the tunnel." I wrapped an arm around Corb's middle.

"What happened to him?"

"Broken neck. He's dead."

And with that, having made my confession, I fell sound asleep.

12

Sleep is something not to be taken lightly, especially if you are over forty. So many things can disrupt it. Aching muscles and joints. The need to pee. Bad dreams. Hot flashes. Dry mouth. A raging werewolf.

That last one I really wouldn't recommend.

"What the actual duck is going on here?" Sarge roared, snapping me out of my deep, relaxing, alcohol-induced sleep. I jerked to one side, my hands going for my knives, which of course I didn't have on me. But score one for me and my training! My roll took me out of bed and onto the floor, away from danger.

Floor. Where the hell was I? I stared at the floor, recognized that I was still in Corb's loft. Only this

179

was not my room. I peeked up over the edge of the king-sized bed—Corb's—to see that he still lay on the other side of the mattress, the sheets pooled around his waist. Shirtless, no less.

"Morning, Sarge." Corb ran a hand over his head. "Can I help you?"

Sarge's eyes glittered with a sharp amber that all but screamed wolf as he glared at Corb. "I came to talk to you, and I find this ducking traitor in your bed."

Sarge shot me a look that had me sitting up and then wobbling to my feet, muscles protesting despite the Advil from the night before, but I knew better than to show any weakness to a mean dog like him. Seriously, what the hell had gotten into him? Then again, it fit with the others. No matter how much I liked this mushy side of Corb, none of them were acting like themselves.

I stumbled around the edge of the bed, struggling to stay upright. "Listen, I know a cranky-ass dog when I see one. Don't make me swat you with a newspaper!"

His mouth thinned, and his eyes glittered with nothing short of hatred. "I'd like to see you try."

I pointed a finger at him. "You want me to stuff my fingers in your nose again? This time I'll yank hard enough to tear you a new nostril!"

Sarge growled at me and I glared in response. What in the world was his problem? Corb swung his legs out of the bed and stood up. "Go easy, man. It's been a rough night. Meow"—he shook his head—"damn it."

I grinned, my mean streak showing up. "I don't think I'll ever get tired of that. Sarge, what do you say when you try to talk about what happened to the mentors and the trainees?"

"What do you mean?" he growled.

Both of my eyebrows shot up. "I mean when you and the trainees got knocked out by Douche Canoe and Sean O'Sean? Also, that is a terrible name, his parents had to know he was going to get teased."

Sarge stared hard at me, his current hatred forgotten for just a moment. "How do you know oink oink oink?" His eyes bugged out and I fell forward on the bed, belly laughing.

Jaysus, my life was complete. I'd heard a werewolf oink like pig and I could die happy now. Which might be sooner than I'd planned given the way my life was going. Someone had shot me, and I currently had two enemies: a werewolf and some powerhouse mage named O'Sean.

I stuffed my face against the blankets, unable to keep back the peals of laughter that would no doubt wake poor Suzy. I couldn't stop them, I really couldn't. When I lifted my head up, I thought I'd be alone in the room, but Corb was still there watching me.

"I'm sorry," I whispered around a last giggle. "I really am, but that was too much. And he deserved it considering what a prick he was yesterday."

Corb shook his head. "It's dangerous not being able to warn you of anything. I tried writing names and information down last night. Same effect."

181

My eyes widened. "You wrote meow, meow, meow?"

His lips might have twitched, but if they did, it was gone very quickly. Speaking of being gone, I did a quick glance around the room for Kinkly. She'd said she would come back after talking to Karissa, but she hadn't. Which meant I was off the hook for missing last night. Crap, I needed all the guard duty I could get now that I was unemployed. Of course, the sleep was good too—and probably necessary, to be perfectly honest.

I blew out a breath. "What is going on with Sarge? Why does he hate me? Honestly, it's like he's a different person now."

"He doesn't hate you." Corb grabbed a pair of pants and yanked them on, his movements jerky. "He's angry with me, and you're just getting the spillover because you're here. But yes, he is more intense than usual, even for him."

"What's he angry about?" I asked, not really expecting an answer.

"Nothing to do with work," Corb muttered. "That would be easier." He came around the side of the bed and touched my arm. "You feeling okay?"

I shrugged. "Fresh as a daisy. But don't change the subject. I'm the one getting my ass handed to me because he's mad at you? That makes no sense."

He bent and kissed me on the forehead, a rather tender move that set off more warning bells. "You don't have to leave if you don't want to. You aren't disrupting my life. I...like having you here."

Well, that was…unexpected. "Thanks."

"That wasn't really an answer," he pointed out.

I smiled and shrugged. "What can I say? I'm a woman of mystery and full of plot twists you'll probably never see coming."

His smile was way too bright, and it struck something in my chest that was a little too close to my heart. "Good. I'll see if I can straighten things out with the other mentors for you and Suzy. But don't hold your breath. Everyone is out of sorts since meow-meow showed up. Stay low until we have a direction, okay?"

I gave him a jaunty salute, and he patted my cheek of all things before turning and heading out into the main part of the loft. Yeah, something was going on with him too. I crept down the hall to my bedroom and let myself in. Suzy was sleeping fitfully, perhaps fighting an unseen opponent. "No, don't!" She flung her hands out as if to stop something.

I touched her shoulder and shook her gently. "Suze, it's just a dream."

She jerked upright and grabbed at my arm, her eyes wide and not really seeing me. "He had me."

"He's gone now." I pulled her into a hug and she leaned against me, not crying but shuddering from the residual effects of her nightmare.

A solid minute slid by, then another, as the shaking in her body eased. "I need to forget about this for a little while," she said. "Just pretend like we're normal, like we didn't get spelled, and we didn't see two dead bodies last night."

"Can we also pretend I didn't get shot?" I suggested. That was weighing heavily on me. Part of me wanted to believe it was an accident, some hunter off in the woods with an accidental discharge. But of course it wasn't.

There were too many shots, and all of them aimed at Eric's house. I knew he'd be safe for now at Gran's place, but for how long? And who the hell was hunting him, anyway? Or was it me they were after?

Crash had gone looking for the shooter; had he found him? Them?

Suzy squeezed me. "You are cooler than I thought. And the first of us to get shot. It'll be a good scar."

I snorted. "What do women do best when they are stressed?"

"Day drinking?" she offered.

"Yeah, that's a no," I said.

"Binge-watch *Sex and the City* while eating ice cream?"

I cringed. *Sex and the City* was not my cup of tea. "Let's pass on that one."

She sighed. "Well, we could go shopping. To be honest, retail therapy is my favorite, so of those three, I prefer the last."

I gave her a slow nod. While it didn't really qualify as lying low, it was probably one of the safer things to do given there'd be people around us. "Why don't we go down to Death Row? We can do some window shopping, and maybe get Annie to give us a better reading? Maybe she can give us some actual direction."

Suzy bobbed her head. "Okay. Let's do it."

"A girl's day," I said. Maybe I would see if Feish would come with us. She could use another friend too. And that would give us another set of eyes on the people around us.

Just in case.

I found some clean clothes, and noted that my leathers were clean and folded on top of the dresser. Corb had stayed up to clean my clothes for me? Or maybe he was looking for clues as to what had happened. Either way, I'd give him a serious amount of points not only for cleaning them, but for having the sense to do so in the first place.

The leathers were probably the better choice than jeans today. Call me cautious, but I doubted things were going to slow down after last night. I'd killed someone. A bad someone, but a death was a death, and Douche Canoe was bound to come looking for Pink Eye's killer.

Gawd in heaven, I was a killer. My stomach rolled hard and I bent at the waist, breathing slowly. I mean, yes, I'd killed Hattie in self-defense, and Pink Eye's death had been an accident, but that didn't make them any less dead.

I frowned and searched through my mind as I pulled my clothes on. I felt sick, but there wasn't any guilt or remorse hanging out in the corner of my brain. No sentiment that death was bad even when it was necessary. Did that mean I was a psychopath? I grimaced and made a mental note to talk to Crash about my lack of feelings. Surely he'd killed a person or two?

I felt a sudden rush of excitement at the thought of talking to him, and not just because I knew he would understand. Which was all kinds of confusing because Corb had hit some seriously good buttons last night. But I suspected those buttons were not really his to push. Corb, Suzy and Sarge…all three felt off. Though looking at Suzy as she got dressed, she seemed much more herself than she'd been the night before.

I made my way out to the kitchen, where Sarge was leaning against the far counter, big arms folded across his chest and a glare etched on his face. Suzy followed me out in her clothes from the night before.

"What are you doing here?" Sarge shot at Suzy. "I fired your ass too."

She cringed a little, which I didn't like. So I put an arm over her shoulders. "Threesome."

Suzy leaned into me, picking the thread up right away, and slid an arm around my waist. Her one eyebrow arched upward, and the sass I knew her for came flooding from her mouth. "You missed out, Sarge. If you'd gotten here earlier, you could have joined in." For good measure, she kissed me on the cheek. "She's good."

I couldn't help but laugh at her, partly because I was relieved a little bit of the Suzy I'd known from before had shown up to the party, even if I didn't understand why. "Oh, please. I'm good, but you were definitely better."

She wrinkled up her nose. "But do you think that last move, with the twist at the end—"

"Stop teasing him," Corb said from the other side of the room. "You're going to send him through the roof."

Defiance ripped through me. "So? He's not a mentor to us any longer. And if he keeps up this bad behavior, I'll call the pound on his furry butt."

Sarge took a half step toward me, which was when Corb stepped between us. "Do not go there, Sarge. Do not come at her."

Sarge glared back at him, but something else flickered across his face, something I couldn't quite pinpoint.

Corb put a careful hand on Sarge's chest and pushed him back. "There was no threesome. They had a rough night, and Breena knows that no matter what, she is always safe here with me. Always."

Wow. That was some serious protectiveness going on, even for Corb.

The werewolf blinked a few times and the lines in his face eased. "Oh. So no threesome."

I threw my hands into the air. "That's all you hear? Jaysus in heaven. No, there was no threesome. Suzy and I are going to Death Row for a few things. Corb, I gave you the details of what happened. Will I get any repercussions from meow-meow?" I winked at him.

"Not right away. Stay together, though. From here on out, we travel in pairs," Corb said. He walked over to us, gave Suzy a quick hug, and then hugged me too. Only he also dropped a kiss. When I saw his mouth lowering to mine, I turned my head quickly so it ended up on my cheek instead of my lips. "Together, okay?"

I bobbed my head, grabbed my bag from the counter, and headed for the stairs. Suzy followed. Her eyes were locked on me. "Are you two a couple?"

A growl from upstairs paused my feet. Sarge could hear us. "I'm moving out today. Moving into Crash's place."

This time it was Corb who let out a growl. Don't ask me how I could tell them apart, but I could.

This time we made it out the front door before Suzy grabbed my arm. "But are you a couple?"

I shook my head, thinking about all the lube in his bathroom, about how pissed he'd been when I'd shown up at his door with a suitcase and interrupted his hookup sesh, and about the kiss we'd shared in front of Himself.

Which was how I found myself thinking of a different kiss, between Crash and me. The kiss that had given me a new standard to all kisses.

"No. I don't think so."

"Huh. He likes you though."

I shrugged. "Maybe. Let's get Feish and go shopping."

Picking up Feish would give me a chance to talk to Gran about the card I'd drawn with the tarot reader, Sean O'Sean. Gran might be a ghost, and her memories could be spotty at times, but she was still the one source I trusted above any other in the shadow world.

I could also tell Eric he needed to lay low until we figured out who the hell was shooting at us.

We didn't bother driving to Gran's place—scratch that, now Crash's place—as it really wasn't that far. Ten minutes of walking through Savannah's squares brought us to the door of the house that I'd grown up in.

"You sure about bringing Feish?" Suzy asked. "Crash is not known for being a good guy."

I'd heard that enough times that I was doing my best to believe it, even if my body wanted me to pour a bottle of Corb's lube out on Crash and roll around on him. "Sure, but Feish is his slave. It's not her fault and she really is lovely. She's helped me out more than once, and I consider her a friend."

Lovely might have been a stretch. I mean, Feish was…well, she was Feish. A river maid who had more than a few fish-like features. But she was a good friend and that was all that mattered to me.

As we stood on the doorstep of my gran's house (I'd decided on our walk over that I was not going to call it Crash's house), I knocked—which felt incredibly odd—and Feish opened the door.

A normal human saw a woman with a harelip and narrowed eyes.

We saw a woman with fish lips, big bulbous eyes, greenish-yellow skin, and a flash of gills along her neck when her high-collared shirt slipped. She had webbed fingers and I assumed webbed toes, though I'd never seen them. "Is this the one from the Hollows?" Feish said, looking Suzy over suspiciously.

I wanted to roll my eyes but contained myself. "You know it is. You were there when she got fired too, so don't be difficult. And she's a friend," I said.

"But I am your friend." Feish looked at me with what could only be hurt on her fishy face. I sighed.

"I can have more than one friend, and so can you. Suzy worked with me at the Hollows, and we had a rough night. She's got siren blood." I hoped that last bit would help, seeing as they were both from water backgrounds.

I took a few steps into the house past Feish. "Corb called you last night? He filled you in?"

Feish nodded. "He did. He was polite. I think he loves you, but it's not real."

My feet stuttered and I cleared my throat. "Right, well, that's a problem for later. Right now I need to speak with my gran. We have problems in spades and no shovels to dig our own graves." That was a saying my gran had pulled out more than once, and it flowed out of my lips before I could catch it.

Feish leaned around to look at Suzy. "You are a siren? Do you know," and then she made a sound that was like bubbles flying out of her mouth.

Suzy gave a slow nod. "I do."

Feish gave a sharp nod. "Good, come in. I'll make tea."

"The good stuff." I gave Feish a pointed look and followed it with a pointed finger. "Not like the first time you met me."

She gave me a wide grin that showed off some stubbly flat teeth. "Ha. Fine, I make good tea." She motioned for Suzy to follow her into the kitchen, where the rumble of Eric's voice called out, "I have biscuits ready. I bake when I'm nervous, and I couldn't sleep, even after we heard from your friend that you were okay."

Suzy glanced at me, and I gave her a nod, shooing her along with a wave of my hands. I trusted Feish and Eric far more than I did Sarge. Suzy was safe here.

"What happened the first time you met Bree?" Suzy asked Feish.

"I tried to give her tea to make her poop a whole lot. Just in case she was there to hurt Boss."

Suzy choked on what was probably a laugh as I took the stairs to the second floor of the house. "Gran?"

Movement in the direction of the sitting room that had doubled as Gran's library turned me in that direction. Gran was sometimes a full-blown apparition so clear you'd think you were looking at a real live person, but this time there were just hints of her—the outline of a body and sway of a skirt. I hurried toward the library. "Gran, are you fading?"

A sigh rippled through the air and her body solidified in front of me. She entered the room and sat in the high-backed chair behind her oversized dark mahogany desk. Her long hair, which usually flew about her face in messy, bright silver waves, was actually swept off to one side. Green eyes that reflected my own were as keen as ever. Today she wore one of her favorite garments, a long flowing burgundy skirt that had more volume than necessary, as if she were doing a throwback to the eighteen hundreds. The fact that she'd paired it with a white blouse that was ruffled at the collar and cuffs only added to the effect. I almost wondered if she was wearing the outfit to freak out the neighbors, which was quite possible. "No, I am not fading really. But it will be better when you are here. You took Crash up on the offer to move in?"

I nodded. "Yes, I'll be here tonight." Well, sort of. Depending on when I had to head back out to the fairy ring for Karissa. *If* she wanted me back. Out of a habit older than I cared to think about, I slid into the chair across from Gran. "Something bad happened. Well, lots of somethings." I told her about the night before, about killing Pink Eye. About being shot in the leg. About losing my job with the Hollows. I started to tell her about Hattie, but she shushed me with a wave of her hand.

"I already knew about that. I watched her spirit get sucked into the darkness." Gran shook her head. "She could have stayed on as a guardian like me if she hadn't decided she wanted to tempt fate. Tell me the real issue, honey child."

"I'm worried because I don't feel bad, Gran," I said softly. "Shouldn't I feel something? It's like the whole Pink Eye thing just blipped on the screen— for all it bothers me, I might as well have squashed a roach."

She steepled her fingers in front of her mouth as she leaned back in her chair. "You did indeed squish a roach, my girl."

I wasn't sure that was the answer that I was looking for. "He was still a person."

"He was evil, Breena. Don't forget that." She wasn't sharp, but her tone brooked no argument. "The O'Seans are power-hungry killers. That they are back in town does not bode well for Savannah."

"You mean they haven't been here all along?" I frowned. "What stopped them?"

"I don't remember," she said with a shake of her head. "That is the curse of being dead. Not everything is linear for me, not everything is where it should be in my mind. I do not keep things from you apurpose. But show me the card he gave you. You said you picked it up?"

I dug into my bag, but the card wasn't there. I tried to remember where I'd left it.

Kinkly. Right, I'd let her take it. "I gave it to someone else. But it was the moon card, only not like I'd ever seen it. It was just a full moon with a big fat wolf's head snarling on it. It had the shadow of a tiny, nearly invisible fairy in the corner. Water behind it." Or maybe the river. To be fair, it could be any body of water.

Gran closed her eyes. "O'Sean spoke truly then. I see many hidden enemies and paths. You must be careful, Bree. Trouble often follows the women in our family. In case you have not noticed. The O'Rylees produce strong, capable women who don't always have the best of luck. But that's part of what makes us who we are."

"Speaking of luck," I said, "losing the job at the Hollows…that is bad. It's the only chance I had to make money to buy this place back." Well, the only steady chance. My words dipped lower as I spoke, drained by sadness.

"And you think you aren't already trained?" She set her hands flat on the desk, which was strange because I could see a pen right through her hand.

"I'm not."

"You are. And you have my book?"

I nodded. "Yes, of course. I used it to help the other trainees."

"Then you don't need them." She waved her hand. "The shadow world is drawn to you, if you hadn't noticed. The jobs will come. Your name alone will be enough to bring you work."

She wasn't wrong. I hadn't found Karissa through the Hollows. A tiny bit of excitement trickled through me. What if...what if I just kept training on my own? I could hire Suzy, and the two of us could work together. There was someone else I could call in to help me too, someone from the past.

Assuming he was still alive.

When I was younger, Gran had arranged for a local police officer to help me with some of my training. On the off chance he was still on the force, he could have useful connections, maybe even some the Hollows did not. Even if he'd retired, he might still be willing to help.

Gran was right. Maybe I wasn't training at the Hollows anymore, but that didn't mean I couldn't work as a bounty hunter in the shadow world. "Is Officer Jonathan still around?" I asked.

"Perhaps. Why?" Her voice was deceptively quiet, but the twinkle in her eyes tipped me off that she knew exactly what direction I was headed. I played dumb, as was my role in this game between us.

I shrugged. "Maybe just to say hello to a friendly face. So, no suggestions on why I feel nothing about killing someone? I mean, let's be honest, I can't go around killing people every day."

Gran smiled. "You are a strong woman, Bree. And I'm not going to tell you how you should feel. But you've always had a strong sense of justice. Of right and wrong. And he was not only going to hurt you, but your friend, too. And from the sound of it, karma is what took him, not your knife."

"You mean he was going to kill us, not just hurt us."

"Yes, I mean kill. So if you don't feel guilty, it's probably because you recognize that his death preserved two lives, and possibly more." Her words eased the fear that had tugged at me. Because more than once Himself (my ex, keep up with me here) had accused me of being crazy. Of being a psycho. Mostly for seeing things that weren't there for him in the beginning of our relationship. He'd held that over me our entire life together.

He'd said it enough that the fear had stuck with me, and it crept up on me in quiet moments. Or, in this case, it had crept up on me because I'd killed someone and didn't feel bad about it. I shivered and rubbed at my arms. "Thanks, Gran. I'll be here tonight after training."

"Be safe, honey child. There is something very wrong with our town. It is in trouble. Beyond that, I cannot see what is coming. But where there is trouble, it will find you."

Yeah, that I could believe.

Which should have prepped me for Death Row shopping.

13

Suzy insisted on walking to Death Row, and Feish agreed, which meant I was outnumbered. Gran said she would watch over the house and let Eric know if anyone was coming close. Given he was one of the only other people who could consistently see Gran, it was a solid plan.

Besides, Eric said he wanted to stay in and keep a low profile and bake.

Bake.

I might fall in love with him just for that. Mind you, I'd end up topping the scale, but would it matter if I had fresh-baked pastries every morning along with my tea? I'm not sure it would.

The walk wasn't far. To be fair, nothing was very far in downtown Savannah, but it was already hot and I'd gotten very little sleep the night before. Not to mention the persistent pull of muscles along my hamstrings and my one calf made me wonder just what I'd done to myself this time. Okay, I hadn't done it, but a gunshot wound was no small thing. Right?

The thing was, morning for us was usually mid-afternoon. Training at the Hollows started at seven and ran till two or three in the morning, depending on how hard the mentors wanted to work us. Of course, we didn't have to train today. But we probably should still train on our own.

Even so, I couldn't keep the yawns away, and more than once my jaw cracked as I let one loose.

Feish walked on my left and Suzy led the way, her perkiness restored now that the night before seemed to have faded from her memory. Neither of them had yawned.

"You're moving in today?" Feish asked.

"Yes," I said. "You still good with that?"

"Boss thinks I would be lonely." She gave a roll of her shoulders. "I think he wants you to spy on me."

A laugh started up in my belly until I saw that she was serious. "Why? Why would he want me to spy on you?"

She shook her head. "I can't tell."

I wasn't sure if she meant she couldn't tell me, or if she didn't know. With Feish, it wasn't always clear. Her manner of speaking was just the other side of awkward.

We'd almost reached the waterfront, with very few words spoken between us—Feish had quickly and efficiently shot down all my attempts to pull information from her—when Suzy spoke up.

"So you really think I was spelled last night?" she asked just as we reached the top side of River Street.

I paused. "I think it happened to everyone at the Hollows the other night, when you all got knocked out. But it was like he set it off in you. You lost confidence. Sarge is angrier than I'd have thought possible. Corb is being so protective and sweet it's even turning my stomach." I paused. "Did you notice anything weird with the others?"

Suzy looked up at the sky. "Luke was even more fearful than usual. But that could just be him."

She wasn't wrong, so I let it go, at least with my outside voice. My inside voice was yammering on at me that I had all the pieces to this puzzle, I just had to fit them together.

We stood there on the top side of River Street, just before we turned into Death Row, and I couldn't help but look down at the water, toward the tunnel where Sean O'Sean had attacked us. Where I'd killed him. The weird angle of his neck, the way his tongue had been sticking out partway between his sharp teeth, the blood. Smell of marijuana and sea water. Saliva rushed into my mouth, not because I was hungry either, though I should have been after skipping breakfast this morning and dinner the night before. Another blow of the ocean wind in our faces brought another waft of ocean and a cascade of images I couldn't dispel.

Oh, I was in trouble.

My stomach clenched suddenly and I swallowed hard to keep the bile down. Nope, that wasn't working.

I turned to the side, up against a building, and heaved until my stomach hurt and I wasn't sure I could stand up. Hands on either side of me helped me stand up, and one of the girls pushed a water flask into my hand. I took a swig, rinsed my mouth and spat. Tried not to notice the tourists staring at me. "Thanks."

"Are you pregnant?" Feish asked.

At another time, I would have laughed. "No, a bad reaction to something," I said. The shaking took me next, and I had to breathe through it, hard as it was.

"Let's go shop, that will help." Suzy tugged me along, and I barely kept up with her as my body tried to shut down and memories of the night before climbed through my mind like monkeys on meth. Feish gave me a look that said it all. She didn't think shopping would help any more than I did.

But we let Suzy barrel us along, into the candy shop—the sweet smells of the sugar making my stomach roll even more—and from there to the hidden door that led to Death Row. There were multiple entrances into the place that was basically a bazaar for vendors of the shadow world. I'd met a number of them a few weeks ago, when I'd first started at the Hollows Group.

But my mind was still focused on the images it had conjured of Sean O'Sean's death. A cold sweat broke out all over my body, and I struggled to breathe normally.

I saw Geraldine—Gerry to her friends—right away, and made a beeline for her as if she were an anchor in a rough harbor. She looked over me and then gave a nod. "Breena." She squinted. "Are you ill?"

I swallowed hard. "Bad breakfast. Trying to run right through me." I blinked back a sudden image of O'Sean's protruding tongue. I squatted where I was and Gerry pushed a bucket toward me as I heaved up nothing. Dry heaves are about as pitiful as they sound. Nothing to show for all that effort but a hell of a lot more sweat.

I sat there on my heels, breathing through the worst of it. A cup was pressed into my hand. "Rinse your mouth out," Gerry said. "Then take a small swig."

I did as she said, the sharp tang of fermented berries warming up my mouth, pushing back the heaves. A quick swig as I stood cleansed the rest of my palate. "Thanks."

"Some days are rougher than others." She looked me over. "Other than the pukes, you look good, toning up well. And the clothing? How is it holding up?"

She'd made my leather pants and boots, which I'd done pretty much all of my training in, plus a short cropped coat that I hadn't worn as much yet given the warm weather. "Good, very good." I pointed at the hole in my pant leg. "Shot, but otherwise holding together."

"I can fix that." She bent with a needle and thread and began to stitch the hole closed. "What are you here for other than the stitch job?"

It struck me as funny that she didn't so much as blink when I said I'd been shot. This was my world now.

"Retail therapy," I said with a smile that I knew was tired. I could feel it around the edges of my mouth, just waiting to sag.

I leaned against her table and turned to watch Suzy work her way through the vendors, flirting shamelessly. Apparently she was back to her usual self. That was good. I, on the other hand, felt like I'd been pulled through a knothole backward and with great vigor.

Feish was even getting in on the act, following Suzy and mimicking her flirting to some strange amount of success if her handful of dried flowers was any indication. I shook my head. "I've never been able to flirt to get my way. I'm terrible at it."

Gerry snorted. "Too strong? Or too blunt?"

I grimaced, doing my best to put my freakout behind me for a few minutes. "Probably both."

Bob-John, vendor of clearing powders, sat at the table to Gerry's right. I gave him a smile. "That clearing powder worked like a hot damn." I almost said I'd used it to drive a demon out of a bigfoot's property, but I wasn't sure I could say it with a straight face even though I'd lived it. Or that anyone would believe me.

Bob-John squinted at me. "I got something new for you then. Since you are the first to appreciate a good powder in a long time."

"Oh, I still have one clearing powder," I said. "I bought two, remember?"

Bob-John ignored me and slid over a red box encrusted with rhinestones. "This is better. Makes you invisible."

Gerry burst out laughing. "You are so full of shit, BJ."

I found myself sliding a twenty across to him while Gerry laughed. Not out of pity. But because his clearing powder really had been a lifesaver. And being invisible could be a pretty good thing with the whole fairy ring deal. Although riding my dead steed had that effect, my butt would be in a world of hurt if I tried to stay on it all night. "Thanks."

He took the twenty and tucked it away. I didn't for one second think that twenty bucks would cover an invisibility spell, but whatever. Maybe it would come in handy, who knew?

Gerry leaned in close. "Be careful. There were men in here looking for you earlier today. Asking if anyone knew a strawberry blonde who worked for the Hollows."

A chill swept through me. It had to be Douche Canoe and his cronies. I swallowed hard. "Thanks for the warning. But I don't work at the Hollows any longer."

"They are bad men, Breena. Not working at the Hollows is not good. You don't have protection now." Her eyes were deadly serious. I nodded.

"I am being careful."

She pulled back and her face smoothed as she shifted the conversation to a discussion of the merits of knives over guns, amongst other topics. Her warning lay heavily on my shoulders, though, and my tension rose with each minute that passed.

An hour slid by while Gerry and I chatted, me with only half an ear on the conversation. There weren't a ton of other customers so I didn't feel bad about monopolizing her time.

Feish strolled back first. "I have tea, much better than before. And more herbs." She held up her handful of what I'd thought were dried flowers.

Suzy came back with nothing but an appetite. "I'm hungry, let's get food."

Once more they led the way, this time going for the stairs that led up to Annie the tarot card reader's shop. A hand on my arm stopped me. Gerry tugged me close. "You need to go. Now."

She tipped her head and her eyes narrowed, focusing on something at the far end of Death Row, and I knew our situation had just gotten a whole lot worse. I did a quick glance to see three robed figures headed our way, and one of them was pointing at me.

"Oh dear."

I jerked away from Gerry and ran for the exit. Stairs, it had to be stairs. Feish and Suzy were taking their time. "Time to run, girls!" I yelped as I all but pushed them up ahead of me.

"Why, what's happening?" Feish tried to turn around.

"Bad men, Feish, very bad men!" I yelled as footsteps sounded below us and a blast of magic rippled by, just missing us, smelling distinctly of lavender. Strike that, just missing two of us. Suzy let out a yelp and froze in place, her eyes closing as she started to slump. I kept her from falling, but I wasn't strong enough to pick her up.

"Let her go!" Feish grabbed at me.

"They'll hurt her!" I made another attempt that worked no better than the last. Feish muttered something and then grabbed Suzy and pulled her over her back.

"Holy Jaysus!" I breathed out as Feish packed Suzy up the last of the stairs as if she didn't weigh a thing. I stumbled after her at the top, spun and slammed the door behind us. Next to the door was a large bar, which I set in place. Annie raced into the backroom, and I smiled at her. "Rodents. Very large rodents."

The door rattled behind us and I pointed at Suzy. "You got anything to wake her up?"

Annie frowned at me. "I am not a spell caster."

Damn it. I opened my bag while the door rattled behind us with a boom that made everyone but Suzy jump. Digging around in the leather bag, I pulled out my remaining container of clearing powder from Bob-John.

"Can't hurt," I muttered as I opened the gaudy, bedazzled container and poured the powder over Suzy's head. The effect was immediate.

She screeched and slapped at her head as if the powder hurt, but at least she was moving. I grabbed her hand and started running. "Feish, let's go!"

"This way!" the river maid yelped back as we burst out of the tarot card reader's shop. Feish pointed to the left, which would take us up to Factors Row. Not my favorite place for a lot of reasons.

"You think Jinx will help us?" Jinx being the big-ass guardian spider/trickster that haunted the area and had a thing for classic books.

"No, but there is somewhere we can hide!" Feish already had some serious distance on me and Suzy as I dragged my young friend behind me. I could barely see for the sweat running down my face, and the nausea had picked a bad time to make itself known. My guts were empty, churning, and my energy was nearly spent.

The cobblestones dulled the sound of our boots as we ran as fast as we could after Feish. Suzy was still yelping about her burning scalp, and a glance behind us revealed we were being followed by three men in black, and not one of them was Will Smith. Hell, I'd take Tommy Lee Jones at that point.

"Here, turn quick!" Feish grabbed my hand as we came around the corner onto Factors Row. Cobblestones under our feet, and a giant black spider covered in bristling hair right in front of us. Her eyes were glued to something she held between two long appendages. A book. She was reading? And she had a red pen in her mouth.

Oh, Gawd, did she think she could edit a book?

Not the time to point out to her that not many people would hire an editor that was also a giant spider. I waved a hand at Jinx. "Out of the way! Eat the ones behind us!"

Startled, she skittered away, her eyes swinging to us as she dropped what she'd been reading. Seriously, a giant spider reading and editing a book. Just when I'd thought this world could not get any weirder.

Feish grabbed my hand and yanked me through a door I'd never seen before, and Suzy spilled in with us. The door slammed behind us, and I would have said we were silent as mice being stalked by three black cats, but there was so much noise in the place we'd stumbled into that I could have hollered my face off and not have been heard.

Music pounded all around us, a bass that drove itself into my chest and made me want to slap my hands over my ears like the old lady I was so often accused of being. How in the world had we not heard that music from outside? Even as I thought it, I remembered a passage in my gran's book.

Within the shadows there are doorways and there are doorways. Some are nothing more than a passage between one room and the next. Some are more than that, and yet there is no explanation for their existence, for they will not always function as such.

"A go between?" I yelled the words at Feish and she nodded emphatically. I wanted to ask her how she'd known it would be there. Go betweens were rare, expensive to make, and based on what I'd read in Gran's book, they didn't last very long.

I made myself look around the room, at the bodies gyrating to the music. Some had clothes on. Some, but not many. Feish pushed against my side. "Oh. This is not where I thought it would lead."

"Where the hell did you think it would lead?" I yelped even as I looked behind us at the door. I was more than expecting the three men to spill in after us. For that reason alone, I pushed deeper into the crowd, ignoring the tug of Feish on one side and the pull of Suzy on the other.

Suzy shivered. "I like this a little too much, Bree. It calls to my siren blood!" She had to shout to be heard, which meant that a few people took note of our passage and her words.

Smiles slid her way, hands following. I smacked a number of them back because she didn't seem inclined to push them back herself. Siren blood indeed. All the way to the back of the club we went, squeezing through the press of bodies, the smell of perfume, cologne, and cigar smoke, and the sounds of laughter muted under the pulse of the music. To say that it was overwhelming was an understatement. But it was a cover for us, and for the moment we were safe. I found a booth at the back of the club with just a single man in it.

"You"—I pointed at him—"out. We're here on official business."

His jaw flapped open. "Do you know who I am?"

I shook my head and let a hand drop to the knife handle on my thigh, just like an old-school gunslinger. "Nope and I don't care. Out."

His eyes followed my hand to the knife. "I see. Well. I know who I can and can't do business with."

Nothing else was said as he slid out of the booth, and I all but shoved Feish and Suzy into the newly freed space. I leaned over the table at them. "Don't leave this booth, don't invite anyone in, and don't go off with anyone."

Feish nodded rapidly, but Suzy was slower to agree. I reached out and slapped her in the face. "Snap out of it. This has got to be some sort of spell." I shivered, feeling whatever magic was affecting her brush against my skin. A flush of heat ran through me, pooling in my nether regions. "I'm going to find the exit. Then we'll go."

Again, Feish nodded, then she leaned forward. "Be careful. Boss would not be happy we are here."

What would I even say to Crash? Yeah, we stumbled into an orgy pit of weirdness? Not likely.

"Boss will never know that we're here," I said, turned around and found myself staring at a man on the far side of the room who hadn't noticed me. A man whom I'd seen wrapped in nothing but a sheet more than once. A man whose kisses had set every part of me on fire.

His head was bowed over a stunning young woman with liquid black hair that rippled down to her too-tiny waist in perfect ringlets. A white dress clung to her every curve, of which there weren't many, and she had not even a single cellulite ripple. What was she, eighteen? Barely legal? Her laughter turned heads.

Crash was making her laugh. I frowned.

Nope, I did not like this one bit. The slice across the mid-region of my heart was not welcome, and I tried to reason the feeling away. So what if he'd kissed me? He could have been trying to distract me, and it had worked.

A tiny voice pointed out that he'd taken care of me after I was shot. That he'd sent me away from danger.

But what if he'd been the one to set the danger in motion?

I was muttering under my breath as I stalked through the room, and people knew enough to move out of my way. I found the bar quickly and the bartender leaned in close. "What can I get you, lovely?"

I put my hands on the bar. "The exit."

He chuckled and I could smell a good amount of alcohol on his breath, beer by the ferment of it. I wrinkled my nose. "What's so funny?"

"You go out the way you came in. Why would you do it any other way?" He polished up a glass and set it on the bar. "Have a drink, take off your clothes, have a good time."

He poured me something from a bottle that glittered. Not in an edible glitter kind of way—this was magic. I grimaced. "I don't do magic I don't know."

Turning on my heel, I meant to go back to the girls. Only now, Crash stood directly in my path. He still hadn't noticed me. And now he had a second girl on his arm, this one with hair the color of mahogany, eyes that matched, and a slinky blue dress fighting a losing battle to cover a pair of boobs the size of melons. Considering how tiny her waist was, I wasn't sure they were real.

He had an arm draped over the brunette, keeping her close to his side as he talked to the first girl in the white dress. Damn it, I did not like feeling this way. The green-eyed monster wanted me to stalk over there and punch him in his family jewels, let him see if he was any good in bed after that.

The old me would never have done it.

The older me was tempted.

I just needed a little stiffening up first.

I turned back to the bartender and snapped back the drink.

"Changed your mind?"

"Yup." I put the glass down and tapped it. One more and I'd still be able to walk. He filled the drink up and I tipped it back like a pro, if I do say so myself. Leaning on the bar, I looked up at the bartender and squinted. "You're not human?"

"Nobody in here is, darling." He winked and the image of him flickered, like seeing two pictures superimposed over one another. One was human looking, the other...the other was covered in fur but still standing upright, so not a werewolf. More like Eric.

"Bigfoot?" I asked, shocked at how numb my mouth felt. Oh no. That numbness spread through my body far quicker than any alcohol should.

"Close. Abominable. You know Eric?" he asked. I nodded, but that made the room spin horribly.

"Good guy, sad about his cousin," I said. With that, I turned and headed out onto the floor where Crash still stood with those two very young and beautiful women.

To be clear, I didn't begrudge them their looks or youth—I just didn't want to feel like I had to compete with them.

"Hey!" I snapped the word out, only it sounded far from snappy, more like slurred.

Crash turned and his blue and gold eyes widened. "Breena. What in Hades's name are you doing here?"

"Never you mind." I pointed both hands at him as if I were doing a sloppy hex. "This is not cool. Just so you know. Not. Cool." I waved my quickly flopping hands in his general direction to take in the two women.

The ladies smiled at me, and the one in the white dress spoke up first. "You think you could handle him? Please. You're human."

I made a pffffing noise. "Handle? Handle? Who says that? Are you twelve? Ten? Are you even allowed in here? Shouldn't you be taking selfies and posting them all over?" Yup, I knew I was drunk as a skunk and didn't care.

Crash didn't take his hands off either woman—girl—they were practically girls. So that was how it was then. I bobbed my head a few times, which made the world spin hard. "Karissa was right about you."

He jerked as if I'd slapped him, which was going to have to be good enough for me. Because I could feel the sparkly drink doing terrible, terrible things to me. And I'd just outed that fact that I knew Karissa. Would he put two and two together and realize why I'd been out in the wildlife reserve?

Tears pooled up in my eyes, damn it I hated crying when I was mad. I stumbled hard, bumped off some guy, and managed to direct myself back toward the booth at the end. I needed to get back to Feish and Suzy. They would look out for me because right then I wasn't sure I was going to be able to see in three, two, one.

Lights out.

Only it was literal.

14

I fell forward as the sparkling magic liquor's potency hit me right between the eyes, and as I fell, the lights and music went out, plunging us into darkness that was only silent for a second before people started hollering, or maybe they were singing? It was hard for me to tell. My knees met the floor, followed rapidly by the palms of my hands. Barely hanging onto consciousness, I knew that if I didn't stand up, I'd face being trampled as everyone tried to blindly find their way out.

The best I could do was wobble forward in a crawl. I don't even know how I found the booth where Feish and Suzy were, only that one minute I was on the floor, the next Suzy was pulling me onto the bench. "What happened, are you hurt?"

"Sparkle juice," I whispered.

"Why would you drink that? It's not for us!" Feish squeaked. "Come on, I can carry her. You two girls, so weak!"

I didn't care, I only knew that I couldn't keep my eyes open, even when Feish slung my arm over one of her shoulders and started hauling ass. "Not the door, they will be waiting there," I mumbled.

Feish didn't so much as give me a one-word answer. Suzy held my other arm and my legs went numb as we pushed our way through the mass of people who were heaving this way and that. Only they weren't really people. They were something else. "People masks," I said. Or I think I said. There were monsters in here. Was I one of them? I glanced at Suzy, seeing the siren in her clearly. Beautiful and terrible all at once.

The doorway we'd come through loomed in front of us. "Why aren't people freaking out?" Suzy asked. "The lights and music stopped suddenly, but they all seem pretty calm."

"I can't say," Feish answered. Again I wondered if it was that she wasn't allowed or she didn't know. She was good at answers like that.

Suzy reached for the door. I wanted to tell her not to open it—those men in black were going to be right there—but I couldn't gather my thoughts in time. Before I knew it, they were carrying me through it onto Factors Row.

"They are gone," Jinx said from the shadows across from us. "You were in there a solid eighteen hours. I hope you had a good time."

I still couldn't feel my legs. "I can't feel my legs," I mumbled.

At least the words came out. Feish snapped her fingers at Jinx. "Don't tell him."

"Oh, being sworn to secrecy is the most fun, but what will you give me for my silence?" Jinx leaned in close and Suzy squeaked. I couldn't blame her.

I did however hold up a fist, the drink still thick in my veins and making me brassy as hell. "A knuckle sandwich is what you'll get! Or another boot to the lady parts!"

Jinx's too-many eyes blinked rapidly. "I don't like to eat humans. You taste awful. Sour. But I do not relish another kick to my lady bits either. I will stay quiet should he ask me anything."

Feish dragged me away, and I barely registered that it was very early morning. Eighteen hours. "We missed training."

"You're forgetting that we don't train there anymore," Suzy said, "which is maybe good, because if we had been training, the rest of the Hollows could have run into the idiots in black too. And if we're all spelled like you think, who knows what would have happened?"

I snickered. "Idiots in black." I was pretty sure that it wasn't really as funny as I thought it was in that moment, but my brain was stuck on that sparkling giggle juice. "Giggle juice."

"Terrible, this is terrible. I need to get tea into her," Feish said. "Fae and their sparkling drinks."

I'm pretty sure I blacked out because between one blink and the next we were inside Gran's house, and I was being laid out on my bed, in my old room. The canopy was the same, there wasn't even any dust on it.

"Here, tip her head," Feish said, and Suzy tipped my head up.

"Only mostly dead," I whispered. Neither of them so much as batted an eye at me. Apparently I was the only one who'd seen *The Princess Bride.*

Before I could say "*you killed my father, prepare to die,*" scalding hot tea filled my mouth. I wanted to yell at them to stop, only Feish plugged my nose and I had no body control, which meant I had a choice to swallow or choke to death on tea.

I swallowed.

The tea burned a hot path down my insides, and not in the pleasant way that whiskey does. No, this was a true burn that left my tongue and the inside of my mouth aching. Which meant the next mouthful hurt even more.

"Drink. You have to drink, or it will be bad," Feish said.

Gran hovered over me. "What did she drink?"

"Potion." Feish shrugged. "I don't know what kind. Fae sparkling drink can be many things. Most not suitable for humans."

Gran tsked at me. "Really? You drank an obvious magical drink and didn't ask what it was?"

"Only one way out with it," Feish whispered. "Sorry."

I looked up at her and then at the tea. "Oh no."

My insides were suddenly on fire in a way that I had never experienced since the food poisoning incident of '99. On the plus side, my body was my own again. I lurched out of bed and ran for the nearest bathroom, where I didn't throw up the tea or the potion. Nope, I was not so lucky.

Feish had finally given me her special tea, and it was burning as badly as if I'd chowed down on candy made of ghost peppers and cayenne.

Sometime later, I stumbled out of the bathroom, sure that I had to have lost fifteen pounds right there. I'd stripped off my clothing and necklace, and showered to wash away the sweat as well as any residual… well, residue. Though I was clean, my butt was still on fire and I wanted to sit it on a block of ice to ease the burn, not that it would work.

Grimacing, I stood next to the bed as I pulled my wet hair back into a messy braid. Feish and Suzy were downstairs now, and it was just me and Gran. Daylight streamed in through the window.

"That should learn you," Gran said without a hint of malice in her voice. I sighed.

"I just…" I didn't want to explain to her that I'd seen Crash fawning over two beautiful young women, less than half my age and probably less than half my weight, and it had stung. That was the truth of it, it had stung. And the worst part was that I'd gone and shown my hand to him. He knew I liked him.

I sighed. "I was stupid."

"Yes, but what were you running from?"

At first I thought she meant my feelings for Crash. Then I realized she likely meant the idiots in black.

I took a step, grimaced at the way my body felt—particularly that awful hot spot that kept puckering in pain—and started moving toward the stairs. Down I went, gripping the banister for dear life. "Doesn't matter."

"I think it does," Gran said, following me. "And those two won't tell me."

I made it to the kitchen, where Suzy and Feish were baking together, Eric overseeing them. It smelled like apple pie to me. My stomach griped that it hadn't eaten in a long time, but the exit area tightened against the thought of expelling anything else.

"You need toast." Feish was already on it, steering me away from the pie I'd smelled. "Come here. I make it."

Damn, she was probably right, but that pie smelled amazing.

Suzy glanced at me. "I called Corb, let him know we were okay. I mean, he'd only left a dozen messages on my phone."

"Did he freak out?" I grimaced as I sat on one of the kitchen chairs, adjusting myself gingerly. Gran's house had been sold with all the original furniture still in it, which meant nothing had changed from when I'd lived in Savannah over twenty years before. The seats were still as hard as they'd ever been. I needed a donut to sit on.

Eric handed me a plate of toast. "Here." Feish glared at him as if he'd stolen her thunder.

I ignored them both and motioned for Suzy to go on.

"After he yelled at me for like five minutes straight, he seemed okay." Suzy cut a piece off the apple she was holding and popped it in her mouth.

Five minutes of yelling? That was not okay. I cringed at the thought of how much he was going to yell at me and then straightened my back. He was not my husband. Or my boyfriend. And really, he wasn't even family anymore. Which meant he had no say over me, other than the fact that he was a mentor of sorts. Or had been. We'd been fired.

Damn, my head really didn't want to wrap around that. I'd spent years thinking of change as a bad thing, something to be avoided, and that kind of hardwiring didn't just go away. Which was why I'd stuck it out with Alan for so long. Far longer than was good for either of us.

A pang from my nether regions made me wince, and I stood up to finish my toast on my feet rather than sitting.

Suzy waved around a second piece of apple, cutting through my minor epiphany. "He said we should head to the Hollows early tonight, plead our case to the other mentors. He thinks they'll reinstate us."

But I wasn't so sure I wanted that anymore. And before I agreed to do anything else, I needed to find out from Kinkly what was happening with the fairy ring. I'd missed two nights in a row, which meant I was out two enormous gems. I needed that money.

Especially now. But how did I contact her? I looked at Eric. "Hey, can you get a hold of Kinkly for me?"

He froze and his face flushed red. "Me? Why? I mean, I could try, but maybe she wouldn't want to talk to me." The words spluttered out of him, and I ducked my head so he couldn't see me smile. He really had it bad for her.

"I just need to talk to her. If you could contact her?" I asked again.

His bowtie bobbed as he swallowed. "Yes, well, I could ask her."

Gran hovered and I just stood there and ate my toast. Neither Feish nor Suzy said anything about the night before, or going through the doorway to what was basically a porn club, or the men in black, nothing. Eric was quiet now too after spluttering about contacting Kinkly.

"Eric," I said, drawing his attention to me, "you know a lot about the shadow world, being a counsellor to shadow creatures. What would happen if Suzy and I broke away from the Hollows Group? Do you think we could make it on our own?"

Suzy sucked in a sharp breath but said nothing, waiting as we looked to Eric. Not because he was a man, but because he was smart. We needed smart. He touched his bowtie and then his glasses.

"You think you might not go back?" He blinked rapidly. "That…would be an interesting turn of events. You'd be free agents, for lack of a better word. That could be good and bad. It would mean you wouldn't be tied to the council like the Hollows Group is, but that might also open you up to shadier people."

I thought about Crash, who was supposed to be one of the bad guys. Maybe he was a dick for messing around with all these women at once, but that didn't make him bad, just a dick. What kind of shady was he talking about?

I sighed. "So you think it's a bad idea?"

"Actually, I think it is a great idea. But I have one question." He cleared his throat. "Could I be on the team? Just as an advisor, of course. I think I could bring insights to the team, and guidance when dealing with different personalities—"

I waved a hand, cutting him off. "I wouldn't do this without you." A smile spread over my lips and then I looked at Suzy. "What about you? Want to start our own club? Keep the money for ourselves?"

She picked up a piece of toast and bumped it into mine. "Done. Girl power, all the way."

Feish's face fell, but I was ready for her. That's what I got for sitting on the throne for the last hour, praying for the end to come. I'd had time to think about how this would go down.

"You'd have to be our secret, Feish. You can be in, but Crash can't know," I said softly.

Her eyes lit up and she threw her arms around my neck, almost strangling me. "We are friends."

"Of course we are." I patted her back.

"We'll need a name," Suzy said. "Charlie's Angels?"

"I think that's taken," I mumbled around my last bite of toast. My guts were feeling better, even if my backside was still miserable.

"Avengers?"

"Also taken." I laughed softly.

"Gran's Girls," Gran whispered. "Eric can be an honorary girl."

I burst out laughing but was rudely interrupted by a sudden banging on the back door. Eric and Feish jumped, lifting their hands as if they were ready to karate chop the would-be invader.

I spun in my seat to see Gran float-running toward the back door, her fingers wiggling like mad as if she could still cast a spell. "I said to stay off my property, Matilda!" she yelled. I pushed out of my seat and hurried after her. Because neither Feish nor Suzy could see Gran. Only Eric could.

They might be able to hear her at times, or get the occasional glimpse, but they didn't *see* her the way I did.

"Damn it, who is Matilda and why is she banging on the door?" Like I didn't have enough problems on my desk. I skidded to a stop at the back of the house as the pace and volume of the banging picked up, and whipped the door open.

"Matilda!" Gran pointed a finger at a woman standing on the doorstep in nothing but a partially shredded nightgown. Blood seeped from wounds all

223

over her body, including a slash that circumnavigated her neck.

I put a hand to my own neck. "Another ghost."

"WHAT?" Suzy whisper-shouted in my ear, making me jump. "What do you mean *another* ghost?"

"Her grandmother lives here still," Feish sniffed, which was a rather wet sound. Maybe she was getting a cold.

"You mean it's haunted?" Suzy was quiet for a breath and then pumped both fists into the air. "YES! I mean, that is so awesome! This team is going to kick some serious ass!"

I ignored her as I stared at the ghost who kept looking over her shoulder, which made her head roll precariously close to the edge of falling right off. Matilda pushed on Gran, who pushed her right back.

"No. You may not come in. You won't bring that darkness into my home!" Gran stomped her foot and Matilda stumbled back, one hand clutching at her neck, the other wrapping around her middle. Tears slid down her pale cheeks, and her dark brown hair hung in messy ringlets. As if she'd had her coif done the day before and slept in it. Only I knew from the style of her nightgown she'd been dead for longer than a day. More likely she'd been dead for a couple hundred years.

Another stomp from Gran, and Matilda floated down the back steps and to the back of the house next door, sliding through the solid brick wall as if it were nothing. Gran sighed. "She is a mess, that one."

My eyebrows shot up. "And this is because?"

"Well, besides the fact that she was murdered? She clings to something that she cannot speak of because of the—" Gran drew her thumb across her throat as she made a 'ggggkkkk.' "—terrible business next door. My gardens always kept it from seeping over to us."

I had no doubt it was a terrible business. The Sorrel-Weed House was known for its hauntings, which had made it a serious draw for tourists, thrill seekers, and true believers hoping to catch a glimpse of ghosts and demons. "Is she going to be a problem?"

"You need to work on the garden," Gran said. "Anyone who lives here needs to keep it healthy. The protection spells I wove around the house are tied to the roots of the plants, and from there to the souls within this house. She and the others will keep out if the garden is maintained. All those idiots wanting to buy the house trampled my flowers and herbs, and that did damage to the spells."

A sigh slid out of me as I thought of all those hot summer hours I'd spent in the garden with my gran. She'd loved it and I'd loved her enough to make the process bearable. But I could already imagine the plants dying off in rapid succession. A green thumb was not a skill I'd ever been able to cultivate. Yes, pun intended.

I backed up and bumped into Suzy. Eric and Feish stood right behind her.

"Was that really a ghost from next door?" Suzy breathed. "I've heard that there is some seriously bad mojo flowing through those walls. Never been inside of it, though."

Feish sniffed again. "Very bad. Even Boss thought maybe too bad for buying this house."

Her lips clamped shut as if she'd said something she shouldn't have. Interesting.

"Yes." I looked at Suzy first. "That was a ghost. Gran ran her off. But I have to keep up the garden here if it's going to protect us from the monsters from next door."

Eric cleared his throat. "I could help with that. I like gardening."

I touched his elbow. "You sure? It's hot out there."

He smiled. "I'm a bigfoot. I like nature and it responds to me. I'll do some baking when it gets too hot to garden."

Was he for real? No man was this good. Of course, then it hit me he wasn't real. He was a damn bigfoot. Downright mythical.

"Thank you, Eric." I gave him a quick hug and he blushed.

"It's been a long time since I've been a part of something," he said. "This is nice. Like a family."

Suzy nodded, and so did Feish. Gran stood off to the side watching us with serious eyes. I clapped my hands together.

"So, since we're all so wide awake, we should get my stuff from Corb's. There's not a lot of it."

Suzy looked around the house with new eyes. "You think there's room for a third? I've always wanted to live in a haunted house. And I'll help with the garden too."

I'd opened my mouth to say no until she mentioned the garden. Any help there would be good.

"If there is room," Eric said, "I could stay too. We are probably all safer together."

He wasn't wrong. The more eyes on this place, the better. Especially considering we'd been shot at out in the bush.

"Agreed," I said. "We can keep an eye out for anyone coming and going. Work together."

I looked at the river maid on my left. "What do you think, Feish? You good with more roommates?"

She pursed those big floppy lips of hers. "Maybe till Boss gets back. When he's back, then he decides."

Back. Which meant he was gone for how long? What had he said the day of the auction?

Up to two months.

Two months in a place like that orgy pit?

Probably. Yeah, I didn't like how that felt on my heart. I was not falling for him, not by any twinkling of the imagination. But I'd thought…

I don't know what I'd thought. That he was different, maybe. That I was important to him?

That he liked me. UGH. I was an idiot. He was a fae king. I was human. This was for the best, it really was. I just had to keep telling myself that.

Suzy and I walked back to Corb's loft to get Suzy's car, Eric already hard at work in Gran's garden as we left, chatting with Gran and getting her advice on how to best remove certain weeds.

Suzy left me at Corb's, took her car, and headed to her place to pack up the room she rented. Which was probably pretty empty considering all the bags in the back of her car.

I let myself into the building, peeled off my boots to carry them in one hand to keep the noise down, and crept up the stairs. Corb would be sleeping now. I was sure of it. Cowardly of me to grab my stuff and run? Maybe. But if he'd yelled at Suzy for five minutes, then I could expect him to yell at me for ten. Especially given the way he'd been treating me. My phone had been shut off, I needed to remind him of that. I'd run out of minutes and hadn't had the opportunity to add more.

Not that I was afraid, I just didn't have the energy to duke it out with him. What I could use was a hot soak in a tub, a full-body massage, and half a bottle of Advil.

Too bad there were only two tablets left in the bottle in the bathroom.

Back in my room, I stuffed my clothing into the one duffel bag I'd brought with me from Seattle. The rest of my stuff—what little there was—I'd put into a storage unit there. But I didn't have the money to get it all shipped to Savannah, not if I wanted to pour every penny toward the house, and the more time that passed, the less I cared. I really didn't have much to my name. I mean, I had the money from Eric and the bounty I'd completed. I touched the leather bag on my hip, where I'd stowed all that money.

For just a moment, a flicker of horror swept through me and I scrambled to open the bag and make sure that the money was still there. I'd totally forgotten I'd been packing it around since the house auction. "Idiot, you're an idiot."

"Oh, I wouldn't go that far," Corb said. "A fool, maybe, but not an idiot. You're too smart for that moniker."

I turned to see him in the doorway. He had on pants and a shirt, so maybe he hadn't been sleeping, even if he had some good dark circles under his eyes. I zipped up the bag with one long swipe. "Well, yeah, today we can call me an idiot." When was the guilt trip coming? The one where he complained that he didn't know where we'd been? Maybe it wasn't coming.

And maybe hell had frozen over.

He looked around me and saw the bag, leaned over and picked it up. "Because you're leaving?"

"No, that's not why I'm an idiot," I said. "There are other reasons. Like packing my money around with me. I need to get it into a bank or something."

He nodded and let my bag go. "Funny. I thought you were going to say you were an idiot for disappearing without a trace for nearly a day," he drawled softly as he stepped into the room and crowded my space. There it was, the guilt trip. And damned if I wasn't feeling it right to my core. "I thought you were going to say you were an idiot because you could have died, and no one would have known where to even look for you." Another step closer, and then he was looking down at me, and not in a condescending way. More like an *I might just eat you* kind of way. Shit, he was super-duper angry.

"Well," I tucked my hands behind me to keep them from touching him. Because despite all the signs that he might be interested, and my hormones' insistence that I should take him up on any and all offers he might be making, I was not a total idiot. I was sure it had something to do with the spell the O'Seans had laid on everyone. "I didn't think you'd miss me. Just a few weeks ago you would have been happy to see me disappear from your life. So why should now be any different?"

His jaw ticked, and the way his chest rose and fell made it obvious he was struggling to breathe evenly. "Is that what you think?"

"I dropped into your life without an invitation." I shrugged. It was hard to act casual when a man of his size was crowding the tar out of you. Especially when my fingers wanted to dance all over him. Bad, bad Breena! He was kind of on the taboo list. Just like Crash. Crap, I'd really fallen into the "I like bad boys" trap. I cleared my throat and dragged my bag across the small bed to my side. "I know that you've got people—sorry, *things*—to do." I made myself give him a casual wink. As if I didn't feel the urge to strip my clothes off and roll around on him—if only to feel sexy and wanted for a change. "You're well stocked, and I don't want to walk in on something I shouldn't."

He frowned. "What are you talking about?"

Oh, Gawd, he was going to make me say it, wasn't he? Well, he'd left me with no choice. Like a Band-Aid I'd left on for long enough it had glued itself to my skin, I was going to have to rip this sucker off. Time to lay it on the line.

"Oink and Boink? Boy Butter? Sorry, but I'm not sure I'm up for the amount of lubrication you apparently require." And just like that, I turned my back to leave before he could notice my red cheeks and realize that maybe I wouldn't mind all the stuff that went with his stash under the sink.

15

I didn't wait around for Corb to come up with some lame excuse for why he had so much lube in his bathroom. I grabbed my bag and my boots and was out of my bedroom, down the hall, and out the front door even as I heard him swear from the bathroom.

Here's the thing, I know what you're thinking. *Get it, girl! Take him up on the offer!* I mean, that's the advice my bestie from Seattle, Mavis, would have given me. And a teeny tiny part of me, right at the center of my libido, was urging me to do exactly that. Buff. Young. Hot. Dangerous. Damn it. He checked all the boxes for a fling, but I was not a fool. He was out of my league.

I'd just been shown how much it hurt to get your hopes up via Crash and his two ladies. Hell, Crash hadn't even spoken to me, as if he'd be embarrassed for people to know he knew me. Whether it was because I was human, or not eighteen going on twelve, I didn't know. It didn't really matter.

But I was not going to fall for another bucket of bruised ego with Corb.

I was across the street and in Centennial Park Cemetery before I heard the door of his loft open. What in the world possessed me to do it I don't know, but I ducked behind one of the bigger tombstones and slid to my butt.

"Are you really hiding from Corb?" I asked myself. "What in the world is wrong with you?"

Movement to my left snapped my head in that direction. "Robert!"

The skeleton swayed side to side as if he were on a ship at sea. "Friend."

"You're okay? I thought you were done for when you got blasted!" I held a hand out to him as if to high five, and he mimicked the motion, only he had skeletal digits and no real palm. I high fived him anyway.

"Okay. Healed," he rumbled. "Friend." He stayed where he was and so did I.

"Yeah, well, your friend is an idiot," I said. "I disappeared for a day and a half. But we were only gone an hour on our end." I rubbed my head. "And I drank something wicked that knocked me on my butt." I winced, thinking about how all that liquid had come out. "I'm still sore." I patted the ground next to me and Robert sat, crossing his bony legs, still swaying.

I sighed and leaned my head back against the tombstone. "What am I doing, Robert? Am I too old for this?" Yeah, that worry was still hanging over me. I couldn't help it. Each day that passed took me a day closer to forty-two, then forty-three, and before I knew it I'd be like Hattie and Gran, unable to stand the heat, complaining about aches and pains and stupid men...I snorted. Who was I kidding? I was partway there already.

A quick peek over the edge of the tombstone showed that Corb's blue Mustang was gone. I hadn't even heard it start up. Then again, I'd been busy feeling sorry for myself. "And then, to top it all off, Crash had two women hanging off him whose combined age is probably still not as old as me. How the hell do I compete with that?"

Robert slowed his swaying. "Don't."

I frowned. "Don't compete?"

His swaying continued. Only it took on a more circular motion as he repeated that one word. "Don't."

Don't compete with them. Damn, when a skeleton had more emotional intelligence than you did, it was a sign that you did indeed have some social issues. I smiled. "Thanks, Robert. You're right, I shouldn't be competing with anyone. That's not why I'm here."

I pushed to my feet, my lower back seizing halfway up. Too many years of hard physical work grooming dogs were catching up to me now. I had to pause there, crouched like Quasimodo, and breathe through the tightness as it slowly released and allowed me to stand all the way up. The first few steps sent tingles up and down my legs, and I hobbled as if I were a heck of a lot older than forty-one. Robert walked with me to the far edge of the park/cemetery and the gate that led out to the east end.

"You coming with me, or staying?" I asked, much to the amusement of more than a few tourists. Of course, they couldn't see Robert.

"Coming." As he finished the word, he collapsed down into that same small finger bone that I scooped up and slid into my leather bag. Hoisting a bag over either shoulder, I stepped out of the cemetery. The walk back to Gran's wasn't long, but felt longer with the duffel bag.

Suzy beat me back to the house, and miracle of miracles, the backseat of her car was mostly empty. I only saw one bag still in it. Damn, she'd moved in fast.

Feish stood on the top step of the house as I let myself in through the wrought iron gate. "She has a lot of stuff. Lucky that I like her."

Eric was in the east side of the yard, working away, humming to himself. "This is great, I love this garden!"

That made me smile. At least someone was happy.

I dropped both my bags at the bottom of the stairs. "I'm going to work in the garden, Feish. We all need to take care of it. If the ghosts from next door can come over now, it will only get worse the more we let the garden slide."

Feish's eyes went wide. "That would be bad."

"Yeah, that's what I think too."

I pulled the finger bone out of my leather bag and set it on the ground. "There you go, Robert." I blinked and he stood there, swaying in the sunshine.

Feish flapped her arms as she all but flew down the steps. "What are you bringing him for?" So she could see him, then.

"Because he looks out for me. And I think he might be lonely." I grimaced. "Don't you think you would get lonely if everyone was afraid of you all the time?"

Her face almost collapsed under the sadness that washed over her. "Yes. I think very lonely."

Crap, I'd stepped in it there. I cleared my throat. "So we stay together, all of us. Friends." I grabbed her webbed hand and gave it a squeeze as Robert muttered "friends" under his breath. Not Friend, singular. Friends, plural.

Before I could acknowledge the tears that welled up in those big round eyes of hers, I hurried into the front yard, which was all garden, all over the place. Feish, I was beginning to realize, had a lot of pent-up emotion that I wasn't always sure what to do with.

My grandmother's garden was made up of four sections, one for each direction on the compass. Not that there was any one type of plant in each section. Nope, far as I could see there was no rhyme or reason to what was growing there.

I recognized most of the plants, if not by sight then by smell. More than anything, I wanted to make sure whatever was keeping the next door monsters out continued to do so. Which meant I started on the fence line against the Sorrel-Weed house. I bent down by a patch of sage and began weeding around the edges of it, stripping the invasive plants out by the roots. The heat of the sun soaked into my back as I gave up and went to my hands and knees.

It was a little weird, and kind of great, to be doing something so mundane when there was so much going on. Being shot at. Killing O'Sean. Losing my job. Falling into a fae orgy pit. Being chased by men in black. It all felt so far away out here.

Feish brought me out a drink, and then she brought out buckets of water that I poured around the sage, peonies, and climbing ivy covered in impossible flowers. A rainbow of colors burst above my head like fireworks as I weeded around the base of the ivy.

Suzy joined me, weeding with me, and Feish kept bringing us water to pour over the roots. A little effort from all made the hours slide by, particularly since Suzy entertained us by talking smack about the Hollows Group trainees and mentors. How Louis thought he was going to be in charge but Eammon wouldn't back down. How the trainees, minus yours truly, had gone out after that first night of passing the entrance exams. They'd danced in a club for supernaturals and Luke had ended up disappearing with someone. No one knew who, but he'd come back a few hours later with a grin on his face. They'd teased him mercilessly about it. She told us how Tom secretly (or maybe not so secretly, seeing as Suzy knew) wanted to bring the Hollows more dignity and respect. "He's tired of us all being the butt of some grand joke," she said.

All good info, but it was that last bit that caught my attention.

"What do you mean by that?" I asked as I pulled a particularly deep weed out. A flutter of wings turned us all to the left as Kinkly dropped out of the branches of the peony tree that sat between the two houses. Eric, who'd joined us from the far side of the garden, slowed in his gardening and blinked rapidly at her. "She did come."

"The Hollows Group is a joke," Kinkly said softly, as she gave Eric a wave. "But seeing as the council ignores the majority of those they are supposed to protect, it's all the rest of us have."

I sat back on my heels, grimaced, and let myself fall back onto my butt, which also made me wince. Suzy snickered. "New definition of having a hot ass, isn't it?"

Carefully I leaned back, doing my best not to react. "So the Hollows is a joke." I turned to Eric. "Why did you come to them for help?"

Eric grimaced and shook his head. "I don't want to say it."

Suzy shared a look with Feish, who shrugged. "You tell her, she might not believe me."

"That isn't fair," I said. "You are my friend, why do you think I wouldn't believe you?"

Suzy sat with her back against the wrought iron fence. "Because she works for Crash, and Crash and the Hollows are known to butt heads. And what I'm about to say sounds like bashing."

As if Crash's history with the Hollows meant anything to me. "Just tell me what you two mean. And why would you want to work for them if they're a joke?" And really, why would Corb? Or Eammon? The remaining mentors all seemed like they had it together, except for Sarge, who'd pulled a Jekyll/Hyde act. Which I was still attributing to some sort of spell with the O'Seans, even if I couldn't figure out why he'd turned on me, in particular.

Something wasn't adding up.

Kinkly landed on my bent knee. "The council has its own police force. Savannah Council Enforcement. SCE. They handle most of the legitimate cases. The ones that intersect with the humans a lot. They get paid well, have benefits, have all sorts of status in the shadow world." Her eyes darted to Feish, who nodded. Interesting. Kinkly tapped my knee, drawing my eyes back to her. "People only come to the Hollows if they're desperate. The jobs they get are on the fringes of even the shadow world, they don't pay well, though they tell the recruits that they do, and they're few and far between. You changed that when you took Hattie out. Not everyone likes that the Hollows Group is gaining some status."

That made me think of Eric's case, of the way he'd been ignored by Eammon and the others. They hadn't wanted to take it on, and not because of the money…because they thought he was full of shit and didn't want to look worse than they already did. How many cases had they let go because of that reasoning? Probably a lot.

Which meant a lot of people had been hurt while they were trying to gain status. Anger thrummed through me as I considered all the implications.

"Then why did you sign up with them?" I tossed the question at Suzy, who smiled, though there was no happiness in it.

"Because I am part siren, the council would never gainfully employ me. They won't take half-men—or women for that matter—or anyone who can manipulate minds. They also don't hire leprechauns. And I wanted to do something for this world of ours. I might be a diva now and again, but this is my home."

I nodded, understanding that reasoning, then frowned. "That leaves spell casters. Necromancers. They're pretty much the only ones the council would be able to hire."

The other three women and Eric all nodded slowly. Feish crouched as if it cost her knees nothing to stay all bent up like a pretzel. "They don't like taking women either," she added, "not just shifter women."

"They make a mockery of the Hollows whenever they can. But your success with Eric caught their attention," Kinkly said softly. "Caught a lot of attention. Everyone has their eyes on you."

"Is that why we got shot at?" I looked at Eric and he pushed his glasses up his nose even though he didn't really need to.

"I don't know about that," he said. "But the rest of what they are saying is true. I'm surprised you didn't know about the Savannah Council Enforcers. Some are even in good with the local human police. I don't know much more than that. They wouldn't consider my case. Told me I was being a fool."

I looked at the ground below me, thinking. I hadn't heard of this police force. But until recently, I hadn't heard of the Hollows either, and I said as much. "Where are they? I mean, I haven't seen any of them around."

"They are secretive, they won't let you see them until they want to be seen," Suzy said. "Likely they are watching all of the Hollows recruits right now to see if any good ones slipped through the cracks."

I looked at her. "You mean you don't know where their headquarters are?"

Suzy shook her head. "If you want an interview, you have to send a letter through the council. If you're chosen to test, then you're taken to their very secret training facility."

Sounded an awful lot like the Hollows Group to me.

As I lifted my eyes, Gran floated into my line of vision. "Neither the SCE nor the Hollows existed before you left." Her mouth twisted into a grimace. "The council decided they wanted more control after the—"

Eric and surprisingly Robert spoke together a single word: "Outbreak."

That set me back on my heels. "What outbreak?"

"'Yellow fever,'" Eric said, his hands making air quotes around the words. "There were a half dozen cases, mostly in the shadow world, but a couple of humans were also infected. The council managed to clamp down on it, but it was a terrifying few months. After that, they decided they needed a new police force. And Eammon and his friends figured there was enough protection and policing work to go around for two groups. And there you go."

This was a good chunk of information to take in all at once. I blew out a big breath. "That's a lot of information. What do you mean by yellow fever in air quotes?" I remembered a couple of the mentors talking about that, but it had happened right after my interview with the Hollows Group, and there'd been enough weird to drive it right out of my mind.

Eric cleared his throat and fiddled with his bowtie. "Have you noticed there is no talk of vampires? Surely your gran told you what happened to them?"

Gran was there, but she said nothing. I frowned and pulled up a few weeds. "Nothing I can recall."

Suzy picked up the thread. "The yellow fever epidemic is the reason those bodies were sunk in the river all those years ago, but it wasn't actually yellow fever that killed all those people. It was a plague of vampirism. The shadow world covered it up—we manipulated the humans into believing they were sick and dying because of the plague, not because of vampire attacks. We wiped out the vampires, but in doing so we revealed ourselves. Which is why so many of us died. It's also why…things are as they are now. Why the two worlds are so separate."

Duck me sideways and upside down. I wanted to laugh and say good one, funny joke. But I could feel the truth of it in my bones, as if I'd known it before she said the words, which was stupid. There was something about vampires in Gran's book, but I hadn't gotten to it yet.

Kinkly flexed her wings. "The shadow world… is not what it once was. Things are changing, and I don't think for the better. Not all the players are here for the reasons they should be, I think—"

Above our heads the loud blare of a crow cut her off and I found myself on my feet, the shovel raised above my head like I was stepping up to bat. Another loud caw and the bird flew away in a burst of movement that left behind a large black feather, which floated down to the center of our little gathering, a chill sliding through the air with it.

I stared at the feather. "Let me guess, that's a bad sign?"

Suzy poked at it with her toe. "Maybe? I don't know enough about signs and omens."

"Me neither," Feish said. "At least not signs that birds leave. Fish, yes, but not birds."

"Kinkly?" I turned to the fairy, but her eyes were locked on the feather. "Kink?"

"You need to be at the fairy ring tonight," she whispered. "Karissa said the card is a warning and you need to heed it. Be careful. Please be careful. They are close."

With a flutter of wings she shot forward, scooped up the feather, paused to touch Eric gently on the cheek, which left him blushing, and then she was gone too. I frowned. "That can't be good."

"The fae are a funny folk," Suzy said, and when I glanced at her with raised eyebrows she shrugged. "I know a little about them, they are close cousins to sirens. Not enough to help you out, though."

A cloud crept over the sun and that little bit of darkness was enough to drive us inside. Enough weeding for one day. Eric hurried ahead of us and went straight for the kitchen. I began to wonder if he baked when he was stressed.

I had no problem with that.

Back inside, Suzy went straight to her phone and scooped it up. "Luke just left me a message. The Hollows isn't training tonight."

"No? Any reason why?" A little chill rolled along my spine. First the raven feather, then the cloud, and now training had been cancelled for the first time in...well, as long as I'd been there. Sure, it didn't affect us anymore, but something strange was happening. I just couldn't put my finger on it.

Look at me go, forty-one and rocking my intuition.

Suzy shook her head. "No reason from Luke. I think we should train here, though. We can use the backyard, practice what we've been learning."

Gran bobbled between us, and though Suzy couldn't see her, she shivered and rubbed her arms. "The girl is right. You still need to train. Your mind and your body." She pointed up the stairs to where I'd left the leather-bound book of her spells.

A smile tried to work across my face. "I'm going to get my gran's book. We can use it and Eric for the not-body training."

They raised their eyebrows at me but said nothing.

"Not body training?" I muttered to myself as I stood at the bottom of the stairs that led to the second level of the three-story house. Standing there, looking up, it felt like climbing those stairs might be a task not unlike climbing Mount Everest. My body did not like all this running, training, digging, fighting, being shot. I sighed and put my hand on the banister as a floorboard above my head let out a low groan.

I might have chalked it up to Gran waiting for me upstairs, except I'd just seen her in the kitchen with Feish and Eric, showing the bigfoot where she'd stashed some good herbs.

Which meant someone else was in the house, someone who shouldn't be. Biting back a groan, I lowered myself into a crouch and crept up the stairs, avoiding the two that squeaked no matter how lightly you stepped on them.

Right hand on the banister, left hand on the knife strapped to my thigh, I popped off the leather strap that secured it in place. Part of me—whatever was left of the Breena who'd lived in Seattle for twenty-ish years—was freaked out at the thought of pulling a knife on an intruder, never mind actually knowing how to use it.

But the rest of me was all outta ducks, and whoever this asshat was who'd climbed into my gran's house was about to get his ass and his hat handed to him.

I stayed in a crouch at the top of the stairs, forcing my legs to take me forward. The creak had come from my room—I would have recognized the timbre of that sound even if I'd been half dead. Maybe that wasn't the best comparison given how my life had been going lately.

Another creak and I stood and pinned myself to the wall next to the closed door of my bedroom. Someone had some serious balls letting themselves in like that. I mean, even if Crash hadn't bought it, the house had belonged to Gran, it was haunted, and there were people living here. People who were currently in the house.

I tightened my hold on the knife and reached across to grab the doorknob as it turned. I jerked back and plastered myself as flat as I could to the wall. The person who stepped out was worse than any monster I could have come up with on my own, worse than a werewolf, a goblin, or, God forbid, a vampire.

I stuck my foot out, tripping his lanky frame as he stumbled toward the stairs. He made a grab for the banister and missed, and I watched with no small amount of satisfaction as my ex-husband fell down the single flight, ass over teakettle, all the way to the bottom.

16

I followed him down the stairs at a slower pace as I tucked my knife away. "Alan, you should really watch where you're going. You could get yourself killed."

"What are you doing in here?" he growled, and I took note of the large rectangular bump under his shirt.

"Are you serious?" My hands went for my knives, but I didn't pull them out. Just let my hands hover over the handles while I stared at what had to be Gran's book under his shirt.

Feish, Eric, and Suzy came running out of the kitchen with all the noise, Gran with them.

She pointed a finger at him. "He has my book!"

"I know, Gran," I said softly. "The question is why. Why would a human like Alan want a book of spells? Hmm?" My mind started rapidly shooting through all the pieces, putting them together as it was wont to do. "Maybe the person who helped you take everything from me, who helped you fool the human court system, wanted a little something in return if you got the house?"

Holy shit, even as the words left my mouth I knew they were true. Even if Alan hadn't lost color and clutched at the book he'd tucked under his shirt. He scooted backward on his butt toward the door, but Eric was there, blocking his escape. Feish and Suzy were blocking his way to the kitchen, and I was on the stairs just above him.

"Alan," I said his name with as much composure as I could muster. "Who are you working for?"

He shook his head.

I couldn't help laughing at him. "That's the best you got? I have a siren here who could just make you speak." I wasn't entirely sure that Suzy could, but Alan didn't know that. "I've got a river maid"—Feish stepped forward—"who could put you through water torture like you've never imagined, and"—I held up a finger and pointed to Eric behind him—"I've got a bigfoot who could literally tear you limb from limb. I don't think you're in a position to—"

Alan's eyes rolled back in his head and he passed out.

"Well, damn." Suzy stepped forward and pushed a boot against his squishy middle. "That was rather anti-climatic."

Alan lay across from me at the bottom of the stairs, kind of crumpled on top of himself, legs and arms akimbo rather like a giant praying mantis. Of course, in that species the female eats the male after they mate.

I can see the appeal of that tradition.

Especially when it comes to Alan or, as I like to call him, Himself. I might have muttered that a little too loudly.

"Why do you call him that?" Feish asked. "It's strange, you know that?"

I stopped a few steps above him. "Because he thinks so highly of himself, he might as well be royalty. And because I fear that if I say his name too many times, he'll appear. Like Beetlejuice. You remember the movie with *Batman* and the *Stranger Things* mom? And look—" I waved my hand over him, "—now here he is."

Alan groaned and slowly opened his eyes. "Just a dream, it's just a dream."

He wobbled up to his feet and scooped up his hat from the third step, just under me. He jammed it on his head, whatever fear he'd been feeling before gone, though the dark spot in his crotch said otherwise.

"If you peed on the floor and wrecked the hard-wood, I'm going to be seriously angry."

I was going to say pissed, but that seemed a bit much, even for me.

He adjusted his hat as if that would make us forget he was bald under there. I settled my resting bi-atch face into place and stared him down. Four stairs above him, I could do just that while I waited for him to explain himself.

Alan glanced over at the kitchen, took one look at Feish and grimaced. This even though he only saw a woman with a harelip. Her shoulders slumped and something in me snapped.

I rushed down the last steps and jammed two fingers right into Alan's solar plexus, driving him backward, basically into Eric's arms. Eric grabbed hold of him, and Alan squeaked like a mouse.

"You're trespassing, and it looks to me like you're trying to steal something." I growled the words, I was so damn angry. "Maybe more than one something? What else did you come here for?" I knew that Gran had secreted items throughout the house, but I needed to find them still. What if whoever had sent him knew about the things she'd hidden? Would foreknowledge of the items allow a person to find them?

He gasped for air as I frisked him, first taking the very obvious leather-bound book out from under his shirt. He'd strapped it to his body, but a quick slice of one of my knives through the thin bindings freed it. To be on the safe side, I continued looking him over. I didn't expect he would actually have taken anything else, so finding my grandmother's talisman in his left front pocket drew a growl from me. I'd left it in the bathroom after my shower, forgetting it in the...heat of the moment, as it were. "Really?"

He tried to take a step back, but Eric held him steady, a seriously awesome snarl on his normally gentle face. Alan was still fighting to breathe so I jabbed him again in the same spot with my other hand for good measure. "Who sent you, Alan? And you'd better talk before I find a spell to make your dick fall off and your balls shrivel into raisins."

His face drained of color, and Suzy grinned. "Oh, I've been meaning to try that one out. Is it as good as I think it is?"

"Better," Feish said. "I know of one man who lost his dick *and* his balls. The spell made it so he was horny all the time but couldn't do a thing about it."

Alan's feet scrambled hard as he tried again to escape. "Men gotta stick together. Let me out, man!"

"Not a man," Eric said. "Bigfoot."

Alan squeaked again, but his bravado hadn't faded yet. "Crazy-ass women."

I looked at my friends. "Think he can say the name of his boss?"

It was Gran who slid around Alan, her hands brushing over his body. I watched in fascination as the hair on his arms rose, his eyes locking onto her location. I didn't know if he could see her or not.

"You could throw him in the basement," Gran said, "and let him rot for a bit. But I think he's been spelled to secrecy. I doubt he'll be able to speak the person's name."

I grinned, deliberately showing all my teeth even though I was seriously frustrated. "Crazy indeed. I don't think you should try to do a break and enter again, Alan. Because next time, there'll be a spell waiting for you, and it will make the rest of your life seriously miserable."

Eric let him go and stepped aside as Alan all but threw himself out the door, fell through the opening, and stumbled all the way down the steps to the rock walkway. Feish stood to my left, Gran somewhere beyond her; Suzy was to my right, and Eric stood behind us—the five of us a united front against Himself.

As he ran down the street, continually looking over his shoulder until he was out of sight, I felt a powerful bond with these people I knew very little.

"Was he any good in bed?" Feish asked.

Suzy let out a peal of laughter. "Even I know the answer to that, Feish. No. The answer is no."

"He's rather self-centered. Which left me—" I gave an exaggerated sigh and slumped forward, "—perpetually disappointed."

Feish's grin was as wide as her face as she gave me a wink. "Boss is good in the sack. All the ladies say so. You should try him out!"

Well, so much for all the good feelings. I cleared my throat. "I'm sure he is."

Eric grumbled. "Men like that"—he gestured dismissively in the direction Himself had run—"give the rest of us a bad reputation. I would never treat a woman I cared for so horribly. I'd shower her with affection, and make sure that she knew I cherished her."

A chorus of awws slid from four very female throats. I mean, what woman wouldn't want a guy like Eric? He was a bit on the nerdy side, but he was tall, super cute and super sweet, and he baked a mean pastry. I cleared my throat to speak, and noted that Suzy had all but locked her eyes on Eric. As if she were seeing him for the first time. Of course, she probably hadn't noticed him mooning after Kinkly.

"I'm going to double check my room, see if, Alan"—gah, I had to force myself to say his name—"took anything else."

I turned away as Suzy took a step toward Eric. "Do you know anything about sirens?"

Holy crap, she was really going to make a move on the bigfoot? Was that even allowed, interspecies dating? Not my place, and they were both adults. I hurried up the stairs, forgetting the burn in my body as I moved on nothing but adrenaline and the desire to check my stuff.

I let myself into my room and looked through my meager belongings. Nothing else was missing, and I set Gran's book back on the dressing table. The window was open and a sharp gust blew in and flipped the pages open. The particular page that it opened to had a scrawled notation about making sure spelling pots were properly cleaned after each use, and according to Gran, the repairs needed to be done by no one but Crash. There was that name again, written in her handwriting, yet I now knew it was just a pen name of sorts. I sighed and closed the book.

The image of him—the Boss, Crash, handsome-as-sin blacksmith and probable bad guy—with a beautiful woman on each arm had burrowed into me in a way I didn't like. In some ways it bothered me more than it had to find out Alan was a cheater—which was crazy. But at the same time, learning the truth about Alan had been a bit of a relief. It had made the divorce clear cut. Because our crappy marriage hadn't really been terrible in an obvious way. Looking back, I could see the mental and financial abuse for what it was, but in the thick of it I'd told myself I didn't have enough of a reason to be unhappy. I'd believed it was just crappy. Crap, crap, crap. And it had been difficult to weigh the value of escaping that crappiness at the cost of destroying all we'd created together, of making us both start over, of failing a marriage that from the outside looked fine. All because I'd robbed myself of the ability to see clearly, in more ways than one.

With him cheating, I'd had an easy out, even if that out had cost me everything. A very small part of me was incredibly grateful he'd done what he'd done.

I sat down at the dressing table and stared in the dusty mirror. It needed to be cleaned, but even so, I could see myself clearly.

I was not ugly.

I was not stunning.

I was average. I put my hands to the sides of my face and lifted, grimacing at the way my skin moved. I bit my lower lip, thinking. Crash must have known that I was attracted to him before he kissed me. I mean, what woman wouldn't be?

I swallowed hard, making myself be logical. "What if he used your attraction for him against you, as if you were a schoolgirl with her first crush? What if there is some fae magic going on here?"

The ground seemed to move under my feet, and I lowered my head to the table as the truth hit me square between the eyes. Who was I kidding? Corb was out of my league, yes, but Crash was in a class all his own. It was ridiculous to imagine otherwise. He hadn't needed any fae magic to manipulate me into finding him attractive—he was freaking fae royalty.

Fantasies, they were both fantasies and they would both remain as such. I gave a sharp nod to myself and nearly banged my head on the mirror.

Big girl panties were a bitch to put on some days. But I yanked those proverbial panties up and got to work. Because work was something I could control, something I was actually pretty good at.

I grabbed a piece of paper and rummaged in the desk until I found a pen that worked.

Forget men and the effect they had on me. I had better things to do, despite what my libido wanted from me.

I started a list.

Figure out who/what Douche Canoe is. Assuming an O'Sean? (Ask Feish?)

Why did Alan want Gran's book and talisman? (aka, who sent him?)

Talk to Officer Jonathan. (A connection for us?)

Weed the garden.

Find a man in your league, you idiot.

I smiled at that last one. I might be an idiot when it came to men, but I was going to blame it on my hormones. I looked over the list. We'd worked on the garden, and I wasn't about to go man hunting.

I had a few hours before I had to be out at the fairy ring, which meant I had time to take at least one thing off my list.

I tapped my pen on the third item. A visit to Officer Jonathan was in order. If I was really going to go it on my own, we needed connections.

Which was how I ended up at the front desk of the Savannah Police Department wearing one of Suzy's dresses. One of her less scandalous dresses, to be clear. I was shocked that I'd been able to zip it up. Then again, it was tighter in the waist than I'd normally wear, the skirt flaring out over my hips and touching the tops of my knees. That length was the most important part of the ensemble as it was long enough that I was able to wear my knives underneath it.

"Officer Jonathan?" The very young, ridiculously perky girl with perfectly tamed bright red hair and flawless skin spoke slowly, as if I were hard of hearing. I frowned and drew myself up. If I was going to be the old lady, I might as well be the one she took seriously.

I leaned over the desk, tapping it with one finger. "I know he might not work here any longer, but I was hoping you might have a forwarding address. If you can find it in your files."

She blinked fake lashes at me—not bothered by me in the least—and gave me a smile just as fake as the hair on her eyelids. "Does he have a last name?"

Oh. Crap.

I dredged my memory banks and couldn't come up with one. "That's all I knew him by. He was a family friend when I was a child. I've just moved back into town and wanted to catch up with him."

She brightened up. "Oh! Well if he's been around that long, it can only be Officer Schmitt."

"That *long*?" I tipped my head. "How old do you think—"

She was already on the phone. "Officer Schmitt, you have a visitor."

That stunned me. "So he does still work here?" I remembered him as a man in his fifties, and he had to be closing in on his eighties now.

"We can't get rid of him." She leaned forward. "You know how it is with the old ones, they just won't let go, even when they're not needed any longer. They've tried giving him retirement packages three times. Keeps turning them down."

She might as well have slapped me. I reeled back as a wiry man in uniform with short, bright white hair strode down the hallway. Well, maybe strode is a bit of a stretch. He limped on his left side as if he either needed a hip replacement or had just had one. His dark eyes locked on me like a hawk.

"Celia?" He breathed my gran's name, then shook himself. "Wait, no, you're Breena?"

I smiled, and he scooped me up into his arms and squeezed me hard enough to make me decide he wasn't so feeble in spite of that bad leg.

"Officer Jonathan!" I squeaked out his name and he set me down, a hand on either side of my body. "I thought I'd better come see you."

His bushy white eyebrows went up. "You did? Any reason you're here now and not when Celia passed?"

More than a little air fled me with that comment. I swallowed hard, once, twice, before I could get the words together. "That is unfair when you have no idea what my life has been like."

His dark eyes didn't leave me. "Is it?"

Damn it. He wasn't going to let up, and I doubted this would be a happy reunion after all.

My jaw ticked. He wasn't going to send me running. "Perhaps we could speak in your office?"

His bushy white eyebrows shot way up. "This way."

Officer Jonathan led me to the back of the police station, through a door, through what looked like a storage space stacked to the ceiling with boxes, through yet another door, and then into a very small room.

He motioned for me to take a seat in one of the two chairs. "Relegated to the very back room in a bid to make you leave?" I slid into the chair and crossed one leg over the other.

Officer Jonathan sighed. "What can I do for you, Breena?"

I took a slow breath. He was not happy I hadn't come back for my grandmother's funeral. I wasn't happy about that either.

For the first time, I spoke words I didn't ever want to have to utter again, the shame accompanying them hot on the back of my neck. "I was in an abusive marriage. That was why I couldn't come back. He wouldn't let me leave. But I'm here now, and I am fighting to keep this town safe, the way my gran taught me." I kept my eyes locked on him, refusing to look away. "I want to know if I have someone here in the department I can turn to for help. For inside information. If not, I do understand."

He leaned back in his chair, clasping his hands in front of his chest. My memories of him surged to the forefront of my mind. He'd taught me how to use knives and guns, how to fight and fight dirty. *You will always be the smaller opponent, and being a woman, you will be underestimated. When you fight, fight with everything you've got and let them think you're crazy. Let them fear the fact that you're a woman. That you are unpredictable.*

I smiled at him. "Some of the shadow people out there are afraid of the crazy woman you helped train."

He didn't so much as crack a smile back at me. "I loved your gran. You broke her heart when you left."

If he'd slapped me, I couldn't have been more shocked or hurt. I swallowed hard. "I was young and stupid. I can't make you believe me, but I don't regret anything as much as I regret leaving like I did. I am here now, Jon." Jon, that's what Gran had called him. How many times had I noticed them smiling at each other, or her touching his arm?

A lot.

A helluva lot.

"This is my last day," he said quietly. "I am leaving Savannah."

I leaned forward. "What? Why?"

He shook his head, took a piece of paper and scribbled two words on it.

Shadow world.

His hand trembled as he picked up his phone. "Officer Burke, could you come back to me, please?"

Jon hung up before the other person could answer. "Officer Burke can help you, I think. She worked with me on a few cases in that…area." He gave me a pointed look.

"Did someone spell you?" I whispered. Holy crap, had Douche Canoe paid him a visit too? How deep did this thing go?

His head didn't move, but his jaw ticked and he blinked once, slowly. Yes. Someone had spelled him, someone was pushing him out.

"Are you okay?" I continued to whisper, afraid that I'd trigger some sort of booby trap.

He did nod in answer to that, just as the door behind me opened, banging into my chair.

"Ma'am, I'm sorry, I didn't realize that Jon had company." The heavy Southern drawl was thick with irritation.

I stood, turned, and put my hand out. "Officer Burke, my name is Breena O'Rylee. I'm an old friend of Jon's."

Officer Burke was a woman about my age, the lines at the side of her mouth and eyes deeper than they should have been. Her chestnut hair was pulled back in a tight French braid, not a single strand out of place, and not a single one of them gray. Sharp brown eyes regarded me, sweeping me over from head to toe and obviously finding me lacking.

"Jon, what do you need help with?" Her voice had that deep Southern swell that I'd had at one point in my life.

"Ms. O'Rylee might need information from time to time. Pertaining to certain things."

I watched Burke's eyes, seeing the way they sharpened further, even though she didn't so much as blink.

"I see."

Yeah, I didn't think I'd be getting any help from this quarter. Damn it. If I didn't know better, I'd say someone was actively cutting off any and all help I might have. But why, when no one really knew who I was? Or was this all just a coincidence?

First the Hollows.

Now Officer Jonathan.

And maybe...maybe even Gran? My heart constricted. "My gran's death, it wasn't natural, was it? Hattie said it wasn't. I thought she was just being mean, but now...I'm not so sure."

Jon's eyes shot to mine, his mouth working soundlessly, and then he gasped and clutched at his chest. "Jon!" Burke yelled his name, and we both shot around the desk, getting him to the floor.

She pressed the button on the walkie-talkie attached to her shirt. "Officer down, we need medic in Jon's office!"

I didn't wait for her to tell me we needed to perform CPR. I pulled a knife, cut his shirt open, and started compressions, counting them out loud, pausing for her to give him mouth to mouth, then starting up again.

I counted through three rounds before the ambulance attendants showed up, pushing us out of the way and taking over. For a few minutes, the room was an assault on the senses: people moving around and directing traffic, furniture screeching as it was shoved out of the way, and the gray pallor of Jon's face.

Then quiet fell on the room, and suddenly Burke and I were all alone.

"You moved quick," she said, the hardness slipping from her eyes and her voice.

"Jon trained me." I scooped up my knife, lifted the side of my skirt, and put it away. "Let's hope we moved fast enough." I would not cry, I would not cry, I…

Damn it. I dashed a few tears away and took a hard, trembling breath.

Burke cleared her throat and her eyes were watery. "He trained me too. If there is something I can help you with, I will try."

I swallowed hard. "I think my gran—Celia O'Rylee—was murdered. And I think he knows who did it."

She gave a slow nod. "He's been dabbling in the dark stuff too long. He knows more than he's able to let on, I'd agree with that." She paused and looked me over again. "You aren't human, are you? You moved too fast, you knew what was happening almost before it did. And you're far too pretty for just being human."

I startled. "Of course I'm human. I'm forty-one and feel every inch of my age. And I wouldn't say I'm pretty. I'm probably average at best. But thank you?" Maybe I shouldn't have said all of that, but her comments had caught me off guard. It was funny she should see me that way. Maybe a bit of Gran's magic had rubbed off on me after all.

A card appeared in her hand and she snorted as she gave it to me. "That's my private line. It's secured so you can speak freely on it."

The card was thick, made of a heavy cardstock with raised bumps all over it but no written words. Braille. Clever.

I didn't have a card. "I'm next to the Sorrel-Weed house, if you need me. No phone on me. I'm out of minutes."

"I'll be in touch." She turned her back on me, pausing in the doorway. "Soon as I know how Jon is."

17

Stunned by the events in the police station, I all but stumbled out, shock rippling through me. Jon had been on the verge of saying something about Gran's death before he'd had what looked like a heart attack. Only I wasn't so sure.

What if it had been a spell? What if I'd triggered it by asking him that question he'd wanted so badly to answer? My thoughts raced along with my heart.

Which is my only excuse for why I didn't notice the broad chest in front of my face until I slammed into it, bounced back, and would have ended up tumbling onto the pavement if not for the strong hands that caught my wrists and held me upright.

I blinked a couple times to make sure that I wasn't imagining things. "Corb?"

He pulled me upright and looked me up and down. "What are you doing here?" No doubt the flowy, flowery dress was throwing him.

I shook my head. "Nothing. I'm doing nothing here."

"Good, I was just headed out to grab an early bite. You hungry?"

I shook my head again, but my stomach betrayed me, growling so loudly that there could be no doubt it was empty.

Corb laughed. "Come on."

Which is how I ended up having dinner with Corb. Of course, with my life, nothing could be that simple.

Corb took me to Vic's above River Street, the same restaurant where I'd met the fairy queen what seemed like forever ago. I couldn't help but look around for her, wondering if she was a regular.

Window seats looking out over the river with a pomegranate mojito in my hand, the smell of mint curling up my nose and drawing some of the tension away. Hell, it could have been a date if it hadn't been Corb sitting across from me.

"Keep them coming," I said to our waitress as I downed the first mojito like it was water and I'd been in the desert for three weeks. I wanted a good buzz on to banish all of the chills this day had rolled over me.

"Easy there," Corb said, "or I'll be carrying you home."

I looked up at him, saw nothing of his cousin in his face, and wondered if this energy between us meant anything. If it was a spell. If it was a game. If it was maybe a little real.

I took a sip of the second drink, a chunk of mint leaf lodging itself at the back of my throat, which set off a spate of rather unladylike coughing. I excused myself as Corb stood, his voice reduced to a buzz in the back of my head as I tried to get the coughing under control. I made it to the bathroom before I coughed up the offending mint with a gack that left my eyes watering.

"Are you all right?"

I wiped my eyes and nodded as I turned around. "Yeah, thanks." Blinking, I stared at the woman behind me, at her plaited hair and the same damn pantsuit as before. Did she not realize I'd notice? "Karissa? It's really not a good look for a queen to just hang out in the bathroom here."

She smiled. "It is a rather convenient meeting place, especially if you do not want a man to overhear your conversation." She tipped her head to one side. "Do you find that your period has changed now that you're over forty?"

I stared at her, my jaw only partially hanging open because she tipped her head toward the door with a little more meaning. As if someone were standing there, listening in.

"A little," I managed to say, though I had to admit discussing my flow with a virtual stranger felt weird, even for me. "Some days are worse than others."

What sounded like footsteps hurrying away from the door made my jaw drop. Had Corb been listening in? Well he wasn't there now. A little lady-talk was all it had taken to remove him from the situation.

She laughed lightly. "Isn't that the truth?" Her eyes fluttered to half-mast and she leaned in close. "The timeline has been sped up. Things are getting far more dangerous at the fairy ring. I want you there full time. I will of course double the pay."

She was so compelling, I found myself staring into her eyes and nodding before my brain caught up. "Why not send Kinkly to tell me?"

"I needed you to understand the importance of this." She added softly, "Crash cannot have what his fae are digging out of my tree. You can stop him."

My eyes about bugged out of my head. "Um, no, I can't stop him. Have you seen him? He's massive and has muscles all the way out to here!" I spread my arms as wide as they would go. "And why the hell didn't you tell me right off the bat that he was the one leading this whole shebang?"

Her eyes swept over me. "You intrigue him, and he likes you well enough that he won't hurt you. I need you to bring me the item as soon as they dig it out. But they cannot see you, and they cannot know you are bringing it to me. Can you do that?"

I thought about the powder that Bob-John had suggested. His clearing powder had worked well enough, why not the invisibility powder? If I got desperate, I could always call on the skeleton horse for a quick escape. It struck me that the task had changed—it wouldn't take as long, but now she was asking for an extraction, risking a possible fight with Crash, as well as guard duty. "You need to up the pay. Significantly."

Now, now was the time to get her to sign something, but the thought fluffed out of my brain like a cloud on a summer day.

Her smile was sharp. "You will get all that I was planning on giving you for the full ten days multiplied by two."

That was good enough for me, and the desire to close the deal and move on was strong. "Okay. Deal."

"Good. Go there straight away." Her eyes narrowed on me. "You aren't who you think you are, Breena."

She kissed me then, not on the cheek but on the lips, catching me off guard as a rush of energy whipped through me. "That will help," she said as she stepped back, leaving me more than a little wobbly. "But it will only last while you are on the job for me. After that, you will feel every ache and pain you've gained, so be careful."

I touched my lips. "What?" It only occurred to me then that I hadn't stopped to ask how I was supposed to watch the fairy ring 24-7 when I was only human. When I was still in Suzy's dress with nothing more than the two knives on me.

"You have to go now. Corb cannot follow you, and trust me, he will try. I will create a diversion, wait for it." She patted my cheek and brushed past me. What did this have to do with Corb? Unless he was helping Crash? Shit, what if the two guys my libido was hot for were working together? Wouldn't that be a kick in the lady bits.

I stood there and stared at the still-swinging door until another woman came in. She took one look at me and gasped. "Lordy, girl, you look like you've seen a ghost."

"Maybe." I gripped the edge of the counter as the other woman tittered next to me, whispering about Vic's being haunted.

What the hell had just happened? The gig had changed, that was what had happened. But I'd get more pay, which meant I'd have a much better chance of getting Gran's house back. Even if I had to face down Crash.

Jaysus lord, how was that going to work out if he found out I was the one who'd helped Karissa?

I frowned until the first *BOOM* shook the restaurant and a roar echoed through the walls, plaster and dust filling the air.

Well, I'd bet that was my distraction.

I bolted out of the bathroom with more pep in my step than I'd had in a long time. My lips tingled, reminding me of the kiss Karissa had bestowed on me.

Above all the screaming, through the dust and kerfuffle, Corb was yelling for me. I didn't look for him, but headed straight for the front door of the restaurant, the light from the window guiding me out. I pushed my way through the people, not caring that they yelped and pushed back.

I felt none of it.

I burst out of the restaurant, dust flying around me as I paused just a moment to get my bearings. Kicking off my heels, I bolted down the walkway and raced across the main road, dodging cars like they were standing still, my skirt flaring and flashing the knives strapped to my thighs.

Whatever pep juice Karissa had given me burned through my veins. Minutes later I was back in front of Gran's house, barely breathing hard.

Up the stairs, into the house, and up to my room, I'd stripped out of the dress and was yanking on my leathers by the time Suzy found me.

"Holy shit, what happened to you? You're covered in dust and plaster!" She brushed some off the top of my head.

I grabbed her by the arms, my mind racing a thousand miles a minute, and in that moment I knew exactly what I needed to do.

"You need to keep the guys at the Hollows busy. Keep them there, all of them, but especially Corb. I've got to get out to the job I'm on. I'll be staying there until it's done, but it's a good job, and it will give us the start we need for our group." I yanked on my pants and grabbed my thigh holsters for the knives, strapping them on so fast that even I could feel my vision blurring over my own hands.

Suzy's eyes went wide. "Okay. Will your gran watch over Eric again? We shouldn't leave him alone for that long with a shooter on the loose."

Gran appeared beside her. "Bring him with you," she said.

I grabbed my leather bag and stuffed Gran's book into it, then double-checked that I had my silver talisman, settling it over my head. "I'm going to take Eric and Robert with me," I said.

"Why not me?"

I frowned. "Because I'm pretty sure Douche Canoe put a tracking spell of some sort on you. O'Sean was following you that night at the caves."

"What about the Hollows?" Suzy asked. "Should we go to them for help?"

I paused, for just a flash. "Eammon wants me to do this job. I don't know why, but he knew I could do this." That last bit was pure conjecture. But it felt right.

"Well, what if Eammon is in on this? We might not be able to trust him," Suzy pointed out in a quick reversal of opinion. "You could be walking into a trap."

Both good points.

I fought to slow my breathing down, struggling. Whatever Karissa's kiss had done, I could feel it pushing me to my limits. "I know for sure that Robert and Eric aren't affected. I don't know with you, and Feish is tied to Crash."

Feish stepped into the doorway. "I can try and slow the Boss down. He's on his way here now."

I swallowed hard. "Then I need to go. Eric!"

"I'm ready," he said softly, "though I don't know what good I can do."

"You're my hide-and-seek champion." I smiled at him. "We need to stay hidden; you can help me with that, and you can come back for help if I get in too much trouble."

"You don't want me to fight?"

"Do you want to fight?" I lifted both brows, already knowing the answer as he shook his head no.

I grabbed him by the arm and ran down the stairs and out the front door. Eric skidded to a stop beside me. "What the hell happened to you?"

"Fairy queen kissed me," I said. We needed a way to get to the fairy ring fast. Before Crash realized where we were going.

I thought about the skeleton horse, but I wasn't sure we could wait for it to pull itself out of the ground. That wasn't quite right, I knew in my gut it wasn't, but I hesitated on calling the horse up for whatever reason. I sensed it would be best to wait.

"We need a way out to the wildlife reserve. You got a boat?" I asked.

I knew Feish had a boat, but if Crash figured out where we were, that we'd borrowed the boat, he'd be on us in a flash.

Part of me didn't mind the image that whipped through my head of Crash being physically on me, the other part reminded me that I was working against him. Again.

Eric tugged me forward, and in no time we were running through the streets of downtown Savannah, our feet a blur. "This is much easier now that you can keep up!" Eric yelled with a grin as we passed the

Hanging Tree square, the resident demon watching us go by.

I couldn't resist, I flipped him off. He snarled at me, but we were gone before he could attach to us.

"Yeah, this rocks." But Karissa had warned me that it would hurt once I was done. At least I wouldn't have to pay the price until later.

Eric skidded to a stop at one of the outer banks of the river, away from the downtown district, and pointed to a small boat with a large motor on it. "I don't come in and out through the downtown like Feish does."

I wondered out loud how he had a boat here.

"Oh, that's not mine. It's a friend's boat," Eric said. He held out a hand and helped me in, and then he got it going. The engine was a beast, and we started flying up the river at a speed that Feish's boat couldn't match. Which was good.

Because I was pretty sure that it was behind us.

I watched as the boat that I was sure was Feish's pulled out into the river—the prow of it curved like a diving dolphin—and headed our way. I ducked down. "Eric, I think that's Crash behind us. Can this thing go any faster?"

He squeezed the handle, and our boat picked up even more speed, the spray of river water soaking us, but that was nothing to what would happen if Crash caught us and we had to explain our way out of this. I wasn't a hundred percent sure that he was even following us, but it was safest to assume that was the case. For all I knew he was just going out to the fairy ring to feel up the tree again.

That set off something low in my body and I squeezed my knees together.

"You gotta pee?" Eric asked.

I shook my head rapidly. "Nope, all good."

I was, in fact, not all good. The idea of Crash had taken root in my mind and my body was reacting way too strongly. Side effect of Karissa's kiss? I was betting so. I put my head down and tried to breathe through the waves of oh-baby-take-me-now that were rippling through every inch of my muscles and nerves.

Shit. I had to stop this in its tracks. Think of something else. Think of something scary or bad.

Like being shot at again. We were headed back to the wildlife reserve; what if the shifter who'd been shooting at us came back to try again? That cooled my libido pretty ducking quick and I was finally able to lift my head and see where we were.

"Overshoot the normal docking place," I yelled to be heard over the engine and the slap of water against the hull of the small boat. We were skipping and bobbing along so fast that we were bouncing.

Eric took us around an extra couple of bends in the river before he pulled the boat to the shoreline. He hopped out first, but I was right behind him. Hopping out like I was twenty again.

We pulled the boat up onto the shore, far enough that it wouldn't be seen from the water. I worked with a couple of thick branches to sweep the drag lines.

The sound of the second boat had me scrambling backward, falling on my butt as I slid in the slick mud.

"So you're faster, but still clumsy." Eric grinned as he helped me to my feet. I grimaced, and then we were off and running again. Yeah, this was going to hurt me later.

But in no time at all we were approaching the massive oak trees at the far side of the fairy ring. The problem was that I wouldn't be able to see how far the yellow and black fairies had gotten in digging through the one tree unless I circled around. With it being close to dusk, there were no fairies here yet. The Unseelie were active from three in the morning until noon, which meant they should still be asleep. This was the perfect time to set up camp to watch them.

"Stay here," I whispered to Eric as I crouched and crept my way around to the side where I could see the action.

The sight of the tree trunk made me gasp. I could almost see through it. Like a piece of stained glass, the striations of wood were barely there.

Did I dare get a closer look? "Eric, you can hear me?" I glanced over to see a single hand emerge from the trees, the big thumb pointing to the sky.

"I'm going to get a better look."

Thumb turned down.

Too late.

Staying in a crouch, I hurried forward and pressed my hands on the trunk of the tree. Karissa wanted me to bring the relic to her. What if I could take it now? I pressed my hands to the hole in the trunk and the tree shivered away from me, the bark turning black under my hands, and the remainder of the trunk peeled away leaving a perfect hole, just big enough for my hand. Inside the circle of trees, on a bed of brilliant green moss, lay a solid quartz chunk of stone in the shape of a cross.

I reached in and pulled it out, and tucked it into my bag. As I pulled my hand out, the circle of trees began to droop, black rot spreading from the tree through which I'd reached the cross, traveling in curling tendrils that cracked the trunks.

I'd done that? It had to be from Karissa's kiss. That's what I told myself, anyway. But something inside of me said it was more complicated.

You must protect the cross now. From all that would take it and mean harm. Keep it safe, Guardian.

The voice rippled through the air and I stumbled backward, running for Eric, forgetting all about being quiet.

He grabbed me by the arms. "What happened? Why are the trees dying?"

"Um, I touched the tree and then it started dying. The other ones seem to have caught it." I opened my bag and he looked in.

"Holy shit, that's a relic of the fae. Why did it let you take it?" he whispered.

"That's an excellent question." Crash's voice thumped into me and I spun to see him across the small clearing.

Lordy Jaysus, he was hot, even more so when he was angry. What the hell was wrong with me? My legs shook, and not out of fear. I took a step back.

"You're working for Douche Canoe, so no, you can't have this." I put my hand on the bag and tucked it behind me.

Crash's eyes narrowed. "Who the hell is Douche Canoe?"

"Sean O'Sean's pop. O'Sean senior," I said. "They spelled the Hollows Group, worked with Hattie, and threatened my life, and you're working for them." Not to mention that he obviously had terrible taste in women if he thought those two young thangs were all that and a bag of potato chips. I glared at him. "And you are a cradle robber."

That last comment seemed to throw him for a loop, but he shook it off. "Sean O'Sean is dead. There are other forces at play here that even I don't understand."

"Yeah, because I killed him when he attacked me and a friend," I said, widening my stance, my hands dropping to my knife handles. Was I really going to take on Crash? Holy shit. Holy shit. My palms began to sweat, and I think I may have peed myself a little.

I slid my bag off my shoulders and handed it to Eric. "Hang on to this for me."

"You can't fight him," Eric whispered. "He'll kill you. He's way stronger than you."

"I know," I said, and I did. He was the bad guy, remember, that's what I had to keep reminding myself. "You get that to Karissa if he kills me."

Crash's eyes went wide and then narrowed. "You're working for my *ex-wife*?"

"You bet. Lady power and all that jazz."

"She's using you," he said.

I snorted. "And you weren't trying to?" His jaw ticked and I nodded. "That's what I thought." I pulled both knives from their sheaths. By all that was holy, I hoped that this was going to work.

"Wait," I breathed the word to Eric, who startled a little but gave a nod.

Then I rushed Crash, pulling up every last ounce of training I had in me.

And prayed I wasn't about to die.

18

My knives hit a resistance as I'd expected; I mean, I didn't think Crash would actually let me just stab him without fighting back. He spun lightly on his feet, a sword just appearing out of seemingly nowhere as he caught my blades and pushed me back.

"Breena, you don't understand," he growled. "You are deliberately putting yourself in danger!"

"So why don't you cut the whole mysterious act and tell me what the hell is going on?" I snapped as I whipped my left blade across in a slash, following it with my right in a stabbing motion. He grunted, the tip of the right blade just missing him, as he was only able to block the first.

I let the magic that Karissa had kissed into me flow through my veins. This was everything youth was supposed to be, power and strength and stamina. But youth was also incredibly cocky, and young people so often thought they were immortal.

I knew better.

So as he stumbled back, his blade still on the upswing of blocking mine, I dropped my left knife to the ground, grabbed his shirt and pulled him in hard for a kiss that I hoped would literally knock his socks off.

All that magic that Karissa had given me? I pushed it into Crash, with a thought that he needed to sleep.

He grunted, his mouth moving over mine with a possessiveness that I wanted but knew better than to believe in. The magic pulsed out of me and he slumped to his knees, his mouth slipping from mine.

"Breena. Don't. You'll get hurt. Or worse."

"I won't help the O'Seans ruin this town, Crash. I won't. Not even for—" I was going to say *for you*, but he didn't want me. Not really. I was just a pawn, a way to piss off Eammon and the Hollows.

Yeah, that stung more than a little.

As he toppled over to the side, unconscious, I scooped up my blade and cursed at the pain that shot through my back. Yup, that was going to be a bitch.

I limped—freaking limped—over to Eric. His eyes were wide. "You…that was amazing. You didn't even kill him, but you beat him. *Nobody* beats Crash."

I shrugged and he handed me back my bag. A slight buzzing filled the air, and I found myself pushing him forward from what I imagined to be a horde of seriously pissed off yellow and black fairies. They'd attacked the trees with fervor and messed with Kinkly's wings. I could only imagine what they'd do to us. If they were awake now, it had to be because Crash had called them.

Eric half dragged, half carried me to the boat and shoved me in. "Look at that, we didn't even need Robert," I mumbled as Eric turned the boat and sent us out into the river once more.

I wasn't sure this was what Karissa had planned, but seeing as the item was now safe with me…I put a hand to my head. "What the hell was I thinking? I didn't even want to take it!"

"I did give you a thumbs-down," Eric yelled over the rushing wind and the slap of the water against the small boat's hull.

"I know, I know!" I rubbed my face vigorously. "It's like…" Like whatever juice I'd been running on from Karissa had robbed me of my better sense.

Eric scooted us back to River Street, and I all but slithered out, my legs jelly. I wasn't even sore, I was just…jelly. "Come on, we need to get to Forsyth Park and the fountain."

Thank all that was holy, Eric didn't so much as blink. He got a hand under my one arm, and once I was up, I was able to move on my own.

"Why aren't we running?" he asked as I forced my legs to work.

"Running people attract the attention of the supernatural; have you not read *The Last Unicorn*?" I smiled up at him and he laughed.

"Okay, so that part of the book was correct, but not much else," he said.

So just like that we went from stealing a fae artifact to going for a stroll through town as so many couples did this close to sunset.

Just another day in the life of Breena O'Rylee. I lifted my face to the last rays of the sun and dared to close my eyes for just a second. "If Crash didn't hate me before, he will now," I said as I opened my eyes.

"I don't think he hated you at all," Eric said. "From what I've heard, he's never so much as blinked in the direction of women other than for temporary pleasure."

A snort slid out of me. "You should have seem him in the orgy pit."

Eric choked back a sound. "I'm sorry, the what?"

"The doorway we went through to avoid the idiots in black was an in between, and it took us to what was basically a fae orgy pit. He had a brunette on one side and a raven-haired girl on the other, and it looked like they were maybe eighteen at best."

"Well, shit," Eric muttered, and coming from him, a bigfoot who looked more like a professor, it made me snicker.

"I don't think I've ever heard you swear before."

He patted my shoulder. "I don't often. It's a bad habit in my profession."

We were quiet for about half a block before I asked a question. "Who do you think is behind all this weird stuff, Eric? I mean, we've got the O'Sean family. Karissa and Crash are obviously fighting over…maybe territory? And obviously this thing," I put a hand on my bag as I looked up at Eric. He shrugged, so I went on. "The idiots in black, who may or may not have something to do with that, and then someone shot at us, but who?"

"Hard to say. All of it is a tangled mess." He paused and turned to look behind us. I looked with him.

There in the distance was a broad-shouldered figure I knew all too well. "Oh shit. That spell didn't knock him down for long."

"Do we run now?" Eric breathed out.

"Just walk faster," I said. I mean, Eric was hardly the one to blend in at over seven feet tall.

We picked up our pace, weaving our way through the next square, doing our best not to look like we knew we were potentially being chased.

"How close?" I asked quietly.

"He's not hurrying to catch us, so either he doesn't see us, which I doubt is the case seeing as he's not blind, or he wants to see where we're going," Eric said softly.

I took the next right, and we broke into a run as soon as we were around the corner, heading for our house. For Crash's house.

Gran's house.

Crap on crackers, he was going to kick me out. I was going to lose my gran's house completely. He'd never agree to sell now.

A flutter of wings caught my attention over the ragged sound of my lungs working overtime. "Kink! Are you okay?"

Tears streaked her face. "I'm sorry," she whispered. "I should have warned you that she'd use you. I thought you were like the others, but you're not. You're my friend. She kicked me out for standing up to her."

I wanted to ask her a question, but I didn't dare. If I did, I feared I wouldn't have enough air left to keep going. We reached Gran's house and I bolted through the gate and up the porch steps. "Kink, meet me out back!"

As soon as we entered the house, I sent Eric to the kitchen with a hand motion, as I ran through the house to the back door, and right out into the backyard. I wanted to catch my breath, but I had more problems than a woman could count, and having all the time in the world wasn't one of them.

"Kinkly!" I whisper-yelled her name and a moment later she buzzed down to me. "What the hell are you talking about? Is Karissa one of the bad guys?"

"No." She shook her head and then nodded. "Maybe. She's working with the O'Seans. They told her they'd help her secure her territory if she got them the fairy cross."

Now that set me back on my heels. Because I knew Crash was working with them too.

Or at least he was making a crucible for Douche Canoe.

Now, if I'd been twenty years younger, I might have lost my mind right there.

But I was not.

And I would not.

I turned around and marched right back into the house in time to see Crash barrel through the front door. I pointed a finger at him. "You. In the kitchen, now."

His jaw dropped and I lifted both eyebrows at him, not even trying the one brow trick. "Seriously. In the kitchen."

"Give me the cross," he growled.

"IN THE KITCHEN!" I yelled and he took a half step back. My heart was beating hard with a mixture of anger, hurt, and sheer exasperation. I went into the kitchen first, part of me expecting a blow from behind, but trusting Crash just enough to give him my back.

Eric, Suzy, and Feish were already crowded up against the far wall, like kids whose parents were really scrapping it out. I pulled out a chair and sat down at the table. Waited for Crash.

A full minute passed—which is a long time to wait, let me tell you, but I refused to back down. Not today.

Not tomorrow.

He finally came inside and sat across from me, his eyes flashing with anger. I glared right back. "You are working on a crucible for O'Sean Senior, are you not? I assume you need the quartz for it, as I believe I recall you saying it would take some time. Are you supposed to make the crucible out of the cross?"

Guessing, I was guessing, but the tightening along his neck told me I was spot on. Score one for me. Unfortunately, I had a feeling I wasn't going to score any other way any time soon.

Before he could speak, I held up a finger. "I don't want the O'Seans to have a leg up. Pardon me, *the* O'Sean to have a leg up."

He frowned but kept his mouth shut. Look at me go. "The younger of the two is dead, and it looks as though your ex-wife is also working for O'Sean Senior."

That frown of his deepened. "Damn it. Damn her."

"Yes, well, seeing as I took on a job for her, I am the one cursing myself. You are somehow both working for the same asshole. How's that for a pickle? I'm not interested in giving *either of you* this quartz fairy cross."

"I'll kick you out of your gran's house," he said.

I leaned back in the chair, having already guessed he'd say that. "My gran would prefer for me to lose this house permanently than to help an O'Sean hurt this town, something she is very sure will happen if they have their way. Savannah is mine to protect, as it was my gran's. So if you want to intimidate me, keep trying."

He mimicked me. "Why aren't you still running away?"

"You want to run around in this heat? Bless your heart, I thought you knew better than to risk heat exhaustion."

Suzy snickered into her hand, but quickly covered it up. I glanced over to see my three friends eating some concoction Eric had whipped up earlier. Like they were spectators at a bull fight. I frowned at them and the jerks all shrugged in unison.

Back to Crash, I put both hands on the table. "We are at an impasse."

Gran floated to the left of me. "My book, you read in my book about fae, about how to bind them, forcing them to heel."

What the hell did that have to do with Crash right now? Yes, he was fae, but…had they made him sign some sort of contract?

Oh.

My eyes widened. "Are you being forced to help the O'Seans?"

His blue and gold eyes closed and he leaned back in his chair. "I am a prisoner to them, far worse than Feish is to me."

Well duck me sideways.

19

Sitting in my gran's kitchen, across the table from Crash, I just stared at him, gobsmacked by the words that had fallen out of his mouth. He was something like a slave to O'Sean Senior?

"Seriously?"

His jaw flexed, but not with anger, more like he couldn't answer me. I'd seen enough of that lately to recognize it for what it was. Feish gave a burble off to my left. "I can speak for him. He will have to punish me later, but you must know, I think, or we will all walk off a cliff that can't be seen in the fog."

I swiveled in my seat to look at her. "What kind of punishment?"

"I'll yell at her," Crash said softly, "and throw things around."

Basically, they'd put on a show for whoever was listening. Clever.

Feish pulled out a chair and carefully lowered herself into it, her bulbous eyes blinking rapidly. "Boss was caught sleeping two years ago, and they spelled him to stay asleep and inked him. They forced him to sign a contract too, threatened my life if he didn't. No one else would have dared. His magic is dulled right because of their hold on him."

Suddenly her fierce protectiveness of her boss made even more sense. He'd given up his freedom to save her. Karissa's words about the Unseelie flowed through my brain.

I whipped around to face Crash. "Let me guess, they gave you the mark of a crescent moon?" He leaned back in his chair and gave me a slow nod.

Karissa had said it was a sign of Unseelie, the bad fae. Had she told me that so that I'd distrust Crash if I saw it on his neck, not realizing that it was a mark of slavery to the O'Seans, and had nothing to do with being Unseelie? I was guessing the answer was yes.

Setting me in direct opposition with Crash. "Would you have killed me if you could have back there? Because of whatever magical hold they have on you?"

Another jaw tick. "I was holding back the best I could. But yes, they want you dead now that they know you were the one who stopped Hattie. Even though they still got what they want."

Did that mean the ceremony that had cost Eric's cousin his life had let through the demon Hattie had wished to summon? Had the demon been wreaking havoc in New Orleans all this time? Now that would make for some seriously shitty irony.

"Won't help if they figure out you killed Sean O'Sean," Suzy said, ever helpful.

Crash's head whipped around to look at her, then back to me. "Pardon, what?"

"Old news. Kinda," I muttered. It seemed like weeks since Suzy and I'd been fired, since we'd been down in the enslaved quarters. Since Sean O'Sean had attacked me.

A string of curse words floated past my gritted teeth as I realized how close I'd come to dying when I'd gone up against Crash. Of course, I'd felt invincible with Karissa's magic floating through me.

"Boss. How did she beat you?" Feish asked.

I put my hand up like I was sitting in school. "Karissa kissed me. I was full of—" I lifted both hands up, wiggling them.

"Youth," Eric said. "Vitality. Strength."

I waved a hand at him. "What he said."

Feish was frowning. "Boss, Karissa's magic does not hurt you. It wouldn't have worked on you that way."

Crash stared hard at me, his blue and gold eyes sweeping over me. "Because it wasn't just her magic. Some of it was from Breena."

Gran puffed away in a quick movement that I did not miss even as his words sank into my mind. *Not just Karissa's magic.*

Hadn't Officer Jon's friend told me I was something different? That I didn't look like I was human? What the hell was happening to me?

"GRAN!" I twisted about, but she was gone. Sort of.

"I don't want to talk about it!" Her voice was faint, but I still heard it and I followed the echo.

I was up and out of my seat, running for the stairs, forgetting that there were maybe more important things to deal with than my potentially questionable heritage. Except that my heritage (parentage?) could potentially help or hurt me in this particular situation.

I skidded to a stop in my bedroom, shocked at how fast I'd gotten there after the day I'd had.

But maybe I shouldn't be so shocked if there really was something inhuman inside of me. Something that was waking up?

Why would it come out now, though? Why not when I was younger and training with Gran and Officer Jon? Why not...any time in the last twenty years when I could have used a shot of confidence? When I could have used a little magic to put Alan in his place?

Gran paced inside my old bedroom. "I didn't know it would be like this, Bree. I really didn't. I was doing my best to protect you from those who would attempt to use you."

"Spill it, Gran, who knocked boots with someone in the shadow world?" My parents had died in a car accident when I was barely ten. Another wave of intuition passed over me.

"My parents. It wasn't a car accident, was it?"

Her lips trembled. "No, I don't think it was, but I've never been able to prove it. Jon could never find anything."

"Just like it wasn't a natural death for you?" My guts were churning. Who the hell was killing my family and why?

She closed her eyes. "I truthfully don't remember my own death. I opened my eyes, and I was standing over my body. Whatever happened to me is gone from my mind."

"I *will* find the people who killed you and my parents, but we'll circle back to that. Gran, what the hell am I?" I took a step toward her and she sank to the bed. I had the urge to do the same. I wasn't human.

"Your grandfather was fae."

Her words like a slap to the face, I took a step back as my brain did the math. I was a quarter fae?

She looked at me. "I did the best I could to keep you hidden, and honestly, when you left Savannah and asked to be blocked from the shadow world, I figured it was the best way to keep you safe. As much as I hated for you to be gone, it meant there were no fae looking for you, no one wondering at your fast reflexes or your flashes of intuition. So long as you were blinded to the shadow world, no one was looking your way, no one was thinking about using you. Like Karissa would. Like Crash might."

Gran's hair swirled around her, buffeted by an unseen wind. "Your grandfather was fae, and your father was from the supernatural world too. I can't remember what he was, Bree, and I've been trying!" She swung her arms above her head in obvious frustration. "But he was strong. And that strength, along with your grandfather's bloodline, is what makes you who and what you are—unique in the shadow world. When you asked for the magic back, it came quietly that first night, but it has been growing ever since, and it will continue to grow."

I blew out a slow breath. "So whatever magic I've got, I asked for it back, and just like that it's here?"

Gran gave me a smile that was somehow both sad and proud. "You released yourself from my spell, Breena. You opened yourself up to your full potential by shedding the past that had shackled you. You had to want it."

I didn't think she just meant the spell. She meant Alan. She meant my lack of confidence in myself. She meant everything I'd lived up until this point. I straightened my back and gave her a nod. "Okay, Gran. Okay. All this is groovy—" Actually no, no it was not groovy, but I would deal with the mental fallout later. "—but we've got to figure out what exactly we're doing with the quartz cross and that mark on Crash's neck."

Because I couldn't give the cross to Karissa, no matter what I'd promised her. And I couldn't give it to Crash, because he'd be forced to give it to O'Sean.

A knock on the front door snapped my head around.

I hurried down the stairs to the door just as Suzy rounded the corner, a gun in one hand and a knife in the other. From the front hall I could just see Crash, sitting quietly at the table, his eyes the only thing that moved as they tracked me.

I grabbed the door and flung it open to see Officer Burke standing there, her fist raised to pound again. "Is that a knife?"

I looked at my right hand. "Shoot, yes it is. Cutting vegetables, and I ran for the door." I tucked the knife into the sheath on my thigh, which might have slightly undermined my cover story.

Officer Burke gave me a tight smile. "I came by to tell you that Jon is doing okay. Or at least he's stable and the doctors think he'll pull through."

I blew out a breath of relief. "I'm glad to hear that. Thank you for coming by to tell me, I appreciate it." I swung the door shut, but she put her foot in the doorway, stopping me.

"About your Gran's death. I took a quick look into it after you left the station. When you're ready, come on down, and we can discuss what I found." She pulled her foot back and turned around. I opened the door and stared at her back.

"My parents were killed too. Thirty years ago," I said softly. "In an apparent car accident that probably wasn't. But it would be dangerous to look into it. I don't want anyone else to get hurt."

Officer Burke paused, but didn't look back at me as she spoke. "You know, the files from your parents' accident might just end up with your grandmother's files. Paperwork can get mixed up like that for people in the same family."

"I see," I said. "I'll keep that in mind. And thank you. Again."

Officer Burke strode down the narrow walkway and let herself out the gate without ever looking my way again. I shut the door and leaned on it a moment, breathing in deep.

With my eyes closed, I let the problems at hand fill my mind in the hopes that the puzzle pieces would click together. Crash was under the sway of O'Sean. Karissa was working for O'Sean. O'Sean wanted to do bad, although unspecified things to Savannah. I had someone shooting at me and Eric, most likely a henchman of O'Sean's. Everyone in the Hollows Group was under an enchantment set by O'Sean Senior.

"Eammon wanted me to work for Karissa," I breathed out the words and took a step back, turning to the kitchen. Crash was watching me, his eyes unreadable.

I cleared my throat, not entirely sure who I could fully trust, but knowing who would tell me the truth if not always as expected. "Feish, is there a way to take the mark off Crash, freeing him?"

"Your grandmother could have done it. It needs to be a spell caster with great power," Feish said softly.

I grimaced, already knowing that there was one spell caster we could ask. Whether she'd help, I wasn't sure. "Crap. Okay. And once you're free of that mark, you don't have to do what they want?"

"I've already asked Missy to remove the mark. She refused," Crash said. "'Just penance for a life-time of sin and debauchery' were, I believe, the exact words she used."

My lips curled up. Suddenly their interaction at the auction made much more sense. He'd asked her, and she'd refused, but I wondered if it was because she wasn't strong enough. Knowing her, she would have wanted Crash to owe her a favor.

"Yeah, that sounds like her. If I manage to free you from it, will you promise to help me stop O'Sean?"

Crash gave me a nod. "You have my word that if you free me of this mark, I am yours."

Feish sucked in a not-so-silent gasp. I chose to ignore the potential innuendo in his wording, because it was Crash. Besides, I'd already come to the conclusion that he was not for me. No matter how hot he was.

"Crash, I need you to go outside a moment while my team discusses what we're going to do." I locked eyes with him. "Because for all we know, O'Sean can control you even now. Maybe he can even track you."

"Like he tracked me," Suzy said.

I thought Crash would get all stupid manly on me, that he'd scoff and say he was stronger than that. But he stood up and went to the door, his eyes find-ing mine for just a moment before he left. "That is smart. You decide how to move forward, and I will trust you to tell me my part."

And then he was out of the kitchen and the front door was clicking shut behind him. I could all too easily imagine him sitting on the front step. Waiting.

"Holy crap, the heat between you two is going to light *my* panties on fire," Suzy said. "I mean, he's so damn comfortable in his skin, he's not only letting you lead, but letting you boss him around? Hot. That's hot."

"Stop that." I waved a hand at her, choosing to ignore what she was saying rather than digest it. "Here's the thing. We have the quartz fairy cross. And I want to hide it in a place no one will ever think to look." I grabbed a piece of paper and started writing. Suzy, Feish, and Eric leaned over my shoulder. "We'll need Robert's help. Eric, I'll need you here, at the house. Suzy, you'll bring Missy to meet us at the Hollows. Feish, you go to Karissa." I sketched out my idea on the paper, lest anyone was listening, and Eric clapped me on the shoulder.

"That is an excellent plan. Very twisty."

I smiled up at him. "That's the idea. Confuse the shit out of everyone else." Hopefully not my team, though.

With the plan laid out, all we had to do was wait for midnight to roll around.

And for me? It was time to ask Gran the really hard questions.

20

"Gran." I sat on my bed in my room, in a house that wasn't mine, trying to tease information out of a ghost who sometimes couldn't remember the most important details. "Can we trust Missy?"

Gran paced the room from door to window and back again. Night had fallen, but we were waiting for closer to midnight to kick our plan into action. Which meant we had some time to prepare and I had time to talk to Gran about some of the things that were tugging at me.

"Missy and I were not friends, you have to understand that," Gran said softly. "We—along with Hattie—were guardians of Savannah. Three kinds of abilities, tied together by our oath to protect the city.

I know Missy went out of her way to hurt you when I wasn't looking. I wasn't blind to it."

"And you let her?" I couldn't help the pain in my voice. That my gran would have knowingly allowed someone to hurt me when I was just a child was unfathomable to me.

"No, of course not! In private I put her in her place more than once. She was behind me in strength, but not by much. Hattie was the weakest of the three of us, but even so she was not weak." Gran sighed heavily. "I ignored Missy's behavior because she was in her own way trying to waken your powers. Pain… sudden and sharp pain can crack open abilities. It is how many of us in the shadow world were trained. I was much softer with you."

Just like that, Missy being a shit to me made more sense. Even so…"But she didn't like me."

"No, she didn't. She's always known you have the potential to be stronger than her."

I scooped up my bag, which I'd set on the bed, and pulled out Gran's book. "And this? Someone was trying to steal it, you saw that. Missy wants it. Could it have been her?"

Gran sat beside me and settled her hand on the red leather-bound book. "Perhaps, but she hates humans, and Alan is very human. No, I think someone else wants it. There are spells within spells in this book. Pages that aren't what they seem."

I didn't even fight the eyeroll. "Of course there are. Jaysus lordy, Gran! Can you at least tell me which pages?"

"No, I can't," she said, "and not because I'm dead. My memory was struck from me—by myself—so I couldn't pass on that information under duress. But know that there are spells in here"—she stroked the cover—"that can't be found anywhere else."

"I need Missy to remove whatever spell O'Sean put on the Hollows Group, and to remove that mark on Crash."

"She can't do either," Gran said.

Hope fled me like a balloon deflating, right down to the raspberry my lips made. "Well, fuck."

"Watch your mouth." Gran snapped her fingers in my face and I sighed again. No matter how old I was, Gran would always be Gran, and the F-bomb was just one word she didn't tolerate well.

"There is a way to release them all, but it is dangerous. And they must all be in very close proximity." She told me how to make sure the spells were removed from everyone.

Gran was not wrong. Not only was it dangerous, but the very thought of it made my stomach roll. Even so, I adjusted the plan I'd been making. I'd learned not to question her wisdom.

I hurried downstairs to the front door and opened it. Crash was sitting there, staring out at the garden. He turned at the sound of the door opening. "Would you come and talk to Gran with me?" I asked.

He stood and followed me inside without a word.

All the way up to my room, where Gran waited quietly.

"Are you planning to have one last toss before the fight?" Gran asked. "That's a good idea. I'll leave you to it."

"GRAN!" Okay, so apparently I *could* still be embarrassed by my dead grandmother. "Crash," I turned to him, deliberately putting my back to my gran. He was grinning, though. Of course he was.

"I think she's right, one last toss." He winked and I lifted both eyebrows.

"I think not." Even if my libido was screaming at me to ride him like a pony. "I'm not interested in competing for your attention with women less than half my age and with tits that defy gravity. Can you get O'Sean to the Hollows by midnight? Tell him we have the cross there."

Crash shook his head. "Wait—"

"Can you get O'Sean there?" I asked again. I didn't want to repeat the rest, my ego was bruised enough as it was.

"Yes, I can get him there, but the two girls—"

I pointed at the door. "You said you'd listen to me, so go. Get O'Sean to the Hollows just after midnight."

Crash's eyes narrowed. "We're going to finish this discussion later."

I shrugged. "Far as I'm concerned, we've already finished it."

I expected him to spin around, to stomp off in a huff, because the man I'd lived with for twenty years would do just that. Then again, Himself didn't have the confidence to own his actions.

Not so much with Crash. He stepped into me, tipped my face up with one hand and placed the softest of kisses on my lips, sending little bolts of energy across my skin, right through to my belly. I might have gasped. Gran might have sighed.

"We are far from done," he said, his words tingling all the way through me. "But I'll let it go for now."

Then he did turn and left me standing there in my room, my legs shaking from a simple kiss that should not have made me feel like that. I slumped to the bed. "Gran."

"Yes, it was that way for me with your grandfather. Kisses like fire, those fae men."

Not fire exactly. More like electricity and storm waves and lightning bolts, night wind and moonlight, it was all there in his kiss and his touch, and I wanted him in a very, very bad way that made my heart race as uncontrollably as if I were closing in on a heart attack. I dropped my head between my knees and did some slow breathing until my blood cooled.

A few minutes later, I heaved a sigh and got up to finish my preparations for the night, which took some time. I pulled a few books off the shelves of my room before making my selection. I went to work on the spine, taking the pages out, and more than a few fluttered to the ground. After much sweating and cursing and, let's be honest, a bit of a mess, into my bag went Gran's book of spells. Next to it was Bob-John's invisibility powder, my flashlight, and an extra shirt.

Around my neck hung the talisman that Alan had tried to steal. I didn't know just how it was important, but I knew that it was and there was no way I was taking it off.

"Ready as I'm going to be," I said more to myself than Gran as I looked at the clock. Eleven-thirty. "You look after Eric, watch out for eyes on him," I said as I headed down the stairs. Suzy stood in the entryway, as did Eric and Feish. I pulled Robert's finger bone out of my bag and set it on the floor. A blink and he was there, swaying side to side.

"Robert, can you call the skeleton horse up in the garden? We need a ride out to the Hollows without being seen," I said.

"Friend. Horse," he said as I opened the door, and he stepped out, his bones clacking on the steps as he went down to the garden.

I put a hand to my back, reassuring myself that it was there. That this wasn't all part of some strange out-of-body experience. I looked at my friends. "Be careful, all of you. We still don't know who shot me the other day. We could have more than O'Sean to deal with tonight."

Eric pulled me into a sudden hug. "You too. You'll be taking the brunt of this."

Hugs all around, then Suzy and Feish hurried off, one going toward the water, the other toward Forsyth Park. I waited until they were gone and then gave Eric his final task beyond staying hidden in the house.

I wrapped my hands around his as best as I could. "Gran will help you. But you have to hurry, and cover your tracks well."

He swallowed hard. "I won't let you down."

I left him there and pulled myself up onto the back of the skeleton horse, a little more gracefully this time. Robert climbed up behind me and then we were off, leaping over the garden gate and racing down the streets of Savannah, heading for the Hollows and a showdown I wasn't sure I was ready for.

21

The horse under me seemed more solid than the last time Robert and I had ridden it. If Robert were capable of more than one-word answers, I would have questioned him about my suspicion that the horse was—for better or worse—becoming more alive. More real. But he wasn't likely to say anything more than "friend," so my thoughts branched in a different direction as we galloped the streets of Savannah.

If everything came together according to plan, then we'd free the Hollows Group and Crash from O'Sean's machinations, and the fairy cross would be safely hidden from any other idiots wanting it for nefarious purposes.

Maybe we'd even stop the shooter who'd come after Eric and me, although I wasn't so sure on that one. Crash had said it was a shifter.

I let my mind mull that over. The only shifter I really knew was Sarge, but he wouldn't shoot at me.

Would he?

"Oh duck me," I whispered. "What if it was Sarge?"

He'd been coming at me hard lately, and that spell had made everyone in the Hollows Group act so weird…

As my mount leapt the fence surrounding the Hollows graveyard, my suspicions were confirmed.

A bounding black shape with shaggy fur ran straight for us. Jaws wide open, snarling, slavering tongue.

The really bad thing? Luke was behind him, trying to stop him, tears running down his face. "Breena, he's going to kill you!" Luke screamed. "Get out of here!"

I vaguely wondered how he could see me on the horse but didn't have time to question it. Maybe it was a shifter thing? Because Sarge could see Robert. There was no time to wonder more than that.

I pulled a knife and threw it, hitting Sarge in the right shoulder. Down a leg, he howled and snarled. I pulled the solid stone out of my bag and gave it to Robert. "Go, bury it deep!"

Robert slid off the horse.

I had one knife left. And a spell I couldn't break on Sarge. Which meant I had to try reasoning with him.

"Sarge, this is insane, what the hell is wrong with you? We're friends!"

His teeth snapped as he lunged at me, and it was then I realized that Luke had a rope around his neck like a leash, although it was barely holding the big werewolf back. With a yank he pulled him off balance, toward the right leg I'd hurt.

"I'll kill you, he's mine! I love him!" Sarge snarled, snapping his teeth again.

Crash? "You want Crash, you're going to have to come through me first, dude. Me and two stupidly beautiful girls with unreasonably perky boobs." There. I'd said it. I did want Crash, damn it. Jealousy was not a good look on me.

Sarge paused, confusion rippling over his face. "Crash? Not Corb?"

"What the hell does Corb…have…to…do… with…this?" The words kind of floated out of me. The conversation with him about unrequited love floated back to me. Sarge wanting me to move out and into Crash's place. Corb's attention to me. Suzy's loss of confidence. Luke being more afraid than usual.

The spell took their weaknesses and amplified them, or maybe twisted them. "Holy shit, you really did shoot me, you asshole!" I slid off the horse, strode over to him, and kicked his furry butt as hard as I could. He turned and snarled, and I grabbed an ear. "Listen here. Corb might make a move on me, but he is not for me. You got that?" I tugged his ear hard for good measure. Luke curled away from me like I was scaring him. "You're acting this way because of a spell that O'Sean put on you. It's making you an even bigger asshole than usual."

Sarge tried to pull away from me, but I hung on tight. "I love him. And you're in the way," he whispered.

My horse gave a low, wet-sounding nicker that was sort of gross, but it had me lifting my head in time to see Corb himself running our way. "Well, shit."

Corb tried to hug me. "You're okay? Jesus, Breena, I've been searching the rubble of the restaurant with the emergency crew. I couldn't find you!"

I grimaced. "Yeah, sorry about that."

Sarge growled and I twisted his ear further. "Everyone go to the Hollows, okay? We need to discuss a few things."

Corb tried again to hug me, but I sidestepped him. "Take Sarge and go. Wait for me there. Please get all the mentors and trainees up by the angel. Okay?"

"Yeah, okay," Corb agreed slowly. "You're going to tell us what's going on?"

"Yes, just ducking go!"

Gawd in heaven, it was like herding cats!

The three men left me there at the gate, and I pulled myself back up onto the horse's back. "You need a name. How about Skeletor?"

The horse snorted. I'd take that for a yes. "Let's find Robert."

Skeletor—yes, that definitely worked—turned on his haunches and leapt to the right, running out to the middle of the graveyard, where Robert stood next to a tombstone. I slid off the horse's saddle and went to stand next to him. "You think this is a good spot?"

"Friend," he said softly and tapped the tombstone. I bent to read the name, which was surprisingly still there.

"Evangeline L'Andre." I didn't know that name, but I trusted Robert if he thought it was a good place. He wrapped his hands around the stone and slid down into the soil. Minutes ticked by before he pulled himself back out and stood next to me. It had to be closing in on midnight.

"Time for trick number two," I whispered, pulling my bag around to me and flipping it open. Bob-John's rhinestone-encrusted box felt heavy in my hand. I lifted it over my head and opened it up.

"Please work, please make me invisible."

A tingling sensation started at my scalp and quickly shifted downward, rolling down my body like droplets of water instead of powder. I held my hand out and stumbled backward. I couldn't see me. I closed my eyes and grabbed my bag, then opened my eyes and held the leather surface up to my face. Only I couldn't see the bag either.

A string of curses left my mouth that made Robert and Skeletor stumble backward. "No, no, I'm not mad. Just shocked. Can you see me, Robert?"

"Friend," he said.

I'd have to take that as a yes. I didn't know how long the powder would last—it had only cost twenty dollars, after all—so it was time to hurry. "Come on then. Douche Canoe O'Sean should be there by now. Skeletor, you stick close."

Robert and Skeletor followed me as I jogged across the graveyard, heading for the angel tomb leading down to the Hollows. As we went, I slid my bag over Robert's head. "You hang onto this for me."

As I drew close I counted the people there. The four trainees, five mentors, Missy, Crash, and O'Sean.

"Why the hell are we here?" O'Sean yelled at Crash. "You said that you were taking me to the cross?"

"He did," I said, knowing that they couldn't see me. I motioned for Robert to stop. O'Sean whipped around.

"Who said that?"

Trick number three. I softened my voice, allowing the accent I'd lost to crawl back over the words. "Celia O'Rylee. I've come back to make right what you've wronged for my town."

O'Sean stumbled back a few steps. "You're dead."

"Yes, and you are going to join me," I said as I worked around the one side of him. He stared at the place where I'd been and threw a spell of black magic that stunk like death. Oh crap. Then it was the worst of the worst, if Gran's book was right.

"No!"

"Free the Hollows Group from the spells you cast on them," I whispered right in his ear, then ducked down. He twisted, stumbled back over me, and fell onto his ass. "Free the fae king."

"No!" he screamed. "You aren't real." He scrambled backward, scuttling on his ass. His fear was a palpable thing and hope surged through me. This was going to work. He'd free everyone, and we could all just go home. Hot damn for a plan going right!

"Crash, protect me!" he screamed.

Oh. Shit.

For some reason I hadn't expected that, and it most surely was not in the plan.

A blast of magic whipped through the air, stripping me of my invisibility.

Douche Canoe stared up at me. "You! How are you doing this?"

"Breena, I can't defy him! You have to get out of here!" Crash yelled. I twisted to see him pulling his weapon. A sword that was easily four feet long, silver and shining in the darkness.

Well, two could play at this game. "Corb, keep him busy while I deal with Douche Canoe! But don't kill each other!" I just needed enough time to make Douche Canoe break the spell.

Corb stepped between me and Crash and the clash of weapons rang through the air. I pulled both of my blades and charged O'Sean, who was on his feet once more. He flung a spell at me that smelled like lavender.

Why the hell would he want to knock me out?

To use you, just like Gran warned. You're a new weapon and he wants whatever you are.

I twisted to the side and brought both blades cutting through air, dispersing the spell into nothing but a few sparkles. "That's a no from me."

311

We sidestepped each other as if were in a ring. "You killed my gran, didn't you?"

"No, but I was there when she died." He smiled. "And I know who did it."

"Mother ducker!" I lunged at him and the tip of my blade slashed through his right arm, drawing blood.

He snarled and flung a spell at me, this one sticky and pink. It hit my feet and locked me in place. A second spell shot at me right after the first, this one that lavender scent again. I barely managed to knock it back as I struggled to stay upright.

"Let us see how you protect your friends then?" Douche Canoe was out of reach of my blades as he prepped a spell that smelled like brimstone—another really bad one. Duck my life. Gray tendrils curled around his hands. "A slow death for them all, yes?"

"No!" I slashed down at the spell that held my legs to the ground, desperation making me sloppy. I cut into my own leg, the wound shallow but deep enough for the blood to flow. Pain rippled through me, and I fell forward onto my hands and knees. My one foot was free. The one I'd cut. I didn't hesitate to reach down and nick my other leg.

The blood burned away the spell, and I didn't question why as I scrambled forward. Douche Canoe must have seen me coming at him from the corner of his eye. He twisted, the grey magic hitting me right in the middle of my chest, but I was still moving and I tackled him to the ground.

My heart stuttered. Douche Canoe's eyes wid-ened as I drove both blades into him at the same time. Heart and neck. We fell to the ground together, and I sat on top of him as the life bled out of him. The same magic I'd seen hit the Hollows Group just a few nights before whipped around him, dispersing in the night air as if it had never been.

I pushed the blades deeper even as my own body began to scream for oxygen. I wasn't breathing, I knew I wasn't. But I had to see this through.

Someone behind me was yelling my name. "Free him," I said the words, and the mark of the crescent moon bloomed over Douche Canoe's head, dispers-ing in the same way.

The light slid from his eyes, a film of white roll-ing over them as the last breath escaped his mouth. He smiled up at me. Because, of course, not all of his spells had been broken. Gran had thought his death would nullify them, but she'd been wrong.

The gray tendrils wrapped tighter around me.

I was pulled off O'Sean's body. Hands touched me, and frantic voices filled my ears as someone tried to push their magic into me. Missy's voice snapped above all of them.

"Your fae magic won't save her now, Crash."

I mouthed a word, a name.

Robert.

A skeletal hand clutched mine and I stood up, only I was looking down on my body. My friends had gathered all around me, Corb doing chest compres-sions as Crash breathed for me. Suzy held one of my hands, tears streaming down her face. It was all very sad, but I wasn't really dead. Was I?

I turned to the hand that tightened on mine. Robert stood next to me. Only he wasn't a skeleton. He was a man. About my height with long black hair tied back in a ponytail, sharp angular features, and eyes like ice. "Holy shit, Robert?"

"You are the first to know my name in a very long time," he said, then shook his head. "You aren't going to die. They will think you are dying. They might even bury you if we don't get you back quickly. But this is the first threshold."

I tightened my hold on him. "You mean I'm going to come back like a skeleton? Like you?" I wasn't sure that I was ready for that.

"No. You're going to go back, but things will be different. You will see more like me. More like... Skeletor." He laughed. "That is a good name for the horse. He likes it."

"Oh, well that's good. Um..." I looked at the frantic energy rolling around my friends. "Can I go back now?"

Robert pulled me into a quick hug. "Go. And know that you are loved, and you deserve that love. Accept it for what it is. I will be with you."

He shoved me hard, and I stumbled, flipped over backward, and hit the ground hard enough to pull a gasp from my body. I sat up, head-butted Crash, shoved Corb off me, and was up on my feet in a flash.

My entire body shook as I turned to look at my friends. "Hi."

22

Suzy was the first to grab me, pulling me into a tight, slobbering, sobbing hug. "Oh my God! Breena, your heart stopped!"

I hugged her back, though I'll admit I didn't have a ton of energy for it. "Right, well, I'm back. I'm good now." And, strangely enough, it was true. Energy flowed up from the soles of my feet through my limbs and the fear and exhaustion slowly peeled off me. I stood a little taller. Around me the tombstones seemed to light up, like they had LED lights embedded in them and I wondered if that was where the energy was coming from. "Honest, I'm okay."

Corb stared at me like he was seeing a ghost. Crash seemed…bothered by the fact that I was standing there, fresh as a ducking daisy. I gently pushed Suzy off me. We still had Missy to deal with, and while I had very little left to bargain with her, I was still going ahead with it. Knowledge was power in this world, and Missy had knowledge I needed.

"Robert, bring me my bag please." I held out a hand to him, but my eyes were on the old woman, who watched me like a hawk eyes a bunny rabbit. Only this rabbit had fangs. The bag strap settled in my open palm and I closed my fingers over it. Suzy gasped, which told me that the bag had just reappeared.

"Cool trick," she whispered.

I pulled the bag over my head and flopped it open, pulling out the book. "If you want this leather-bound book, then you need to give me something for it," I said.

Her eyes narrowed. "What, pray tell, would that be?"

"Three answers," I said.

"One," she fired back.

"Two it is," I said, and she nodded.

"Are you still a guardian of Savannah?" I asked, and her eyes bugged wide for just a moment. Obviously that was not the question she'd been expecting.

"In my own way, yes," she said. "I am not Celia."

"You sure as hell aren't," I muttered, took a breath, and asked the next question. "How many bad guys are we dealing with?"

Her lips twisted upward. "We?"

I nodded. "We."

"So you fancy yourself a guardian of Savannah now?" One of her eyebrows twitched upward. Curse her—of course, she could pull off that trick.

Suzy stood beside me. "I'm with Breena. We are guardians of Savannah now."

"How many?" I asked again. "I'm making this easy for you. All you have to do is give me a number, no names."

I held the book out to her and she put her hands on it, but I didn't let go. Her eyes locked with mine. "You are a fool."

"Why, because I'm giving you this leather-bound book?" I asked.

"Because you are not what your grandmother believed. You are a mutt with blood that is too diluted to be anything more than a thorn in my side." She tried to pull the book from me, but I held it tight.

"True enough, but I stopped Hattie with nothing but a pair of knives and my wits, so maybe I'm not like you. Maybe I don't need magic to survive in the shadow world."

She hissed at me, freaking *hissed*. "There are five that battle for Savannah, and you killed a pair who made one of them."

Four baddies left then. Damn.

I let the book go, and she stumbled backward with a glare. Tucking the book under her arm, she left the cemetery.

Eammon stepped in front of me, watching her go. "Terrible idea, lass."

"Probably one of my best, actually," I said. "She might not have given me any truly useful information, but then again, I didn't give her a terribly useful spell book."

Eammon whipped around to look at me. "What did you give her?"

I smiled. "A little switcheroo. *Spells for Beginners* is about as thick as my gran's book. Take pages out of one, stuff it with the pages of the other. And I of course signed it over to her."

All the best with your casting of spells. I hope this helps as I thought it fitting to your skill level. Love B.

Louis and Tom looked at me as though I'd been speaking in tongues. But Louis had a strange, assessing look on his face. It was Louis who was really looking at me. "You...I watched your spirit float above your body. Who were you talking to?"

Right. "Well, that's Robert. I still don't get why you can't see him. He's very nice." From the corner of my eye, I could see Robert swaying on his feet, a skeleton once more.

"Friend."

The mentors didn't seem to know what to do. They sent the remaining three trainees home, and then they all looked at me. I looked back. "What?"

"What are you going to do next?" Eammon asked softly. "You need to be dealing with Karissa yet. My fault, that one. Damn spell made me weak to her again!"

Karissa. I'd sent Feish to her to keep her busy, because I knew that if all the players showed up at once, the shit show would have been beyond any sort of control. But that Feish hadn't come back—her job had been to deliver a message and then return—meant things had gone very sideways.

"Hells bells, I gotta go!" I turned to Crash. "You good? The mark is gone?"

He bowed at the waist. "It is gone. With my thanks." Very formal, but whatever, I didn't have time to figure out what was going on with him.

I'd left Feish with Karissa long enough.

"Skeletor!" I yelled for my horse and the mentors laughed. Until he pulled himself from the ground. They all stumbled back.

"What in the world is that?" Louis breathed out, shock making his French accent heavier than normal.

"Oh, so you can see him but not Robert?" I pulled myself up onto Skeletor's back and patted his neck, noticing that his flesh was indeed firmer. Plus, he'd been invisible to other people before. He was changing, although I didn't understand how. Maybe it was because of me and my near-death experience? I shook my head, not knowing, and at the moment not needing to know. Later. I would figure it out later.

Louis put his hands in the air like he was doing the Y in YMCA, his eyes wide and brows high. "*C'est quoi ce bordel?*"

I blinked and looked to Eammon for an explanation, but it was Crash who translated. "What the duck?"

Yeah, he didn't say duck, and I gotta say, hearing him drop an f-bomb sent a rather strong shiver through me. "Look, I gotta go. I've got to deal with Karissa. Suzy, you get back to Eric, and lock down the house till I'm back."

Suzy gave me a quick nod and took off running.

Crash stiffened. "I should come with you. I can help you deal with Karissa."

I snorted and Skel—see, shortening it already—scuttled sideways. I clamped my legs tight around the horse's middle. "Yeah, because your ex-wife is going to be easier to deal with while you're there? Every other man here knows that's a terrible idea, Crash."

All the other men nodded in unison. "She's not wrong," Eammon said. "I should never have encouraged her to help Karissa." He rubbed at his head. "She's always been a weak spot for me, but I thought I'd put her behind me." His weak spot. So, I'd been right, the spell O'Sean had put on the Hollows had latched on to their weaknesses and amplified them.

But wait, if Karissa was Eammon's weak spot...I had to blink a few times before the meaning sunk in. "WAIT. You and Karissa?"

Eammon winked up at me and touched his nose. Holy hot damn.

And just like that, the animosity between him and Crash made total and complete sense. It didn't matter which of them had come first—Eammon was still pissed that she'd picked Crash at some point.

Crash growled something under his breath, but I was done with the drama. I turned Skel, and Robert scrambled up behind me. "Okay, enough of the gossip, fun as it is. I've got to wrap this day up." Fatigue was biting at me, and the ache in my low back was throbbing.

A hand settled on my calf, and I looked down to see Corb there. "Look, you should take someone with you. You…you were dead just a few minutes ago, Bree." His concern was touching.

"You want to help? Find out who Alan is connected to in the shadow world. He used magic to claim the house, and he tried to steal my gran's book from me." I dug my heels into Skel's sides and the horse leapt forward. This time I was a little more ready for the rapid motion as we raced away from the Hollows.

"We need to get to Forsyth Park, to the entryway to Faerie!" I yelled into the wind.

Skel turned to the left, just a little, hooves making no sound as he led us through city square after city square. Still, there were no humans that noticed us, the few that were out. Some of the squares we passed through felt dark, like the entities bound to them would reach out and take your soul if you let them, and others felt light as a feather.

But all had restless dead in them. That much I knew. I shook my head at the fancy that rolled through me. "Robert, lots of dead here."

"Friend. Not dead."

"No, not dead, not today." I smiled as the wind pulled at my hair. "And we have to save one more friend before we can go home and get some whiskey."

He let out a soft sigh. "Whiskey."

"Yeah, whiskey." I'd pick up my own bottle, see if I could get some good Canadian Rye. Smoother than my usual, I could use smooth at that point.

Skel plunged through a waist-high line of deep green foliage, and then we were there in Forsyth Park, heading straight for the fountain.

I leaned over Skel's neck. "Slow down!" Only the horse didn't slow down. Skel leapt over the fountain edge and did a dive straight for the opening I'd passed through before. Even so, I wasn't totally prepared.

Eyes closed, breath held, I felt the water pass over me, and then I was dry and the wind around us was blowing. I opened my eyes. Skel danced underneath me and I considered getting off, but it would feel unsafe to touch the ground here in the night. To walk through those long grasses that could conceal so much.

"Okay, well, let's go find Karissa," I said.

"Not friend," Robert whispered.

"Yeah, that's what I'm worried about," I muttered as Skel picked up speed until we were bouncing along through the grass. The night here was clear, the moon high, and the light from it cast long shadows across both the land and the glittering sea out to my left.

I will say that part of Faerie called to me. In that moment, I just wanted to stand around and look at things. To wonder at the strange beauty of it. I turned away from the sea and, like before, there was the wood calling to me, the viewing pool, and the queen of the fae standing next to it.

No more pantsuit this time. She was dressed in a flowing red dress that split up one side, showing off a long, pale leg. The top was loose, and it hung to just above her nipples. My first thought was how in the hell was she keeping the dress up? My next was to wonder if she and J-Lo were related what with the impossible dresses that no mortal woman could pull off.

I shook my head. "Where is Feish?"

"That slave? She is here." Karissa waved her hand to the left and Feish stepped out of the circle. Her bulbous eyes were wide, and I saw the fear in them as clear as day. Karissa ignored her. "You have the fairy cross?"

I opened my mouth and a buzzing like an over-sized mosquito thrummed up behind me. Kinkly landed on my back, right in the middle where Karissa couldn't see her. "Ask for payment first. Or you'll have no chance of getting anything. If you can get her to hand it over first, then you can make a run for it."

In other words, I needed to find my opening to make that happen, and that meant talking to Karissa, in order to find that opening.

I cleared my throat. "Where is my payment?"

Karissa's face didn't so much as twitch, yet I knew in my gut she was peeved I'd asked for the payment upfront.

"How many nights did you watch again?" she asked softly.

I smiled. "Actually, it doesn't matter how many nights. You agreed to pay me double what you would have paid for the entire ten days, regardless of how many nights I was there. And of course, Feish will come with me."

Now her face did tighten, just at the corners of her mouth and around her eyes. "I would like to see the fairy cross."

I kept on smiling, although I felt the negotiations sliding in an undesirable direction. "And I'd like to see the payment first."

Really, it was a matter of who could hold out longer. As much as I needed this payday, I'd walk away from our negotiations if I had to in order to keep me and Feish safe. "And Feish can come on over this way."

"The filthy river maid stays here," Karissa snapped, her façade breaking. "She has kept me occupied and I would like to know why."

My own smile shifted until I was baring my teeth at her. Skel snorted and stomped a foot, and Robert tapped my shoulder. "Not friend."

"Feish is coming with me. And she kept you occupied so you would stay the duck out of my way." I slid off the saddle and landed on my feet without so much as a wobble. Mind you, I was mad as a wet hen and about as ready to peck her eyes out for trying to keep Feish.

I stood there, fingers brushing lightly against the handles of the knives. "I suggest you send her over, or you can kiss these negotiations goodbye."

Karissa blinked. "You would throw away your payment for a slave? You are no better than Crash."

"For a friend," I said. "No amount of money is worth her life."

Feish's big lips bobbled and a tear slid down her yellow-green skin. I looked back to Karissa, who was watching me.

Kinkly tugged at my shirt again. "She won't give you payment. I think…I think she might try to kill you and take the fairy cross."

"Bless your heart," I said softly, a part of what I'd read about dealing with the fae coming up from my memory banks. I just had to get to Feish and get back to Skel and Robert. Easy peasy, right? "You think you can keep my friend, the fairy cross, and all the payment you owe me?"

Karissa smiled wide, her beauty still there, but I suddenly knew why she and Crash hadn't worked out. She really was not very nice.

"I'm quite sure I can. This is my place of power, and you came willingly," Karissa said softly. "You can't escape now unless I give you free passage."

I was within about ten feet of her now, and Feish was just to the left of her. "You know that thing about making deals with the fae?" I asked.

Karissa laughed. "Yes, you didn't put it in writing, you foolish child."

I laughed right back at her. "Right, which means I don't owe you shit. The fairy cross is mine, and by all rights, I don't have to give it to you."

Her face flashed with shock first and then anger as she processed the double-edged sword. The no contract thing worked in my favor too. She locked eyes with me with an intensity that made me think she had to poop. "You will give me the fairy cross."

"That's a no from me." I took a step to the left, closer to Feish, as I pulled one knife clear of its sheath. "I mean, a really large no, if you want to be exact. You were never going to pay me, were you?"

I was within distance of Feish so I reached out and pulled her hard behind me. Karissa just gave me that same poop stare as though she couldn't believe what she was seeing. "Give me the cross!"

"Nope." I kept my eyes on her and pushed Feish behind me toward Skel and Robert. "Also, you can get a great laxative to fix the constipation. I think my ex used one with a purple cap."

She threw her head back and a scream of pure rage erupted out of her mouth. I shoved Feish up onto Skel's back, not caring if she could see the beast or not, and climbed on after her.

"Go. Go! Back to Forsyth Park!" I yelled, and Skel leapt forward. Feish bounced along in front of me, Robert behind, and Kinkly clinging to my shoulder.

"You have to hurry! She'll close the opening!" Kinkly yelped.

"Can we slow her down?" I yelled back.

I twisted to see Karissa headed our way on the back of a large stag, her hair swept out behind her and a literal storm cloud in her wake. There was no way we'd make it all the way to the gateway if we didn't do something. If *I* didn't do something.

"Get them home, Kinkly!" I yelled and pushed myself off the saddle. I tucked myself into a ball, rolling with the fall but feeling every bounce in my bones.

This was really going to be a bitch tomorrow.

23

I didn't bother to pull both knives. Her power was pretty obvious, and I knew I couldn't fight her and win. But I could buy my friends the time they needed to get out.

"You know," I said as she slowed to a stop in front of me, "I thought you were pretty cool when we met. But you're just another mean girl, aren't you?"

The stag lowered his head as if he would impale me and I took a step back. "Look, you don't have to be like this."

Karissa held a hand out and bands of air wrapped around me, pinning my arms to my sides. "You are causing me no amount of grief."

I didn't panic, didn't attempt to escape from the hold she had on me but instead went limp. "You don't seem to understand. I am looking out for my friends, and for Savannah. That's my job."

Her eyes narrowed. "I want to hate you."

"Why?" I spluttered. "I did nothing but try and help you until it became apparent you were a two-faced liar."

Her jaw jutted out. "Because."

I blinked up at her. "That's a child's answer." Okay, in retrospect, perhaps that wasn't the smartest thing to say given I was already in a boa constrictor's hold of air bands I couldn't see. She tightened her hold and I squeaked. "Are you one of the four baddies?"

Her hold on me loosened. "What?"

I sucked in a deep breath, and I'm not sure why I asked the next question, only that it seemed like a why-the-hell-not kind of moment. "Four, there are four more assholes who want to do damage to Savannah. I've killed the O'Seans, so that takes one off the list. Are you one of the remaining asswipes?"

Her eyes cleared of some of the anger. "You really think you are protecting Savannah? That you are like Celia? And the O'Seans are dead?"

The bands loosened, and I drew another good breath. "Look, I don't know why you wanted that fairy cross. I can't believe you really intended to give it to the O'Seans in the first place!"

"To keep it from Crash," she said softly. "The O'Seans wanted him to make a crucible for a ceremony, and I told them I would retrieve the cross for them, but I fully intended to give them a fake."

"I hid it," I said.

The bands relaxed completely. She slid off the stag and walked toward me. "Why did you not give it to Crash then? Was he not able to woo you?"

I snorted. "Same reason you weren't going to give it to O'Sean. I didn't want them to be able to do whatever it was they planned on doing. Because I doubt very much it was going to be anything good."

A sigh slid from her. "I really want to hate you."

I laughed. "Why?"

Her lips pursed. "You are the first one Crash has had real interest in since our marriage ended."

And how would she know that if she weren't spying on me? Kinkly seemed to pick up my thoughts.

"Sorry, I had to tell her," she whispered.

A snort escaped me before I could catch it. "Please. You should have seen him with a girl under each arm in the go between I stumbled into."

Her eyebrows went up. "You went into a go between?"

"Some idiots in black were chasing us." I held up my hands. "Look, I suspect Crash is using me, okay? I think—" Gawd in heaven, I did *not* want to say this out loud, especially to her.

"—that he knows I have a crush on him, and he's using it. But I'm aware. Okay?"

She lifted a hand and put it on my shoulder. "You will keep the fairy cross hidden somewhere safe?"

"I will," I said. My mind was already putting pieces together, and I knew that what I was about to ask next might not go over well. "But...I think you should let Kinkly stay with me. She could report back to you if you like."

A quick nod from her surprised me. "Excellent."

I took note that she wasn't offering me any payment.

And just like that, I was leaving on foot, with my head still attached, and although the fairy queen was not exactly on my side, she wasn't fighting me either. I'd take that as a win.

Even if my body was suddenly remembering my age and lack of fitness. I stumbled through the fountain and out into the water on the Savannah side. Through the mini-waterfall and then a pair of very strong arms scooped me up.

"How the hell did you get away?" Crash's voice rumbled through me as he dragged me out of the fountain. "You've been in there for two days, and the entryway was blocked even to me!"

Did that mean he'd waited out here for two days?

I gave him a hug back and put my head against his chest, thinking about what I'd said. That I thought he was using me. I wanted to trust him, I wanted to believe that he wanted me, but I was no child.

I was a grown-ass women who knew better. Fairy tales didn't come true, I wasn't going to get the prince (or the king in this case), and I wasn't going to magically get the house back in my name. But we were all alive, and no one was currently gunning for us, and I'd take that much as a small win.

"We came to an understanding, Karissa and I," I said as he put me down. I looked around to see that we were alone—or at least none of my friends were there. The sun was high in the sky, just past noon on whatever the hell day it was.

Robert and Skel were gone, but that was a good sign. It meant I wasn't in trouble.

For the moment. "I'm tired," I said. "Tell me I can sleep now?"

Crash scooped me up as if I weighed nothing. "You can sleep now. You're safe. I...you're sure you're okay? What do you mean you came to an agreement?"

"We are both grown-ass women, who can actually have a conversation rather than spitting and hissing at each other." I leaned my head against him and closed my eyes. "The Hollows Group? Are they all okay?" I was worried that Sarge might come at me again. Or that Corb might make another move, and I didn't know if I had it in me to fight off either of them.

"You were right about the spell latching on to their weaknesses. Your interactions with Suzy seemed to have dispelled the effects on her, and likely if you'd spent enough time with the others you could have done the same for them. But killing O'Sean was a much quicker way of releasing all of us from our ties to him."

I mumbled, "Sarge?"

"Sarge admitted to shooting at you. He doesn't remember much of the last few days, like he was dreaming. He's been in love with Corb a long time, and they both knew it. But Sarge didn't realize how deep it went until now. The wolf in him has claimed Corb as an unofficial mate, so he'll have to work on that. Corb, on the other hand, is mortified about the moves he made on you. He says he pushed you when you were scared and drunk." His arms tightened around me, holding me impossibly closer. "Expect an apology from him." I wondered just how Corb had been convinced to give an apology.

"And the others? Eammon, Louis, Tom?" I kept my eyes closed, just enjoying his warmth and his scent of fire and steel. He might try and use me someday, but I'd give him credit where credit was due—in his arms, I was safe as I was going to be.

"Same thing," he said. "They've all been struggling with things that could be considered weaknesses. In fact, it's why Eammon agreed to O'Sean's demands. The first spell was subtle, and no one would have realized that it was even happening. His weakness has always been trying to keep the peace to the point of making mistakes. Same reason why he okayed your arrangement with Karissa, I think."

That made me open my eyes as a thought rippled to the front of my fatigued brain. "You didn't find the fairy cross, did you?"

Crash looked down at me. "Someone saw you go to the Hollows graveyard. Whoever O'Sean was working with, they know it's there. And they are looking."

I sighed and closed my eyes, unable to keep the smile off my face. A few minutes passed before I let the one word slip out of me. "Good."

"Good? How can that be good?" His hands loosened on me, and I found myself standing upright. The smell of Gran's garden circled around me, along with several sets of arms, and I opened my eyes to find myself home.

Feish, Suzy, and Eric held me tight, and I held them back. "Hey guys."

"I never doubted," Feish said softly as she pulled back. "I knew you'd get out. You are my bestest of friends." She gave me a big double blink that maybe was supposed to be a wink, I'm not sure.

Suzy clapped me on the back. "We were prepping a rescue mission. Eammon was even going to help."

I grinned, although it felt like a struggle. "Thanks. But it was better this way. Me and the queen bee had a good chat. Talked about all sorts of things."

"Like men?" Suzy offered.

I laughed. "That was one of the subjects." I could almost feel Crash stiffen next to me.

"Look, look at the new little oak tree I planted." Eric tugged me to the side of the garden he'd been working in. Kinkly fluttered around in front of us, dancing in the tree's leaves.

"This is my favorite, Eric!" she said, her long legs flashing as she hopped from branch to branch.

I smiled as he blushed. Looked like I wasn't going to get sleep any time soon so I gave the tree my attention. "It looks great! Imagine how good it will look when it's been here a few years." I gave him a wink, and he winked right back. Our secret.

The fewer people who knew where the fairy cross was really buried, the better, and the fact that everyone thought Robert and I had buried it in the graveyard solidified our ruse.

Kinkly danced over the leaves. "Here, I can speed up its growth!"

A sprinkling of fairy dust fell from her, and the oak tree rose underneath her, the trunk thickening even as it stretched taller, leaves bursting out and creating a stunning canopy that would have taken many, many years.

Now a huge oak stood where there had been nothing but a sapling moments before. I reached out and touched the trunk, feeling a tiny thrum of magic deep below, there and then gone.

I stepped back. "It's perfect, Kink. Thank you." She spun down and gave me a high five. I sighed. "I'm exhausted. I'm going to bed."

Suzy looped an arm through mine. "Come on, I'll tuck you in. Seeing as you looked after me, I'd like to do the same."

I leaned into her. "Sounds good."

Half an hour later, I was showered and literally tucked into bed. Suzy patted my head hard, like I was a dog. She needed to work on her maternal instincts a little, but I appreciated the effort. "Go to sleep. Everything is good."

I closed my eyes and waited for her to leave the room before I sat up. "Gran?"

Gran slid through the door and sat on the end of my bed. The room was dim, with all of the curtains drawn, and she looked like more than a ghost. "Breena. You did it. You stopped the O'Seans."

"I had a lot of help," I said.

"That's the best way to face challenges. Not alone, but with your most trusted people at your sides and your back. This world isn't meant to be faced alone." She patted my foot, and I could almost feel her touch.

She was right, but I already knew that. Having my friends around made me feel more powerful. "You were right, there is something happening in Savannah. Something bad." I yawned.

Gran smiled. "What did Missy do when she realized that the spell book wasn't what she thought?"

I leaned back into my pillows. "No idea. She didn't look in the book right away."

Gran tsked. "That one, she is not bad, she is not good. She is a true neutral, and if she believes one of the four who are gunning to take over Savannah will suit her purposes, she will align with him or her."

I yawned again. "I'm going to sleep now, Gran."

"Before you do." She stood and I tracked her movement with my eyes as she headed to the door. The desk next to it had a thick manila envelope on it. "The detective dropped this off for you."

I closed my eyes. "Sleep first," I said.

I drifted off, safe and warm, the double dose of Advil and lovely heating pad doing their job to keep the aches and pains at bay. Whatever little bit of fae I had in me, and whatever else my father's line had brought to the table, they didn't bring what Advil did.

Somewhere around midnight I woke up. Keeping my eyes closed, I listened as footsteps walked toward my bed. My blood pounded and I reached slowly under my pillow for the knife I'd stashed there.

Just in case.

"I can't protect her, Celia. I know you want me to, but she throws herself at challenges in ways I don't even understand. And comes through them just as inconceivably," Crash said so softly that I shouldn't have been able to hear him.

"She has always been a tiger," Gran answered just as softly. "But for years she's been told she was a sheep. She's finding her claws again. That's good. It makes her stronger."

"I know, but that's part of what worries me. Her feistiness is like a beacon." A hand brushed over my face, tucking my hair behind my ear. "I'm afraid that she'll take on more than she can handle on her own. That she'll end up…"

"Like me and get herself killed," Gran said and sighed. "Then it's up to you to help keep her alive."

He sighed heavily and stepped away from the bed. "I'm trying, but part of that is keeping my distance from her. Protecting her from the fae who would use her."

"Did you at least put her on the deed?" Gran asked and I almost sat up right there. Put me on the deed? As in deed to the house?

Crash's hand brushed over my hip. "She's been on the deed since I bought the house. You know that I can't outright give it to her. But she paid in full when she removed O'Sean from this world."

Gran sighed again. "So you're still leaving?"

"I have to figure out who is behind this. Who is pulling the strings, Celia. You know that."

"I don't always remember," she said.

Jaysus on a winking donkey, I was getting more information asleep than I could have imagined.

It took everything I had to stay still. "How long will you be gone?"

"I don't know." His hand slipped off my hip. "I don't know."

"Well, don't dilly-dally...she is going to need you...." Gran snapped. Their voices faded as they left my room, and I sat up slowly, with only one groan, thank you very much, to stare at the closed door.

My heart raced from their words, and from Crash's touch. Was he telling the truth? Or was it another twist? Was I really on the deed? That would mean I could start searching for the things that Gran had hidden.

I knew what I wanted to believe. That he was telling the truth. That I could have this house in my name.

Like a beacon glowing, on the table by the door, the yellow envelope that held information about both Gran's death and my parents beckoned to me.

Whatever was coming for me, I knew that opening that envelope would start it all up again.

I pulled myself out of bed and picked up the envelope, tucked a finger in the edge and took a deep breath.

I had friends at my side. A new lease on life. And a job to do.

All outta ducks to give, I needed to know who was hunting my family, no matter what the cost was to my own life.

I tore the envelope open.

Check out the third book in "The Forty Proof Series"

Midlife Demon Hunter

Need more than that to tide you over? You can check out more of the amazing authors in paranormal women's fiction genre at:

www.paranormalwomensfiction.net

OR you can check out my big list of books at:

www.shannonmayer.com